*"And what do y____
Erica asked int___*

"A woman's mouth... ___ ___ was a low rumble of sound that echoed through the airwaves and touched all those secret places within her.

"And I have a weakness for silky, thick hair," he continued. "There's something incredibly erotic about having a woman's hair wrapped around my hands and being able to hold her where I want her."

Images flooded Erica's brain. Of him coaxing her down the length of his body. Of being pinned beneath him. Of fingers tangling in her hair, holding her as he ravished her neck.

"Most of all," Ian said, "I like a woman who's sensual and willing to try new things...."

Erica's lashes fluttered closed and an image of a naked couple making love in carnal, wanton ways flashed behind her eyelids.

"A woman who isn't afraid to tell me what she wants." Ian paused for a long moment. Then, in a husky timbre, he asked, "So, Erica, what turns you on?"

Blaze™

Dear Reader,

Harlequin Blaze is a supersexy new series. If you like love stories with a strong sexual edge then this is the line for you! The books are fun and flirtatious, the heroes are hot and outrageous. Blaze is a series for the woman who wants *more* in her reading pleasure....

This month bestselling Harlequin Presents author Miranda Lee delivers #9 *Just a Little Sex...* about one night of passion that turns into much more! Rising star Jamie Denton says you need to break the rules in #10 *Sleeping With the Enemy,* a story with sizzling sexual tension and erotic love scenes. Talented Isabel Sharpe takes us to #11 *The Wild Side,* a fun, lusty tale about a good girl who decides bad might be better. Popular Janelle Denison rounds out the month with #12 *Heat Waves,* another SEXY CITY NIGHTS story set in fiery Chicago—where the heat definitely escalates after dark....

Look for four Blaze books every month at your favorite bookstore. And check us out online at eHarlequin.com and tryblaze.com.

Enjoy!

Birgit Davis-Todd
Senior Editor & Editorial Coordinator
Harlequin Blaze

HEAT WAVES

Janelle Denison

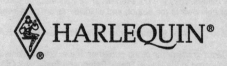

HARLEQUIN®

TORONTO • NEW YORK • LONDON
AMSTERDAM • PARIS • SYDNEY • HAMBURG
STOCKHOLM • ATHENS • TOKYO • MILAN • MADRID
PRAGUE • WARSAW • BUDAPEST • AUCKLAND

To Leena Hyat and all the lovely ladies at www.heartratereviews.com who've made the Internet a much nicer, romance-friendly place to visit!

To my husband, Don, my inspiration and research partner. Keep up the great work! <g>

ISBN 0-373-79016-3

HEAT WAVES

Copyright © 2001 by Janelle Denison.

A NOTE FROM THE AUTHOR...

What a thrill it is to be a part of the new Harlequin Blaze launch! I always enjoy writing supersexy books for Temptation, and it's wonderful to now have the luxury of exploring deeper layers of sensuality with Blaze, along with more erotic premises. If you're looking for fantasies come to life, mixed with a generous dose of red-hot sexual tension, then Blaze is for you!

Wild. Sexy. *Sizzling*. *Heat Waves* is all that and so much more. Take a sassy radio deejay heroine, whose on-air persona tempts and teases her listeners with provocative topics, throw in a sinfully sexy hero who challenges her issues on the air and off, and the result is a scorching, wickedly satisfying affair that will leave you breathless!

I hope you enjoy my first book for Harlequin Blaze. There are many more Blaze novels to come, so be sure to check my Web site for updates at www.janelledenison.com. I'd love to hear what you think about these groundbreaking books. You can write to me at P.O. Box 1102, Rialto, CA 92377-1102, or e-mail me at janelle@janelledenison.com.

Enjoy,

Janelle Denison

1

IAN CARLISLE WAS OBSESSED with a woman he'd never met. A woman who seduced him every night with her alluring voice, fired his interest and libido with the provocative and sometimes erotic topics she discussed on the air, and aroused him with their sizzling banter and sexy debates.

Lately, she'd become a part of his dreams and fantasies, too, and that's when he knew he was in deep. It wasn't enough that he came home to her every evening, now he was taking her to bed with him every night. Unfortunately, he still woke up alone, and most times hard and aching for that illusive fantasy. She provided an irresistible attraction that kept him coming back to her night after night.

With ten minutes to go before her radio show time, he stepped into his glass-and-chrome shower stall. He welcomed the cool rush of water on his taut, heated skin after spending an hour working off the stress of a long day negotiating a major deal for his investment firm. Now his head was clear, his body relaxed, and his thoughts focused solely on *her*.

He soaped up his body, scrubbing across his chest and torso, and down to his thighs. Anticipation rippled through him, heightening the need to hear her sultry voice and discover what she had planned for tonight's show and her audience's listening pleasure. Excitement unfurled deep in his belly at the thought of yet another night of teasing debates and sexy challenges.

Their nightly ritual was like an illicit affair, verbally risqué and physically arousing. The kind of flirtation that was fun, frivolous and daring. A playful, lively distraction that took his mind off work and the painful memories that had a way of creeping up on him in the evenings when his penthouse was too quiet.

That's how he'd come across Erica McCree's radio show nearly a month ago. Desperate to fill the oppressive silence in his huge, empty house, he'd flipped on his stereo for music and instead he'd found *her.* Amusing, sassy, seductive, she not only made the hot summer Chicago nights hotter with her candid talk about sexual issues, she inflamed him, as well. And it had been a long time since any woman had affected him so strongly and on such a basic, masculine level.

Not wanting to miss Erica's opening intro, he shut off the water, stepped out of the shower and dried off with a fluffy forest-green-colored towel that matched the bathroom's decor. Pulling on his favorite pair of sweat shorts, he headed into the living room and turned on his stereo system with a flip of a switch on the wall. A serious male voice filtered from the speakers placed strategically throughout the front rooms with a brief up-to-date newscast, which would then segue into Erica's evening talk show, *Heat Waves.*

Taking advantage of the extra minutes, Ian padded barefoot across the polished hardwood floors leading into the kitchen to retrieve a cold beer. Grabbing a long neck of his favorite brew, he shut the refrigerator and twisted the cap off the bottle. Unerringly, his gaze was drawn to the piece of paper attached to the surface of the white enameled door by a magnet for pizza delivery. The color publicity photo of Erica McCree he'd printed from the radio station's website stared back at him, eliciting a slow burn of desire he was accustomed to feeling when it came to her. After enjoying Erica's company on the air and candidly debating intimate issues with her as if they were old lovers, he'd been curious to see what she looked like, to know if her appearance matched her incredibly rich voice and uninhibited personality.

He'd been surprised, but not at all disappointed with his discovery. He liked what he saw, was fascinated by the contrast of the unabashed image Erica projected on the air and the photo of the real woman. While she came across as an experienced sex critic on her show, there was something soft and feminine about her in the picture, coupled with an underlying mystery that captivated and intrigued him. Deep brown eyes highlighted with gold flecks sparkled with an abundance of amusement, and the sassy tilt of her head caused silky waves of honey-blond hair to brush her shoulders. Without a doubt, the mischievous smile curving her glossy lips gave him the impression she was hiding a wealth of secrets from her listening audience.

And he wanted to unveil every single one of them and discover who the real Erica McCree was—talk-show vixen with experience to back up her provocative topics, or a sensitive woman masquerading as an accomplished siren? It was a question he didn't have an answer to—yet.

The newscaster finished his update and weather report, informed listeners to stay tuned for the upcoming segment of *Heat Waves,* then made a smooth transition into a jingle for a local furniture store.

Ian headed back out to the living room, stopped by the floor-to-ceiling windows dominating one long wall and took a swallow of his beer. At sixteen floors up and just off Lake Shore Drive, he had a million-dollar view of Grant Park and Chicago Harbor. The twinkling lights of sailboats and yachts drifting on Lake Michigan were an awesome sight to behold, especially at night. A wry smile touched his mouth when he considered his choice of drink and the old, threadbare sweat shorts he wore, both of which were at odds with the luxury and opulence surrounding him.

He shook his head, still amazed that he'd come so far. From a scrappy, poor kid whose mother was more interested in her next quick fix rather than the welfare of her son, to a wealthy CEO of an investment firm that had been turned over to his care when David Winslow, his mentor and surrogate father, had retired. Poverty was far behind him now, yet Ian still couldn't quite get used to the fact that he had more money than he knew what to do with. How he'd gotten to this point in his life sometimes seemed like a blur, most likely because he'd allowed the guilt and pain of a more devastating, personal loss to blunt his emotions.

For years after his fiancée's death, getting through each day had been a laborious task of forcing his mind to focus on nothing but stocks, bonds, mutual funds, and making big money for his clients. He hadn't realized the tedious, monotonous rut he'd dug himself into...until Erica McCree. Their on-the-air connection and chemistry gave him a boost of energy and enthusiasm that no investment deal could compare with. She gave him something to look forward to at the end of a mentally exhausting day— excitement, thrills and a physical craving that made him feel alive again when he hadn't even realized just how dead he'd been inside.

With a deep breath, he finished his beer and turned

back to the living room just as Erica announced her intro and the topic of her show.

"This is Erica McCree, and you're listening to WTLK and Chicago's most titillating talk show, *Heat Waves,* which pretty much sums up the weather lately. Hot. Sultry. Humid." Her voice grew soft and seductive, her next words rolling off her tongue like a satisfied purr. "Hmm, sounds like a night of great sex, doesn't it?"

Husky, feminine laughter drifted around Ian, courtesy of his sound system, warming him in a way the outside weather couldn't. Awareness and heat made a mockery of the cool shower he'd taken and the air-conditioning lowering the temperature of the air swirling around him.

"I'd like to share a story with you, which will lead into tonight's discussion. Recently I went out on a date and the guy I was with spent most of it on his cell phone," she told her audience, her tone more amused than annoyed. "And when he wasn't talking to a third party, he was checking out other women. However, at the end of the date he expected more than a good-night kiss. He didn't get it, by the way."

This time Ian chuckled, at Erica's impudent attitude and the fact that she seemed to take delight in rejecting the other man's advances after being ignored most of the night. Not that he could blame her for turning the guy down. Indeed, the infatuated part of him reveled in the knowledge that she'd spent that particular night alone.

"The whole incident got me wondering, what does a man find sexy about a woman? What catches his interest, what keeps him calling, and what ultimately turns him on—in bed and out? So, guys, what turns *you* on about a woman and keeps you coming back for more?"

She let the dangling question ignite imaginations as a light jazz tune rolled into another advertisement. Ian set his empty beer bottle on the end table, grabbed the portable phone and settled himself on the couch. Luxurious brushed-suede fabric caressed his bare skin and added to the anticipation within him as he contemplated Erica's question. What made him return to her show night after night? What kept him calling? What ultimately turned him on?

She'd find out soon enough, when it was their turn to debate tonight's topic.

Minutes later she was back on the air with a caller. "So, Derek, what grabs your interest and keeps your fire burning when it comes to one special woman?"

"Long legs that end in stilettos and big breasts in tight shirts rock my world."

"I take it you're not concerned about intelligent conversation at this point," Erica commented jokingly. "Do her breasts have to be real, or can they be artificially enhanced?"

"Doesn't matter. The bigger, the better."

"Hmm, well, I think you just took half the female population out of the running, myself included." Humor infused her voice, making Ian imagine an indulgent grin spreading across her face. "Thanks for your opinion, Derek. Next up is Larry. What turns you on?"

"I like a woman who's a quiet, demure lady in public, but a slut in the bedroom."

"So, you want your cake and be able to eat it, too?" Erica said without missing a beat.

"That's one way of putting it," Larry replied, his voice gruff and macho. "Women should be seen and not heard in public, and accommodating to my needs in bed."

"I didn't realize some of us were still living in the Dark Ages," she replied lightly, in a way that couldn't be construed as insulting. "I'm sure the woman you're looking for is out there somewhere, so keep up the search. Good luck, Larry."

She disconnected that line and picked up another. "Welcome to the show, Kent," Erica continued, introducing the next caller and keeping the flow of conversation upbeat and lively. "What's your opinion on this subject?"

"I'm attracted to the way a woman walks, which is what grabbed my attention with my current girlfriend. If she's confident and secure about herself it'll show in the way she holds her head high, her straight shoulders, and the subtle sway of her hips. Confidence is a huge turn-on for me, especially when that assertiveness carries into the bedroom and sex."

"Wow, I like that," she said sincerely, seemingly mulling over her latest caller's perspective on what turned a man's head. "Ladies, take note. I think Kent has a very valid point you might want to consider in your own attempts to catch a man's eye. Let your body do the talking. Confidence *is* sexy, especially when it's worn on the outside. It'll make him wonder what's beneath that layer of confidence, and it wouldn't hurt to back up that self-assurance with something equally confident and sexy when he strips away that outer layer. Garters, teddies, barely-there panties—the possibilities are endless, and without a doubt he'll appreciate the extra effort."

Unbidden, images of Erica in sinful, sensual lingerie projected in Ian's mind like an intimate centerfold. He envisioned her lying across his bed, silk and lace contouring to gently rounded curves, and sheerer material caressing her soft skin and accentuating everything feminine about her—breasts, hips, thighs. Her rich hair would flow over his pillow, and the come-hither look in

her eyes would match the inviting smile on her lips that
said, *I want you.*

The fantasy teased Ian's senses and his blood pumped
heavily in his veins. Shifting on the couch as his body
responded to that visual stimulation, he shook those
erotic thoughts from his head and continued listening to
the show. He found himself entertained and enlightened
by the various responses other men offered Erica—along
with a few women who deemed it necessary to share their
point of view about the question of the night. The callers'
answers were diverse and insightful, and Erica's come-
backs were playful, spontaneous and sometimes a little
outrageous.

At ten-forty-five, Erica broke for a commercial. Right
on cue, Ian picked up his cordless phone to call into the
station. It was his turn to state his opinion on the matter
and seduce Erica's imagination with his definition of
what he found sexy about women—about *her*—and what
kept him coming back for more.

He hit the speed dial and waited for the fun to begin.

ERICA TURNED OFF HER MIKE, slipped off her headset and
leaned back in her chair with a long sigh. She lifted her
hair off the back of her damp neck, hoping for relief from
the stifling air in the small, crowded soundproof studio
where the DJs broadcasted their shows. The station's an-
cient air conditioner was on the fritz again, which wasn't
a surprise to any of the employees on the fifth floor of
the downtown Chicago building. After chugging all day
to ward off the summer heat wave, the unit was now
spitting out sporadic spurts of cool air, making her body
alternate between gratitude and hot flashes depending on
the unit's temperament.

Right now, she had a sheen of perspiration on her

warm skin, which was sticky and clammy, but felt great when she caught one of those rare gusts of cold air from the cantankerous air conditioner. She'd worn a denim miniskirt and thin blouse, and since no one was left at the station except herself, the station's producer and program director, Carly, and the rent-a-guard outside, she'd stripped down to her cotton tank top. Anything more and she'd be walking the fine line of indecency, not that any of her callers would ever know.

She kept an eye on the computer monitor flashing in front of her, watching the time limit on the current reel of commercials before she had to be back on the air. Opening a side drawer, she found a scrunchie and pulled her hair into a high ponytail, then glanced to the left where Carly occupied the glass-enclosed booth next to hers and was screening incoming calls for the next segment.

The radio station was a small operation with few frills, and everyone had more than one job to perform in order to keep things running smoothly. While the pay was mediocre, Erica was doing what she enjoyed and was completely self-sufficient—unlike her mother and sister, who had no idea how to support themselves. And she was gradually making a name for herself.

Three years ago she'd moved from California to Chicago after breaking off a live-in relationship that had turned too controlling. The relationship had nearly stripped her of everything that was important to her and made her realize she was better off alone. With a degree in communications to her credit, she'd landed her first DJ job at a blues station, working the grueling, 2:00 to 6:00 a.m. graveyard shift. After two years of being blatantly passed up for various promotions and premium time slots, she'd started searching elsewhere for employment. She'd applied at WTLK on a whim and was offered a job.

She'd always wanted to be a radio talk-show host, and the then station's owner, Marvin Gilbert, had given her free rein for her time slot—bless his weak heart that had given out on him three months ago. He'd backed her decision to bring something sexy and fun to the station's program, while Virginia, his snooty young wife of two years had frowned upon airing such a "trashy" show. In fact, there wasn't anything she'd liked about the station, the programming or the people who worked for her husband.

Now that Marvin was gone, it remained to be seen what Virginia had planned for the station and WTLK's employees. Most of them figured they'd be out a job by the end of the year.

"You okay in there?" Carly asked, her voice transmitted through a speaker on Erica's control console.

She checked the advertisement reel and had two minutes left before it was show time again. "It would be nice if Virginia would spring for a new air-conditioning unit so we all wouldn't melt or suffer from heat stroke the rest of the summer."

Carly made a sound of disgust. "Being the tightwad that we always knew she was, she's made it perfectly clear that she isn't going to spend a penny on this station and repairs if she doesn't have to. Not with Marvin cold in his grave and her sitting on only a quarter of the inheritance she believed he was worth."

Unable to help herself, Erica smirked, remembering Virginia's childish tirade after Marvin's will had been read and she'd realized he'd frittered away a good amount of his money. She'd been appalled to discover that the most valuable thing she now owned was a run-down radio station that was barely making ends meet and turned over a very small profit.

"I miss the old geezer," Erica said with a sigh.

"Yeah, we all do," Carly agreed with a hint of sadness, then screened another caller for Erica's show.

Reaching for her water bottle, Erica took a drink of the lukewarm liquid that wet her parched throat but didn't quench her thirst. "Damn, but it's hot in here," she muttered, wishing she had more time to get a cup of ice from the machine down the hall.

"Well, prepare yourself, sweetie. The temperature is about to rise." Carly waggled her brows lasciviously. "Hottie alert on line three."

Erica glanced at the clock on the wall to check the time, and knew immediately who her good friend was referring to. "You have no idea whether Ian is a hottie, or not."

"How can he not be with that deep, orgasmic voice that makes a woman's pulse pound?" From the other side of the thick glass that separated them, Carly feigned a rapturous shiver that made her whole body shimmy. "And I'm not just talking about the pulse in my wrist!"

Erica rolled her eyes, but couldn't deny that her nightly caller had that same effect on her, too. But it wasn't only his bedroom voice that made her nerves tingle and her body crave a dozen shameless kinds of desire. It was his effortless way of making her feel as though she was the sole focus of his attention, that their sensual debates were just a prelude to something more forbidden and satisfying.

A ridiculous thought, considering she had no intention of ever meeting him in person. It wasn't that she considered him an overzealous fan, but she didn't want to spoil the rare chemistry and connection that sizzled between them on the air. He was a delicious, exciting fantasy, one she shared with her listeners. She'd learned years ago that it was safer to indulge in sexy daydreams and erotic night fantasies than to get involved with some men. Her fantasies usually surpassed anything reality could offer. Case in point was the self-centered jerk she'd recently dated who'd inspired tonight's topic.

"You and I both know that a voice can be very deceiving," she told Carly, having met a few of her regular listeners at public relations events. "And a guy with a voice as incredible as Ian's has to have been short-changed in the looks department. He can't possibly have it all."

"You're probably right," Carly agreed with a quick, flashing grin. "But it's a nice fantasy, so I'd appreciate it if you didn't shatter the illusion in my mind."

Erica swiped the back of her hand across her warm, damp forehead and quirked a brow her friend's way. "Hey, you've got your own real-life hottie, so don't be fantasizing about *my* callers."

Carly batted her lashes in return, her expression all too knowing. "My, aren't *we* a tad possessive about Mr. Sexy Voice."

"I'm just looking out for Dan's welfare." Dan was the station's manager, a real gentlemanly prince among men, and Carly's main squeeze. The two of them had been skirting their attraction for months and finally hooked up when Erica had asked Dan to join them for a Sunday evening out at a popular nightclub. Carly and Dan had danced the evening away and had been seeing each other exclusively ever since.

A carefree shrug lifted Carly's shoulder. "Well, if Dan doesn't want me lusting after other sexy male voices, he needs to put out the goods, if you get my drift."

Erica slipped her headset on, her fingers inches away from pressing the button that would put her back on the air. "You haven't slept together yet?" She couldn't contain her surprise.

"No. He said he didn't want to go too fast, and wanted to take things slow and easy. He's got way more control than I do," she said in obvious frustration, which was quickly replaced with an unraveling, fanciful sigh. "On the other hand, the foreplay has been incredible and I'm most definitely more *relaxed* these days, if you know what I mean."

Light laughter bubbled out of Erica. Oh, yeah, she knew *exactly* what Carly was alluding to—orgasms aplenty, no doubt in varied and innovative ways. "I'm truly envious." Erica had been the recipient of too many unmemorable wham-bam-thank-you-ma'ams in her sexual past. While she had nothing against quickie sex, she'd often wished she could find a man with slow hands instead of quick gropes that left her wanting. One of those rare breed of males who appreciated the gradual build-up of a hot seduction.

Someone like Ian...

She rejected the tantalizing thought as quickly as it formed, content with him being a safe, *undemanding* fantasy. She had her own personal illusions she didn't want to shatter. "Enjoy Dan's attention and all that sexual tension leading up to the big night, and be glad that you don't have to rely on battery-operated devices to take the edge off of your physical needs."

"Point taken, but just for the record, I've decided to turn the tables on lover boy until *he's* begging *me* for release for a change." Carly pressed a few buttons on her console and held up her hand, fingers splayed, for Erica to see. "Five seconds to airtime and Mr. Sexy

Voice. Like every one else who's been listening to your show for the past few weeks, I'm dying to hear his take on tonight's topic.''

Erica was equally curious to discover what turned Ian on about a woman, and silently admitted that she'd been anticipating his call and the fun, playful, sensually charged repartee that usually ensued from their conversation. Her heart beat a little faster as she watched Carly count down the seconds on her fingers until her fisted hand indicated Erica's cue to begin her show.

"This is Erica McCree and you're listening to *Heat Waves* on WTLK," she announced into her microphone as the last bit of jazz faded into the background. "We've heard some fascinating comments on what men find irresistible about women. I know tonight's discussion has certainly enlightened *me,* but there's more to come so let's get back to business. If you listen to *Heat Waves* on a regular basis, then you already know my next caller, who's become something of a special guest on my show."

She pressed the button for line three, putting her fantasy man on the air. "Hello, Ian. How are you tonight?"

"Hot," he said huskily.

She laughed as he echoed her current sentiment while she sat in her warm, stuffy booth. "Aren't we all? Is it the heat wave that has you so hot, or something else?" she dared.

"The heat and humidity started it, but I'm in an air-conditioned room so I can't say that my rise in temperature is all weather-related."

She didn't miss the insinuation behind his words, or the frisson of immediate awareness that shot through her. "Sounds like maybe a cold shower might be in order."

"Umm, already tried that." A mischievous note laced

his low, mellow baritone. "It was only a temporary relief."

Oh, he was very bad. And very, very good. "I'm glad the heat didn't keep you from calling. Inquiring minds want to know...what's the first thing that you notice about a woman, and what holds your attention beyond that first glance?"

"Intelligence and a sense of humor gets my initial attention," he said thoughtfully. "I've discovered lately that laughter is a great tension-reliever."

"So is good sex." As soon as the words left Erica's mouth and traveled miles across the airwaves, she dropped her head into her hands and shook it—hard. She wouldn't know good sex if it snuck up behind her and bit her on the butt, not that her listening audience needed to know that. And she hadn't slept with a guy in so long she could almost requalify as a virgin. Amazing the flaws and inexperience she could conceal being sequestered away in a private booth with only a microphone to link her to the outside world.

"I like the way you think." She heard a lazy grin in his voice, felt the vibrations curl through her belly. "Hey, we might have just discovered the ultimate relaxation technique. Can you imagine what laughter and sex together could do for a person's stress level?"

All she could imagine at the moment was sex with *him* and subduing her own spiraling need and deep ache, and knew she had a long, restless night ahead of her. "How about we save that topic for another show?"

"Fair enough. Let's see..." he continued, his voice a low rumble of sound that found and touched all those secret places within her. "I'm also attracted to a woman's mouth. Soft, glossy lips made for long, slow, deep kisses, and sexy smiles that make me feel like I'm the only one she desires…''

Unconsciously, her straight teeth tugged on her bottom lip, and she tasted the remnants of the pale-pink, cotton-candy-flavored gloss she wore. Sweet. Slick. Silky. Liquid heat settled low as her mind conjured images of him nibbling off the sugared taste, his tongue sliding across her parted lips, then delving into the heated depths of her mouth in an all-consuming, electrifying kiss. To her mortification, a small noise, much like a moan, escaped her throat before she could stop it.

"Are you okay?" he asked.

Her face flushed to the tips of her ears. One glance at Carly in the booth next to hers and her friend's comical expression and she knew that way too many people had been privy to that very telltale sound.

"Hot night, dry throat." The excuse was a paltry one, but served its purpose, and she followed it up with a long gulp of her water.

"I also like silky, thick hair," he continued, leaving her embarrassing slip behind, thank goodness. "There's something incredibly erotic about having a woman's hair wrapped around my hands and being able to hold her where I want her."

More images flooded her brain. Of him coaxing her down the length of his body until her lips brushed silken steel and he urged her strokes to a slow, seductive rhythm. Of being pinned beneath a hard, muscular body, the fingers tangling in her hair holding her head back as he ravished her neck and gradually moved lower to take the straining tip of her breast into the heated depths of his mouth…

A shudder coursed through Erica and her too sensitive nipples tightened and rasped against her tank top. She swallowed in an attempt to regulate her breathing, which had become quick and shallow.

"But it's chemistry that will keep me coming back night after night," he added, pulling her from her indulgent musings.

Was that why he called in night after night? Did he feel the sizzle between them, too? The thought was a heady, thrilling one. "Chemistry is always a good reason to keep things going, but how do you keep the initial spark from fizzling?"

"Being spontaneous helps. Not knowing what to expect, yet going with the flow and enjoying whatever happens will keep things between a couple fresh and exciting. Do you like spontaneity, Erica?"

His too-easy shift in topic startled her and made her skin prickle with renewed awareness. "I wouldn't be a talk-show host if I didn't," she replied smoothly, and quickly turned the questioning back to him, before he had a chance to put *her* in the spotlight. "Let's get down to the nitty-gritty of things, Ian. What is it about a woman that keeps you happy in the bedroom?"

While he thought about his answer, her gaze shifted to the phone lines. Only one line blinked, which was amazing in itself since the station had been inundated with calls before Ian's appearance. She'd noticed a nightly decline in calls when she was on the air with Ian, as if the city of Chicago was just as riveted by this man as she was.

"I like a woman who's comfortable enough with her body and sensuality that she's willing to try new and different things."

Erica's lashes fluttered closed, another *huge* mistake on her part, she realized as a silhouette of a naked couple making love out in the open in carnal, wanton ways flashed behind her eyelids. She quickly snapped her eyes back open before she got caught up in the fantasy, and wondered how far Ian was willing to go to try a little spice and variety. "Are you an exhibitionist, Ian?"

He chuckled. "I don't think so. I think it would be fun and a bit forbidden making love in risky places and being a little adventurous, but actually *getting* caught isn't something that excites me."

Catching a movement from Carly's studio, Erica glanced that way and found her friend fanning herself with her hand and mouthing the words *hot stuff.* She smiled, shook her head and turned back to her microphone and Ian. "What else turns you on?"

"A woman who isn't afraid to tell me what she likes and what feels good." He paused for a moment. "I like being a part of a woman's pleasure, and it really turns me on when I hear that she's enjoying herself and what I'm doing to her."

Erica shifted in her seat and crossed one leg over the other. The insides of her thighs were damp from the heat, or maybe something else she refused to think about. "So, you like a vocal lover?"

"Soft moans are nice, so is an occasional 'that feels good' or other sexy talk. It lets me know that I'm doing something right and my partner is having a good time, too."

Erica sifted through her own previous sexual encounters, trying to remember if she was a moaner, or not. She couldn't recall any memorable experiences and was doubtful that she'd been on the receiving end of anything worthwhile or rapturous enough to moan about.

"So, Erica, what catches *your* eye with a man?"

The bold turnabout startled her, but she managed to

hold tight to her composure. "That wasn't tonight's question."

"Turnabout is fair play." His lazy tone was teasing, but underscored with a private challenge Erica recognized. "I'm sure your listeners are just as curious as I am to hear what catches your interest with a man."

As was Carly, judging by her friend's wide-eyed, attentive stare through the glass partition. While Erica hadn't anticipated being on the receiving end of tonight's question, Ian had effectively and brazenly cornered her. To maintain her integrity with her listeners who trusted her with their secrets, she knew she ought to share hers in return.

"I'm attracted to a man's eyes," she said, her voice lowering to a husky pitch. "Not necessarily the color, but the way he looks at me, like I'm the only woman in the room, even if there are a dozen other women around. It makes me feel feminine and sexy and very, very confident."

"And confidence is very good," he murmured, echoing a previous caller's preference.

"It has its advantages, and keeps a man guessing." Absently, she touched the erratic pulse at the base of her throat and found her skin moist and hot to the touch. Desire sharpened her senses, making her crave a more masculine caress.

"What turns you on, Erica?"

"A slow seduction," she said, feeling hypnotized by their conversation, as if she were speaking to him alone. "I like a man who'll take the time to learn what sends me over the edge. Mentally and physically."

"Which, in my estimation, equates to mind sex and foreplay, and lots of it." Humor deepened his voice. "You like *fun* sex."

It's what she *imagined* she liked. "As opposed to serious sex?" A grin quirked the corner of her mouth.

"You want to have a good time in the bedroom," he clarified. "And like me, you're open to diversity and new experiences."

Bingo. Which left the field wide open for her since her sexual encounters were so limited.

He knew her too well, without really knowing her at all. It was as though he'd spent the past month learning everything about her…intimate details he'd coaxed from her while seducing her imagination with provocative, arousing banter.

She was aroused now…hot and aching and wishing for release from all the tension stringing her nerves tight.

Her computer screen flashed the countdown to a commercial break, saving her from having to find a witty comeback when her mind was completely numb and free of any clever rejoinders.

She inhaled deeply and released it slowly and quietly. "As always, Ian, your opinion on tonight's topic has been duly noted by many. This is Erica McCree and thank you for keeping the dial tuned to WTLK," she said to her listeners. "I'll be back with more of your calls right after these messages."

The phone lines lit up again and thrummed to life, putting Carly to work screening calls for the next segment. Off the air, Erica said to her fantasy man, "Thanks for calling, Ian."

"It was my pleasure."

The word *pleasure* held a dozen different connotations, each one an erotic promise that filled her with an intense longing.

"Same time tomorrow night?" he asked.

She grinned to herself, hating to end their brief time

together when she knew she'd be going home in a few hours to a very quiet, empty apartment—with her battery-operated device as company instead of a flesh-and-blood male.

Instead of Ian.

"Yeah, same time tomorrow night," she agreed, already looking forward to the call.

2

"LAST NIGHT'S SHOW was great."

The shy, quiet voice grabbed Erica's attention. Smiling, she glanced up from braiding Tori's hair and met the other woman's gaze in the mirror in front of them. Unable to help herself, Erica inwardly winced at the painful-looking bruise coloring the left side of Tori's cheek and the cut splitting her bottom lip. And those were only the injuries that were visible. No doubt, Tori's heart and soul were just as broken.

Tori Williams was a battered wife, and one of the many women who sought refuge at the Camenson Women's Shelter three blocks from the radio station. Erica had been visiting the shelter for the past eight months, volunteering her time a few days a week in whatever capacity her help was needed. Emotional support and a listening ear seemed to be the biggest necessity. So was just being a friend to the women who craved the kind of understanding only another female could offer.

Erica had never been abused or battered, but when she was thirteen she'd witnessed a volatile relationship first-hand between her mother and a boyfriend. After months of enduring verbal and physical degradation that had escalated to more menacing threats, her mother had finally sought refuge at a women's shelter with her two daughters because they'd had no other place to go.

Unfortunately, that violent relationship hadn't stopped

Sharon McCree's behavior of hooking up with men who were bad for her and took advantage of her insecurities. But the terrifying situation had changed Erica from a naive little girl to a young woman who found herself very cautious when it came to men. The incident had shaken her and cemented her belief that completely relying on a man left a woman too defenseless, vulnerable and needy. She'd seen the pattern with her mother, who was working on marriage number five in her ongoing quest to be supported financially, regardless of the emotional cost to herself or her daughters. Erica's older sister, Daphne, had followed in their mother's footsteps and had married a wealthy older man who placed certain restrictions on his young wife—unrealistic restrictions, in Erica's opinion. Erica could never understand how her sister accepted a loveless, childless marriage. It was a matter of security, Daphne had told her. But to Erica, security came at too high a price—a loss of independence and self-reliance.

Erica had been there once and the experience remained a strong reminder of how important it was for her to be true to herself and make her own way in life. After dating Paul for six months, she'd found herself entangled in a one-sided, dominating relationship that had nearly stripped her of her independence and confidence. Luckily she'd ended things with Paul and moved on after he'd delivered his ultimatum, but Erica now knew how easy emotions and insecurities could get in the way of straight-thinking. Now she preferred being single and self-sufficient. Personally as well as professionally, she alone was in charge of the direction of her future.

Unfortunately some women, such as Tori, didn't realize they had the choice and fortitude to make their futures better and brighter, instead of enduring a controlling marriage. This was the young woman's third stay in the women's shelter in the past six months, which led Erica to believe it might not be her last. Not if she didn't find the fortitude to divorce her abusive husband. And Tori didn't have only herself to consider. She needed to think about the welfare of her five-year-old daughter, Janet, as well.

With an inward sigh, Erica redirected her thoughts back to the present and Tori's comment. "What were you doing up that late?" she chastised lightly as she continued to weave the young woman's brunette hair in a tight braid. "You should have been in bed getting a good night's rest."

Her shoulder lifted in a small shrug. "I couldn't sleep." The angst in Tori's hazel eyes spoke of nightmares that no doubt plagued her. "Besides, it was much more fun listening to you and Ian talk about what's attractive in the opposite sex."

If her evening show took Tori's mind off her grief and problems for a few hours, then Erica couldn't deny her that pleasure. "The man is very opinionated, don't you think?" she asked, to keep the easy flow of conversation going between the two of them.

"I like his opinions," Tori said softly, a rare, impish smile turning up one corner of her mouth. "He seems like a really nice guy. And it's obvious that he has a thing for you."

Erica secured the tip of the braid with an elastic band, intrigued by the woman's remark. "You think so?"

She nodded. "We all do." She nodded toward the other women in the shelter around them. "Me and the other girls can't wait to hear you and Ian on the radio. He's just so…well…"

"Sexy?" A blush stained Tori's pale cheeks at Erica's accurate guess and she laughed. "The man does have a to-die-for voice, but it's just a show, and my debates with Ian are pure entertainment.''

But even she had to admit that at times it felt like so much more than simple, playful fun. Amusing diversion or not, the man stoked a fire deep inside of her and evoked a wellspring of need she had a hard time putting aside after her show ended and she headed home in the early morning hours…*alone.*

"Your conversations with Ian are different from those with your other callers," Tori said as she stood, her expression thoughtful. "It's like the two of you are dating on the air."

"That's certainly an interesting concept." Erica grinned as they headed into an adjoining room furnished with a few used couches, chairs and a big-screen TV that accommodated the women and kids that stayed at the shelter. Catching sight of Janet working on a puzzle in the kid's corner, Erica waggled her fingers at the little girl and received a smile and enthusiastic wave in return.

Tori cast Erica a sidelong glance brimming with curiosity. "Do you ever wonder what Ian looks like, and if he's really such a nice guy in person?"

Erica had to be honest. "Yeah, I've wondered, but it's safer this way, you know?"

Tori's eyes widened. "Do you think he's a stalker?"

"Oh, no. Not at all," she quickly reassured Tori with a shake of her head.

Erica instinctively knew that Ian's brand of flirtation was harmless—the only danger he posed was to her sorely deprived libido and her overactive senses. She believed his interest was just as genuine as hers, but he'd never crossed any professional boundaries that would put her on the defensive or make her worry about his intentions.

"I just meant that Ian's a nice fantasy," Erica clarified. "For me and hundreds of other women who find his voice and on-the-air personality so mesmerizing." She sent the other woman a secret wink. "And there's nothing wrong with fantasies. There's no risk involved, and no expectation from either party, so it's safe to let your imagination sweep you away."

Tori tipped her head, her fingers playing over the end of the braid that fell over her shoulder. "So you don't mind sharing him with thousands of listeners?"

"He's not really mine," Erica said, taking her purse from one of the high cupboards in the living room. "And let's face it, the guy might have a voice that could seduce a nun, but he's probably a couch potato with a beer belly and receding hairline."

Tori laughed, the sound a little hoarse from disuse. "Not in *my* fantasy, he doesn't."

"Exactly." Not that a man's looks mattered to Erica, but reality just couldn't be as good as the mental image she and every female listener had no doubt conjured of Ian. "In our minds, he can be whatever we want him to be. Personally, I'm thinking Tom Cruise." She grinned.

The other woman's eyes sparkled, and she whispered, "Russell Crowe for me."

"Yum," Erica agreed, glad to see a shift in Tori since she'd arrived at the shelter a few hours ago. The other woman's eyes were brighter now, her complexion not nearly as pale as it had been earlier. Her straightened posture replaced the stooped shoulders and the sense of dejection that had cloaked her. The changes were slight, but enough to make Erica feel as though her visit today had served a purpose.

"Do you have to leave so soon?" Tori asked, a thread of disappointment in her voice.

She checked her watch and sent Tori a regretful look. "I'm afraid so. I got a call from my station manager this morning to attend a mandatory meeting at 3:00 p.m. sharp, and I'm already pushing it timewise." Dan hadn't been forthcoming with details of the staff meeting on the phone, but the urgency in his voice led Erica to believe it was very important. "I'll be back this weekend."

"Okay," Tori said softly.

Erica was hoping the other woman would have said, "I'll be here," but the words didn't come. Erica wasn't completely surprised, suspecting Tori would return to her husband out of a sense of obligation and fear, and the vicious cycle would start all over again.

Erica's heart twisted at the disturbing thought, but she knew there was little she could do to sway the other woman's decision if she was intent on leaving the protection of the shelter. Erica could only hope that the resident counselors were able to convince Tori that she had the internal strength to make it on her own. She deserved so much better than a man who took his temper out on her.

And just in case Erica didn't see Tori that weekend, she pulled her into a gentle hug and said, "Take care of yourself, and Janet, too."

"I will," Tori promised, clinging to Erica for a few extra seconds.

Erica said a quick goodbye to the other women, the counselors and the children, then headed out into the sweltering afternoon heat and humidity. Sliding behind the wheel of her compact car that had driven her and her small bundle of belongings to Chicago three years ago and was still going strong, she drove the short distance to the station. Once there, she entered the run-down building and jogged up the five flights of stairs for her daily bit of exercise and grabbed a diet soda and bag of chips from the vending machine. Breathless, overheated, her skin damp with perspiration, she burst into Dan's small office with thirty seconds to spare.

"Leave it to you to make a graceful entrance," Dan, the station's manager, drawled from where he sat behind his small metal desk.

She waved a hello to the rest of the crew who worked various shifts at the station and flashed a grin at her boss. "I've heard that you spank your tardy employees," she teased right back. "And I don't think that Carly would appreciate sharing that punishment with the rest of us."

"Thank God *I* made it in time," Ray, the early-evening disc jockey said meaningfully, which coaxed a round of amused chuckles from WTLK's other radio personalities. They all knew Dan and Carly were dating, and ribald jokes and antics were common between the friendly and outgoing twenty-and thirty-somethings that worked at the station.

"Very funny, guys," Dan replied with a very bosslike frown, though his tone was good-natured and he took their ribbing in stride.

Erica sat down on a foldout chair, sighing as the chill from the metal seat seeped through the thin rayon material of her short sundress and offered a modicum of relief. True to form, the air-conditioning had seized up again. The bank of windows across one wall were wide open, and a fan swiveled back and forth from a filing cabinet in the corner, stirring the warm air and offering whatever respite it could. It wasn't much with all the extra bodies in the room.

Setting her can of soda on the corner of Dan's desk, Erica ripped open her bag of chips and glanced around the room, noting the absence of Mike and Tim, WTLK's afternoon duo who were currently on the air, and one other person. "What do you know, we're missing...*Carly.*"

As if on cue, the station's producer-program director arrived, her face flushed from the heat and her chin-length bob tumbling around her face in silky disarray. "Sorry I'm late. I got stuck in traffic."

"That's okay," Erica said as she nibbled on a chip, which kept her smirk in plain sight for Carly to see. "We've all noted your tardiness, and Dan will deal with you accordingly once the meeting is over."

"Keep the screams and moans to a minimum so they don't travel over the airwaves," Steve added humorously from the other side of the room.

Carly quickly caught on to the gist of their teasing and cast her boyfriend a seductive look. "Don't worry, I'll make sure Dan uses the velvet whip instead of the leather one."

As soon as Carly settled into the vacant seat next to Erica, Jay—the most pragmatic one of all of them—directed the conversation toward business. "Now that we're all here, what's up, boss?"

Dan leaned forward in his chair and folded his hands on top of his desk. His suddenly grave expression turned the playful atmosphere into a serious discussion. "I received a registered letter this morning from Virginia's attorney. She's selling the station."

Gasps of surprise, groans of disbelief and outright curses echoed in the room. They'd all known the possibility of Virginia putting the station on the market existed, but the reality still caused tension, distress and even anger from some.

"What does this mean for us as employees?" Ray

asked, his concern evident. He'd just recently gotten married and had a baby on the way.

Dan sighed, the sound rife with uncertainty. "Honestly, I have no idea. This sale will either make us or break us as a radio station, depending on who buys WTLK and what they plan to do with the program format. We all know we could go from talk radio one day to inspirational the next." His gaze encompassed everyone in the room, but there were no reassurances in Dan's eyes. He was stating cold, hard facts without sugarcoating the harsh possibilities. "If no one buys the station and Virginia decides to take it as a loss, then we're all out a job. Hell, we might all be out a job even if she does sell the station and the new owners decide to bring in their own radio personalities."

Erica rubbed the sudden ache in her temple, hating like hell the thought of starting over yet again when she was just getting a foothold in the industry and getting her name out to Chicago's listening public. But she'd find another DJ job if she had to. If that's what the sale of the station came down to. It certainly wouldn't be the first time she'd started out fresh and new.

"I do have to say that our ratings are up," Dan continued, putting whatever positive spin on their current predicament that he could. "And those ratings can be used as leverage to entice a buyer to keep the format and programming the way it is. Just as long as the ratings continue to climb and we draw in some big-name advertisers."

Dan flipped through a stack of papers on his desk and glanced at Erica. "While everyone is doing well in their time slots, your ratings have jumped the highest in the shortest amount of time, Erica."

She smiled, pleased with that information. "Great."

A wry grin curved the corners of his mouth. "There's been a definite increase in listeners since your mystery caller, Ian, has become a nightly guest on *Heat Waves*. There's been a certain buzz around town about your talk show, and I've had advertisers calling wanting your time slot for their commercials, and that's a *very* good thing."

Erica's elation dwindled to a small frown. The knowledge that *Ian* was responsible for her increase in ratings took some of the wind out of her sails. She wanted her show to gain notoriety and popularity, but on her *own* merit and not because a sexy voice was stirring interest and mesmerizing her listeners. At the same time, she found it difficult to argue success in any form.

Dan addressed a few more questions and worries, doing his best to keep everyone's panic to a minimum. For now, his main concern was to increase their ratings, and that meant making sure their programs and the issues they chose to talk about were stimulating enough to pique listener interest—and keep them coming back for more.

The way Erica saw things, this was her opportunity to take things to the extreme and ride on that "buzz" Dan had mentioned earlier to create an even *bigger* sensation. If for some reason she found herself hitting the pavement for another job, she wanted to use the high ratings on her professional résumé to land something other than a graveyard shift at another station. She wanted, and needed, her name to be a familiar one.

Finished with the meeting, Dan dismissed the group and everyone shuffled out of his office. Carly hung back, and Erica waited for the room to clear, too, then stood and pitched her empty can and chip bag in the trash next to Dan's desk.

"Thanks for the heads-up on the station being put on the market," she said to Dan, appreciating the honesty and open rapport he maintained with his employees. "It's something none of us wanted to hear, but at least we know what to expect."

He nodded in understanding. "With luck, it'll be a smooth, easy transition for all of us with whoever buys the station."

"*If* someone buys the station."

"I'm trying to think positively," he said, absently pushing his fingers through his already mussed dark brown hair. "And we'll do whatever we can on our end to make the station and programming as enticing as possible. The bottom line is ratings. After that, all we can do is sit tight and wait and see what happens."

Carly perched her hip on the corner of Dan's desk and picked up the clipboard that she'd brought with her to the meeting. She thumbed through the first couple of pages, then glanced at Erica. "By the way, I need a topic heading for tomorrow night's show," Carly said after checking her program outline. "And feel free to spice it up." She waggled her brows.

"How do you feel about orgasms on the air?" Erica asked, tossing out one of the ideas she had in mind. An idea that would no doubt be an interesting and sizzling discussion between her and Ian and generate listener reaction.

Carly grinned. "As long as it isn't your own orgasm on the air so we don't get slapped with an FCC fine, then I say go for it."

"Orgasms it is." Erica slipped the thin strap of her purse over her shoulder and headed for the door. "You coming, Carly? I'll walk with you downstairs."

Carly shook her head. "Dan and I still have the issue of me being tardy to discuss, and it might take a while." Sauntering over to the windows that overlooked the rest of the station, she closed the miniblinds so no one could look into the office. "But I will see you tonight."

Erica caught her friend's drift real quick and grinned. "Hmm. Have fun, you two." She closed the door after exiting.

As for her, she had tomorrow night's program to outline for *Heat Waves*. And that meant browsing through the sexual manuals and books on intimate issues she had at home that gave her the verbal ammunition to back up her chosen topics and sensual discussions on-air.

She might not have street experience when it came to her more provocative subjects, but she was definitely book smart about sexual issues.

And that's all she needed to tantalize her listeners.

"GOOD EVENING, CHICAGO. This is Erica McCree and you're listening to WTLK. With this heat we've been experiencing lately, can you imagine how residents felt during the Great Chicago Fire back in 1871? I'm burning up, how about you?" She released a long, slow breath that traveled over the airwaves like a sultry breeze. "Be sure to stick around for tonight's show, because I'm betting things are going to get a whole lot hotter."

At the sound of Erica's opening intro to her show, Ian stopped from grabbing the file folder with the contract he needed to review before attending a morning meeting, immediately transfixed by the woman who'd occupied his thoughts for the better part of the evening. He didn't realize until that very moment that her familiar, feathery voice was exactly what he'd needed to hear after spending the past two and a half hours fending off the not-so-subtle advances of a female client who'd insisted on talking about her portfolio over dinner.

Jill Grayson's request wasn't an unusual one, and

hooking up with her in the evening suited his own busy schedule just fine. He'd accepted her invitation thinking about the stocks, bonds and IRAs that he'd invested in with her recent divorce settlement. However, it hadn't taken him long to realize that she was more interested in getting lucky with him than hearing about the status of her investment accounts.

Ian shook his head in disbelief. While he'd been discussing the decline in her high-risk stocks over appetizers, she'd been rubbing her bare foot up his pant leg and making an "mmm-mmm good" production of appreciating her oysters in the half shell. During dinner she'd insisted that he taste the different selections on her plate and fed him with *her* fork. She'd then slipped the utensil in her own mouth and licked her lips for good measure. After dessert and coffee, when he'd shown her a projected growth chart for her investments, she'd leaned close in the pretense of getting a better look, pressed her hand on his upper thigh and squeezed affectionately, then let her fingers brush the fly of his slacks. When his body didn't so much as stir from the intimate caress, he'd gently removed her hand from under the table before she grew more brazen.

All the signals for a night of no-strings-attached sex had been evident. But none of Jill's antics, not even her blatant "why don't we finish this at my place" come-on could entice the enthusiasm Ian needed to follow through on a night of slaking her apparent lust. There was a time when he might have taken her up on her casual, one-night-stand offer and indulged in a mindless, unemotional release himself, but he'd taken one glance at his watch, noted the time of 9:30 p.m., and knew he had a hotter date waiting for him—one he refused to miss. Not even for uncomplicated sex, which suddenly held little appeal to him.

Much to Jill's disappointment he'd turned down her overture and called it a night, claiming work as an excuse. It was a half-truth, though she clearly didn't believe him. He *did* have a contract to review for a morning meeting, which had brought him back to his office to pick up the paperwork. Knowing he'd never make it back to his penthouse in time for Erica's show, he'd turned on the stereo on his credenza and decided to mix business with pleasure. He'd review the contract during commercials, and enjoy Erica when she was on the air.

"Last night we talked about what men find sexy about women," she said, recounting the details of her previous show. "What catches his interest, what turns him on, and what ultimately keeps him coming back for more. Tonight I thought we'd continue on that same topic, but take it one step further than the initial spark that usually leads to asking a woman out on a date."

Intrigued as always about where her discussion was heading, Ian shrugged out of his suit coat, then sat down and settled into his soft leather executive chair. He loosened the knot of his tie to give himself extra breathing room, and let himself unwind and relax after the trying evening he'd had.

"I've often wondered, what should a guy expect at the end of a first date? A kiss? Sex? And what defines what will happen once the evening is over?" She let her questions linger seductively, giving her listeners time to formulate an answer of their own. "Guys, I'd love to get your take on this question. And women, how do you feel about putting out at the end of a date? What do *you* expect? The phone lines are open, so give me a call and tell me what you think."

Erica's monologue segued into a reel of commercials. Taking advantage of the break, Ian opened the folder on his desk to peruse the paperwork, but his attempt to concentrate on the legal jargon in front of him proved futile. Instead, his mind swirled with other tempting thoughts... the most prominent of which was what it would be like to spend the evening with Erica. On a date. Talking in person. Laughing with her and seeing her brown eyes sparkle with pleasure. Touching her and experiencing the flash of mutual desire between them without any barriers.

And where would all that sizzling chemistry lead? To a sweet kiss? A deeper embrace? Or a hot tumble in bed? Ian had his own ideas of what he'd want out of a first date with Erica, and wondered if she'd be pleased or disappointed with the slow, provocative approach filtering through his mind.

"This is *Heat Waves* on WTLK, and we're back on the air with Rodney," Erica said, interrupting Ian's private musings with her low, throaty voice. "What do you expect at the end of a date?"

"I'm a go-with-the-flow kind of guy," he replied confidently. "A kiss is great, but I'd be lying if I didn't say that sex at the end of a date is better. If she's giving out all the right sexual signals and being touchy-feely, then I'm definitely going to go for it."

"That's understandable," Erica agreed. "Would sex on the first date change the way you think about her?"

"If she's hot to trot from the beginning of the evening, then yeah, it might make me wonder if she puts out for all the guys she dates," Rodney admitted. "It might sound like a cliché, but I might label her as being easy."

"And would that stop you from asking her out again?"

"Not if I was looking for a good time without strings."

Erica laughed, the husky sound warming Ian deep inside. "Your point has been duly noted, Rodney, though I think your ideals might be a bit dated. Women like sex just as much as men and shouldn't be penalized for that. Thanks for your opinion." She paused, connecting another caller. "Hello, Bruce. How do you feel about this issue?"

"Depends on the woman and the circumstance. I don't go into the date with sex in mind, but no healthy red-blooded guy is going to refuse getting it on with a hot babe if it's clear that's where the date is heading."

Ian exhaled a breath, thinking about his own evening and where it could have led—right into Jill Grayson's bed. He had a healthy libido, that much was evident in the way Erica aroused him with her breathy voice, and how she tempted and tantalized him when they were on the air together. Not to mention the mornings he woke up hard and aching from erotic dreams of making love to her.

He liked sex and enjoyed being with a woman, yet he'd just refused Jill's very open invitation for a night of uncomplicated sex. He recognized that something within him had changed. After too many years of casual relationships that didn't demand anything emotional from him, he was beginning to crave *more*. And it had all started with Erica...but where would it end?

The answer to that question remained frustratingly elusive. He didn't make a habit of obsessing over women, and he sure didn't want Erica to think of him as an over-zealous fan, but there was something between them and he was certain she knew it and felt it, too.

He had no idea what would come of his time with Erica. While he looked forward to their evenings together and their sexy banter, more and more he found himself wanting to take that leap to another level. A face-to-face meeting that would either dispel all the sensual fantasies filling his head, or lend credence to the heat and awareness rippling between them.

Maybe it was time he took that chance.

Putting aside the contract he needed to review, he let that appealing thought take hold and flourish as he continued to listen to her show.

"Well, we've heard from the men out there and what they expect at the end of a first date. The general consensus seems to be that there are naughty girls that guys sleep with, and good girls that you date and end the evening with a chaste kiss. We have Rachel on the line with us tonight. How do you feel about women being stereotyped?"

"It's chauvinistic," Rachel replied bluntly, clearly annoyed. "From what I'm hearing from your callers so far, a woman can't have sex with a guy on a first date without getting a bad rap and being classified as easy, but a man can sleep around and be considered a stud."

"Unfortunately, despite how far women have come in today's society, it sounds like that old double standard is still alive and well in America." Erica sighed and connected the next caller. "What do you expect at the end of a first date, Adam?"

"I might be in the minority," he began cautiously, "but the more I like a girl, the more I want to play it cool and give the relationship time to build. It's all about respect."

"That's great to hear, Adam," Erica said, complimenting the man's values. "Your viewpoint gives a lot of women hope that there are more guys like you out there who are willing to wait for just the right moment to take the relationship into the bedroom."

Ian latched onto Erica's comment, catching the underlying note of wistfulness in her voice. Her longing was
slight, but undeniably there, and it made him smile. She
came across as sexually uninhibited on the air, but there
was something about her he couldn't quite put his finger
on that led him to believe she was a woman who liked
to be courted and slowly, gradually seduced. So many
fascinating contradictions he wanted to explore and un-
ravel.

"The time is ten-forty-five," she said, wrapping up the
first segment of her show. "We'll be back with more
Heat Waves after these messages."

A musical score blended into an advertisement for a
local dry cleaners. Turning down the radio behind him,
Ian hit a button on the speakerphone on his desk, then
punched in the station's number. He received a busy sig-
nal on the first two tries, and made it through on the third.

"WTLK talk radio," a familiar, upbeat feminine voice
greeted Ian, her lilting tone drifting through the speaker
on his phone. "Do you have a comment for tonight's
show?"

"Don't I always, Carly?" he drawled, having long ago
dispensed with formalities with her.

"You're one hell of a punctual guy, Ian. We could set
our clock to your call."

Leaning back in his chair, he propped his shoes up on
the corner of his desk. "I hope being prompt isn't a bad
thing."

"Depends on what we're referring to," she said slyly.
"Hang on for a few seconds and I'll put you on the air
with Erica."

She put him on hold, and as he waited for Erica's
return to the airwaves, he glanced out the plate-glass windows in his office that overlooked the Board of Trade

building and Sears Tower. The office building his mentor had bequeathed to him was a prime piece of real estate, the corner office he'd taken over a few years ago as CEO an executive's dream—spacious, luxurious, with the best panoramic view on the entire floor.

David Winslow had given him so much, when there had been so many days when Ian felt as though he didn't deserve any of the older man's generosity and loyalty. David had trusted him with his daughter first and foremost, even before he'd handed over the reins of the investment firm to Ian, and he'd let the older man down in a way that had forever changed all of their lives. Yet despite the tragic event that had cut Audrey's life short and had consumed Ian with guilt for so many years, the Winslow family still embraced him as one of their own, and Ian would always be grateful for their unconditional warmth and support.

"Hello, Ian," Erica greeted. Her sweet voice echoed through his speakerphone, pulling him from his darker thoughts. "Welcome to the show. Inquiring minds out there are dying to know, what do you expect at the end of a first date? A kiss? Sex? Or something in between?"

He clasped his hands behind his head, formulating his answer with *her* specifically in mind. "I like to take things slow, especially if it's with a woman I really like. Don't get me wrong, sex can be great, even on a first date, but once you cross that boundary it shifts the focus of everything to a physical relationship." And he would know, considering he'd spent the past eight years doing just that.

"And that's a bad thing?" she questioned, making it sound as though jumping right to sex was *her* personal preference, which he didn't believe for a second.

"No," he replied, mulling over the rest of his answer.

"Gratuitous sex is easy and all about satiating physical needs, which is all good and fine if that's what you're after. But if your first date ends up in bed, before you really get to know the other person, it's hard to backtrack to romance and seduction, which can be the best and most exciting part of dating."

"Definite food for thought," she murmured, her breathing a bit deeper than before. "So, how would you end the evening if you were on a date with a woman you *really* liked?"

Again, visions of her danced in his head, with her brilliant, golden-brown eyes and soft, parted lips. Lips he wanted to taste. A mouth he ached to devour. "I'd probably end the night with a kiss."

"So, you're a traditional kind of guy, then?"

Her tone was light and teasing, yet he suddenly felt very serious. Inspired by honesty and a deep-rooted longing he'd locked away when Audrey had died, he told the truth. "Yeah, I guess I am one of those traditional kind of guys." He'd grown up without security and stability, and as an adult found himself holding tight to integrity and the kind of values that had gained him respect with colleagues and friends. He'd like to think women, Erica specifically, found those traits appealing, as well.

He went on. "I like romance and the excitement of flirting, and I like to get to know a woman mentally before making that physical leap."

He wanted to get to know *her* better. Her likes and dislikes. And what *really* turned her on. It had been way too long since a woman had been anything more than an evening or two of company, and he saw tonight's discussion as an opportunity to take his interest in Erica one level higher...but only if she was ready and willing to take that step, too.

He'd never know if he didn't take that chance.

And he would, soon. Very soon.

He returned his attention to seducing her mind. "Holding back can really heat things up between a couple. And besides, kisses are the best kind of foreplay to making love. Especially since kisses aren't limited to a woman's mouth."

A few extra heartbeats passed before she spoke. "What if there's an explosive chemistry between you and your date on your first night out together and you want each other really bad?" she countered, raising the situational stakes. "Would you make an exception and go for it?"

He smiled and absently rubbed his thumb along his jaw and chin. "If I'm considering another date with her, then probably not. All the more reason to let things simmer and build. There's a whole lot to be said for anticipation, you know."

"Hmm. So, you'd still end the night with a kiss, even if the woman you were with made it clear she'd have sex with you?" Her question was infused with incredulity, more for her listeners' benefit and stirring up controversy than any real disbelief on her part, he guessed.

"There are varying degrees of kisses, Erica, and some can be just as good as having sex," he said, his voice lowering to a husky pitch. "A chaste kiss on the cheek works if the date was just okay and there's no chance of a second one. But if that chemistry is there—" *like it is between us* "—and the woman is willing—" *like I imagine you would be* "—I'd most definitely indulge in a hotter, deeper kiss. The kind that is intense and passionate and gets all your juices flowing. The kind that will make you restless with wanting and keeps you coming back for more.

"Where do *you* fall in the scheme of tonight's topic,

Erica?'' Ian asked curiously, turning the tables on her before she had a chance to respond to his comment or redirect the conversation. ''Are you naughty or nice on a first date?''

''How about somewhere in between,'' she murmured silkily.

He chuckled, her evasive answer not surprising him in the least. ''So you're a nice girl with bad-girl tendencies?''

''Yeah.'' He detected a grin in her voice, and something much more personal. ''Then again, it all depends on the guy and that chemistry we've been talking about.''

She was flirting with him. Just as he'd done with her moments earlier. Both of them fanning the flames of their attraction in a very public forum, and now he burned for her.

''Like *our* chemistry?'' he dared, taking a huge risk in elevating their debate to a bold and intimate plateau. ''How do you think an evening between you and me together would end? With a kiss or sex?''

He heard a swift intake of breath, which gave him a small measure of satisfaction. He had shocked the unshockable Ms. McCree.

''I...well...'' She paused, obviously giving herself time to gather her composure. ''That's hard to say. We might hit it off well on the air, but there's no telling what the chemistry would be like between us on a real-live date.''

He sat forward in his chair, recognizing her hedging for the diversion it was. And he was feeling spontaneous and wicked enough to issue her a challenge she wouldn't be able to refuse very easily in front of her faithful listeners.

''You've got a valid point,'' he acknowledged. ''So

why don't you and I go out on a *real* date and find out how it would end?''

Instead of the sassy reply he'd expected, she put him on hold and made a not-so-smooth transition into a commercial for antacids.

3

"OH. MY. *GOD!*" Erica sat in her seat, stunned by what had just happened. Her entire body felt flushed and over-heated, and tonight it had nothing to do with the building's faulty air conditioner and everything to do with the man who'd just issued her an on-the-air challenge. She glanced into the booth next to hers where her friend stood with a goofy grin on her face.

"I can't believe Ian did that," Erica said, tugging off her headset as she vocalized her upset. "On the air, no less!" They'd been flirting, engaging in their nightly ritual of scintillating banter and heating up the airwaves, and then *bam!* "He asked me out on a date in front of thousands of listeners!"

Carly shrugged very unsympathetically. "What can I say other than it's about damn time!"

Erica gaped at her in disbelief. "How can you be such a traitor and side with *him?* What Ian did is like…like…" She grasped for the right words and blurted them out in a rush of breath, *"Emotional black-mail!"*

Carly frowned, her expression turning perplexed. "How do you figure that?"

She waved an impatient hand in the air, the gesture doing nothing to ease her frustration, only serving to stir the stifling, stuffy air around her. "He put me on the spot, *knowing* that if I said no and rejected his overture it would bring on a whole lot of sympathy for *him* with my listeners.'' Her lips stretched into a grim line. "This wasn't supposed to happen.'' *Ever.*

"It was a natural progression, Erica,'' Carly said, her tone much too logical for Erica, who was feeling anything but reasonable after being thrown for such an unexpected loop. "Honestly, I'm surprised it took him this long to ask you out.''

"I liked things the way they *were,* thank you very much.'' No pressure, no expectations. Just harmless fun and playful flirtations. Ha! "What the hell am I going to do now?''

"Well…'' Carly's eyes glowed devilishly. "You can always say yes.''

"Are you nuts?'' Jumping up from her chair, Erica paced her small cubicle, keeping an eye on the two minutes she had left before she had to be back on the air. With Ian. Addressing the issue he'd dropped on her and her listeners.

She groaned. "I didn't ask for this. I don't even know the guy. Not really.'' He was a seductive voice she debated with, and a gorgeous, arousing figment of her imagination. A perfect, illicit fantasy she took home with her at night to keep her company in the darkest hours before dawn.

Now he wanted to become flesh-and-blood real. She shivered at the thought.

"You know him, Erica,'' Carly said, trying to convince her. "Better than you want to admit. The two of you have been on the air together nearly every night for a month.'' She laughed with a small degree of amusement. "Heck, the two of you communicate better than most husbands and wives. You're open, and candid. And you have to agree that all your sexy talk is great fore-play.''

Erica rolled her eyes. "It's entertainment, Carly!"

"So is accepting a date with Ian. Your listeners would eat that up."

They stared at each other through the glass partition, neither one willing to back down.

Carly sighed. "What could it hurt to say yes and go out with him? You've been on blind dates before, and this basically would be the same thing."

"All my blind dates have been disastrous," she reminded her friend pointedly.

"You might get lucky with Ian." She waggled her brows in a very suggestive way. "In more ways than one."

Inhaling a calming breath, Erica dragged her fingers through her loose hair, pulling the strands away from her face. How could she explain to Carly that she didn't want to shatter the fantasy she and Ian had created on the air? That a part of her didn't believe that reality could come close to matching the torrid, perfect fantasies she had about him? That meeting in person could destroy the sensual magic between them? That she harbored insecurities that went way beyond that initial face-to-face meeting with Ian?

"The phone lines are going crazy, and you've got about another thirty seconds before you need to get back on the air." Carly's voice gentled. "It's all about ratings, Erica, and you know that can't hurt any of us right now."

She pointed a finger her friend's way. "Now, *that's* emotional blackmail."

"No, it's the cold, hard truth," she stated bluntly. "But imagine what this could do for your name, *Heat Waves,* and the station."

Erica hated like hell to admit it, but Carly was right. Hadn't she, herself, seen the interest in Ian's nightly calls to the show steadily climb? Her devoted fans were demanding more, mesmerized by her on-air relationship with Ian. Now he was offering her the incentive to keep her listeners' interest piqued in a whole new forum. A very *public* forum.

Her stomach twisted in knots and she chewed on her thumbnail. She disliked the thought of depending on Ian, or anyone else for that matter, to raise her ratings. But she couldn't deny that he'd helped to elevate her standing in radio during the past month. And with the sale of WTLK, her future as a successful talk show DJ was on the line…whether with this station, or another.

Bottom line, she needed those ratings. And she needed Ian to help her increase her listener base.

And there was the rub to the situation. Three years ago she'd sworn she'd never *need* another man again, yet here she was, put in the position of relying on Ian to push her career to new heights. She couldn't make that climb without him, not easily, anyway. Not after the way he'd made himself such an integral part of her show. Not after the way he'd endeared himself to her audience.

And especially not after he'd asked her out on a date. Refusing him would cast her in a very insensitive light to the thousands of women who'd accepted Ian as their fantasy, too. Turning him down would be professional suicide, and both she and Carly knew it.

"He's waiting, Erica," Carly said, interrupting her thoughts. "And so are your listeners. Ten seconds to airtime."

Taking her seat in front of the microphone, she adjusted her headset and prepared to sacrifice herself at the proverbial altar…all in the name of ratings and preserving her professional integrity with her audience.

She lifted her chin and bolstered her fortitude. If Ian was intent on taking their on-the-air relationship out in public, then she'd take advantage of the situation for all it was worth and grasp whatever attention and publicity that came her way as a result of their date.

She pressed a button on the control panel that put her back on the air. "Welcome back to *Heat Waves,* and we're definitely sizzling tonight. I apologize for leaving you all hanging. If you were stunned by Ian's proposal, then you can imagine how I felt." She laughed lightly, forcing the tension within her to dissolve. "But that's one of the entertaining things about live radio. It's unrehearsed, and sometimes uncensored. Ian's question was both."

She closed her eyes, and took the big plunge. "I'm sure you're all wondering what I told Ian…yes, or no. Actually, I haven't spoken to him since he popped the big question; he's been on hold all this time. Since you, my listeners, have been following my nightly debates with Ian, I've decided to let *you* decide whether or not I should accept a date with him." She blinked her eyes open again and looked at Carly, who expressed her approval with a grin and thumbs-up sign. Erica wished she felt half as enthusiastic. "The phone lines are open and I want to hear from you, so call me and cast your vote."

By silent agreement, Carly spoke to Ian privately and jotted down his phone number for Erica to call him back later after she'd polled her audience's opinions on the air. Listener reaction to the unexpected twist in her show was enthusiastic and supportive, and the results of her inquiry were concluded in a resounding, unanimous *yes*.

The man had way too much influence over her listeners, who were completely and totally enthralled by him. Not that she could blame them when he'd managed to charm her, as well, over the past month. She'd just never, ever, expected to find herself face-to-face with Mr. Sexy Voice.

She was going out on a date with Ian. She shook her head in final defeat, wondering how tonight's topic had gotten so out of hand. Good Lord, if talk of sex and kisses instigated a date, what would happen when she discussed orgasms on tomorrow night's show? At the erotic thoughts filling her mind, her skin puckered with goose-flesh.

During the next commercial break, Erica took a private, off-the-air moment to dial the number Ian had left with Carly. She assumed he'd been listening to her show during the voting process, knew the outcome had leaned heavily in his favor, and her calling was just a formality to congratulate him and set up the where and when of their date.

Obviously expecting her, he answered with a deep, gracious, "Hello?"

She couldn't contain the smile tugging at the corner of her mouth, despite the turmoil he'd put her through. "Looks like you win, Ian."

"I'd like to think we both win, Erica." His sensual insinuation was unmistakable.

More tingling along her arms, across her breasts, down to the pit of her belly. Oh, Lord, what had she gotten herself into? A big mess, that was for sure!

She rubbed her damp palms down the skirt of her dress and got down to the unavoidable business at hand. "I have a few stipulations I need you to agree to before we take this any further. First of all, this has to be a double date." There was no negotiating that request. She was being cautious and playing it smart. There was safety in numbers, and considering she didn't really *know* him, despite how Carly felt, Erica wouldn't meet him alone and take any chances.

"I understand," he said easily, and without any hesitation. "In fact, I'd be worried if you didn't bring someone along this first time."

This first time. As if there would be many dates to come. Sheesh. The man's confidence amazed her. And excited her.

"It'll be with my station manager, Dan, and Carly, whom you've already met over the phone," she said, reeling in her two friends on this scheme whether they liked it or not. "And we'll meet *you* at a designated place."

"All right," he said agreeably. "Name the day, place and time, and I'll be there."

Without argument, he was leaving all the details up to her. She appreciated the control and his cooperation. It made her feel much more comfortable knowing she was the one in charge of their...*date.*

"Let's make it for tomorrow night," she said, figuring Friday evening before her show would be ideal for all of them. And in a casual setting, too. "Do you know Pizzeria Uno?"

"The one on East Ohio Street?"

She nodded, then realized he couldn't see her. "Yep, that's the one. I take it you've been there before?"

"Umm, they make the best deep-dish pizza in all of Chicago."

He was familiar with the city, at least. She wondered how long he'd lived in Chicago, what he did for a living...the kind of personal stuff they'd avoided talking about on her show, but would now have the time and opportunity to explore deeper.

Oh, boy. "How about we meet there for dinner at let's say, seven?"

"That works for me."

Two thoughts occurred to her at the same time. "Ian?"

"Yes?"

"I don't know your last name." It hadn't mattered before, nor had it been necessary. Now it was one more step to becoming familiar with each other beyond the on-the-air acquaintances they'd been for the past month.

"Carlisle," he said, his voice low and seductively rich. "Ian Carlisle."

Nice. Very nice. She bit her bottom lip, worried on it for a few extra seconds before posing her next comment. "And I have no idea what you look like." She hoped he'd give her *something* to banish the image she'd given Tori earlier that day…of a couch-potato kind of guy with a beer belly and receding hairline.

"Don't worry, I know what *you* look like and I'll approach you when you arrive at the restaurant."

She frowned. "You know what I look like, but I don't even know what color your hair or eyes are." She tucked a loose strand of hair behind her ear, her skin along her neck damp to the touch. "I'm feeling at a distinct disadvantage here."

"You won't be for long," he promised, but offered nothing more.

She accepted *his* terms, figuring he was entitled to a few of his own. "After our date, you can call the station at ten tomorrow night and we'll give everyone details on the air. Will that work for you?"

"Perfectly."

"Great." She swallowed against a sudden fluttering in her throat and sealed the deal with "Then it's a date."

There was only one question that remained...how would *their* date end...with a chaste kiss, or something more?

She'd have the answer to that in less than twenty-four hours.

FRIDAY WAS THE LONGEST day of Erica's life, even though she and Carly spent the better part of the afternoon trudging down the Magnificent Mile on Michigan Avenue. Her good friend insisted that she needed a new outfit for tonight's occasion, and Erica didn't argue. Not only did she need to keep her mind occupied or go crazy, but she figured a new dress wouldn't hurt, either.

Much to her dismay, she'd splurged on more than a soft suede miniskirt and silky tank top at Ann Taylor. After a spontaneous stop at a beauty shop for a manicure and pedicure, Erica hadn't been able to pass up the pretty open-toed sandals she'd been eyeing for the past few weeks that matched her outfit perfectly. And when Carly pulled her into Victoria's Secret for a lacy teddy in Carly's quest to "bring Dan to his knees," Erica hadn't been able to resist buying something frilly and sexy for herself, too—something other than the practical cotton underwear she normally wore. With Carly's coaxing, she'd indulged in half a dozen bikini-style panties, and an under-wire bra in sheer chantilly lace that lifted and enhanced her B-cup size breasts and gave her more cleavage than she'd ever had before.

Now, wearing the complete ensemble as she, Carly and Dan crossed the parking lot and headed along the sidewalk leading to the front entrance of Pizzeria Uno, she was glad she'd treated herself to those simple luxuries because it gave her a much needed boost of confidence. Anticipation and anxiety clashed inside her; the butterflies swarming in her stomach were a result of pure adrenaline and frayed nerves.

She had no idea what to expect of Ian, or tonight, and that had her tied up in knots, too. She'd dated a few men since coming to Chicago, but none had had the restless kind of effect on her that Ian did—just from the sexy sound of his voice and the seemingly effortless way he seduced her mind. All of those other men who'd come and gone had been safe, because they affected neither her emotions nor her hormones. Ian had a way of shaking up both, and that was a combination she'd avoided for the past three years in an effort to focus on her career.

She'd be a liar if she said she wasn't drawn to the Ian she'd come to know on the air, and making this leap to something far more tangible and real struck a dose of fear within her. By agreeing to meet with him she was tearing down the barriers that kept her safe and secure behind a microphone. Untouchable. Now there was nothing to stop temptation from taking its natural course. And because she was so strongly attracted to Ian she was afraid of getting carried away into a deeper, more serious involvement. Afraid of forgetting lessons learned and losing herself as she had with her ex-boyfriend.

Never again. She refused to become a carbon copy of her mother and sister—using men for security and sacrificing everything in return. Being meek and mild and always answering to a man. Giving up the freedom to do what you want, be what you want, without having to ask permission or approval.

Banishing those thoughts to the far recesses of her mind, she smoothed a hand down the side of her skirt. Remembering a caller's advice from a few nights ago, she pulled her shoulders back, lifted her chin, and did her best to exude poise and confidence. It was all a matter of keeping everything in perspective. And that meant staying in control, keeping her emotions at a distance, having fun with this and keeping it light.

"You really do look like a million bucks, Erica," Dan complimented from a few steps behind her and Carly on the brick-inlaid sidewalk.

"Thanks, Dan," she said from over her shoulder, and grinned wryly. "That's just about what the outfit cost me."

"It was definitely worth it." His dark eyes took in the little red dress that Carly wore just as appreciatively. "I'm guessing that you spent twice that much," he said to his girlfriend, "because you look like *two* million bucks."

Carly beamed, her skin flushed from his praise. "If you think the dress looks good, just wait until you see what I'm wearing *beneath* it." She wiggled her bottom enticingly.

Dan groaned. "You're going to kill me yet, woman."

Erica laughed, grateful for the lighthearted moment. "Then give her what she wants."

"I give her plenty to keep her satisfied," he replied. "I'm in the same mind as your Ian. Romance and seduction. Besides, she might not buy the cow if she's getting the milk for free."

Erica heard Dan's amusing witticism, but her mind latched onto only one part of his comment. "He's not *my* Ian."

Carly gave her a playful nudge in her side as they rounded the corner to the restaurant. "I'm sure he could be, if you played your cards right."

Erica wasn't sure what cards she wanted to play with

Ian. She supposed it all depended on how tonight went and if their on-the-air chemistry was evident once they met face-to-face. Even then, where would it all lead? She'd find out soon enough.

A small crowd stood out in front of the establishment as people waited for their names to be called for a table. Heads casually turned her way as she approached the entrance, and she found the combination of subtle and bold stares unnerving. Especially since she had no idea who Ian was or what he looked like. He could be watching her at this very moment and she wouldn't even know. A shiver coursed down her spine at the thought.

"Why don't you two wait out here, and I'll go and check on the reservations I made earlier today and see if Ian has checked in with the hostess," Dan said, then left Carly and Erica standing out front while he went into the busy establishment.

The evening was warm and sultry, making Erica's skin shimmer from the humidity. Nervously, her fingers fluttered through her hair to push it away from her face, which she'd left down and slightly curled at the ends so it brushed her shoulders.

Antsy from the anticipation of waiting, Erica shifted on her sandaled feet and glanced at the people around her. Her perusal came to a skidding halt when she met the striking green-eyed gaze of a man standing by himself about ten feet away. Awareness filled her and her pulse quickened. He was gorgeous—from his thick black hair that was cut in a neat executive style, to his broad shoulders encased in a blue knit collared shirt and jeans that molded to an athletic body made for sin. Everything about him was pure, unadulterated male, and he took her breath away.

He was, most definitely, a *hottie*.

He hooked his thumbs in the front pocket of his jeans, his sensual mouth curving upward in the kind of lazy smile she'd imagined a hundred times in her head. A delicious warmth settled low, arousing her as if he'd caressed her with more than just his heated gaze.

She swallowed hard. Unable to look away, she willed him to move toward her and introduce himself as Ian Carlisle...until her attention was pulled away from him by Carly's startled gasp.

Her friend clutched her arm as a choked sound escaped her. "Oh, God, Erica, I'm sorry," she whispered frantically. "Please forgive me for talking you into doing this."

Erica frowned in confusion, having no idea what Carly was talking about until she glanced up again and spotted a portly man who looked old enough to be her father approaching her with a bouquet of flowers in his hand. He stopped directly in front of her, his eyes shining with excitement and awe.

Every fantasy Erica had ever had about Ian withered away in that moment. Her comment to Carly about a guy having a voice as incredible as Ian's had to have been shortchanged in the looks department came back to haunt her. Her prediction had come true.

She gulped, her chest tightening with disappointment—not that she'd let this man in front of her see her shock. She forced a polite smile, even as she wondered how she was going to survive the next few hours. "Ian?"

The man's bushy brows rose high over his whiskey-colored eyes. "Uh, no. My name is Barry, and I'm the manager here. My wife and I listen to your show, *Heat Waves,* all the time and I'm a huge fan. I was talking to that gentleman back there who's here for your date, and told him how much I'd love to meet you and get your autograph, and he said I could do the honors and present you with these flowers while I was at it.''

He brandished the bouquet with a flourish, and she took the floral display from him. "Thank you," she murmured, the scent of roses filling her senses. Still uncertain about who her actual date was, and not willing to assume anything at this point, she asked, "What guy are you talking about, Barry?"

"Ian," he said, as if she should have known. "Your nightly caller. He's right over there." He pointed to the man lounging against the metal railing circling the outdoor seating area.

She heard Carly's breath rush out of her lungs in a grateful sigh, which matched Erica's own relief.

As soon as their gazes meet again, Ian grinned, his eyes twinkling mischievously. The man most definitely had a sense of humor to go with all that devastating sex appeal.

She turned back to the manager of Pizzeria Uno and shook his hand warmly. "It was a pleasure meeting you, Barry. If you have a business card, I'd be happy to send you an autographed publicity photo and other promotional items."

As Barry dug a card from his wallet, a woman standing to her left tapped her on the shoulder. "Excuse me, I didn't mean to eavesdrop, but are you Erica McCree?" she asked while the rest of the people in her party stared expectantly.

Erica smiled and nodded. "Yes, I am."

The other woman's face lit up. "Oh, wow, this is so cool! You're here for your date with Ian, aren't you?"

And that's all it took for word to spread. Erica had never considered herself famous before, or even a highly recognizable name, but in the blink of an eye her status as a radio talk-show host had been elevated. And for those who'd never heard of her name and her show, they were quickly filled in on the details of *Heat Waves* and the much anticipated date with Ian.

Everyone watched in interest and fascination as the gorgeous bystander slowly made his way across the distance separating them, his sole focus on her. For Erica, everything and everyone around them faded away as he filled her vision.

"That was a rotten trick," she said when he finally stood in front of her, larger than life and more seductive than in her dreams. Her nostrils flared as she inhaled a subtle but warm and woodsy scent emanating from him.

He gave a one-shouldered shrug, and even *that* nonchalant gesture was overwhelmingly sexy. "You certainly made *Barry's* evening." His voice was familiar and rich, making her burn deep inside.

This man, without a doubt, was Ian.

A smile teased her lips. "It made your night, too, judging by that devious pleasure I see twinkling in your eyes." Incredible bedroom eyes. The kind that could undress a woman in a single, calculated glance.

He didn't deny her claim, making it obvious that he'd enjoyed the mix-up.

"Thank you for the roses," she said, motioning to the bouquet in her hand. "They're beautiful. I can't remember the last time someone gave me flowers." She licked her bottom lip, feeling another bout of nerves swell within her.

"You're welcome." His gaze dropped to her lips, caressing them as intimately as her tongue had, then slowly lifted back to her eyes. "I can't remember the last time I *gave* a woman flowers, and I wanted to make sure I made a good first impression."

She laughed softly at that. "Considering who you sent to deliver them, you made an impression I'll never forget." She extended her right hand for him to shake. "It's nice to finally meet you, Ian Carlisle."

"Likewise." He slipped his hand into hers. His palm was large, his fingers long, his grasp engulfing her in startling heat. "Your publicity photo doesn't do you justice. You're beyond beautiful."

Then he leaned forward and brushed a warm, chaste kiss on her cheek, giving credence to the romance he'd talked about on her show. Oh, and the seduction, too. She was halfway there, melting with every touch and every word he spoke.

"Oh, wow," An unfamiliar female voice exclaimed from somewhere behind Erica, bringing her back to the present with a jolt. "If he's starting the date with a kiss, I can only imagine how the date will *end!*"

"Tune into tonight's show on WTLK to find out," Carly said cheekily, stirring interest for *Heat Waves* and taking advantage of the free publicity while she could.

Dan joined them, and introductions were made all around. Barry ushered them inside and away from the eager fans wanting Erica's autograph or a glimpse at Ian. The manager insisted on seating them at one of the tables that was tucked into a corner and away from most prying eyes. As they followed Barry through the dim restaurant, Ian rested his fingers at the base of her spine to guide her. The gesture was polite and gentlemanly, without any sexual connotation whatsoever, yet his touch instigated a conflagration of excitement to flow through her veins.

And that's when she knew she was in big, big trouble. Could she resist this man who made her crave long pent-up desires? And did she really want to? The feverish question preyed on her mind.

After sitting down and agreeing on the Chicago classic deep-dish pizza, the four of them eased into a relaxed, casual conversation about the radio station and the hype surrounding tonight's get-together. The verbal exchange between her and Ian was light and lively, and surprisingly without the reserve or awkwardness that normally accompanied a first date. She'd known him for a month, but it felt as if she'd been with him for years. While there was no denying the mutual chemistry they'd both wondered about, there was also a mental connection between them that transcended their physical attraction.

The arrival of their dinner created a pause in conversation. After a few bites and appreciative murmurs over the delicious flavor, Carly looked across the table at Ian.

"So, Ian, how long have you lived in Chicago and what do you do for a living?" she asked, her inquiry direct and blunt.

Erica nearly choked on the bite of pizza she'd been swallowing, mortified at Carly's not-so-subtle ploy to pump information out of Ian. "Geez, Carly, Ian's not here for an interrogation."

Dan smothered a grin, used to his girlfriend's outspoken ways. Carly blinked at her innocently as if to say "what did I do?" but Erica knew better than to fall for the act. Carly wanted the goods on Ian to size up his suitability.

Erica glanced at the man sitting next to her, who looked more amused than annoyed at Carly's third degree. "You don't have to answer those personal questions."

"I don't mind," he assured her easily, and swiped his napkin across his mouth. He met her gaze and smiled. "A first date is all about getting to know each other, isn't it?"

There was something about his statement Erica wanted to argue. Maybe it was the subtle suggestion that if he shared something, she should offer a bit about herself in return. Intimate details and secrets that would give depth and insight to who she was underneath the radio personality.

She wasn't ready or willing to give him a glimpse into her soul, that part of herself she'd kept private and secure for the past three years. "You already know what *I* do for a living," she said, keeping things superficial. "And I've been in Chicago for three years."

He tipped his head curiously as he reached for another slice of pizza, feeding a healthy appetite. "Where did you live before that?"

Finished with her piece, she pushed her plate aside. "Southern California."

His brows rose incredulously as he chewed a bite. "You left year-round warmth and sunshine for freezing cold winters and hot, humid summers?"

She laughed and stirred her straw in her drink. "You can't imagine how many times I've asked myself the exact same thing when the wind-chill factor has hit below zero. I'm not a winter person at all. But the trade-offs were worth it."

What those trade-offs were she wasn't willing to divulge out loud. She'd been searching for independence and freedom, and a chance to prove herself in her career. Putting miles between the people in her life who didn't understand her drive and ambition had been one of the first steps in gaining what she'd sought.

"So, where do *you* work?" she asked, redirecting the questions back to him.

"I'm an investment broker and the CEO of Winslow Financial Investment."

"That's impressive," Carly cut in, sounding suitably wowed, by his profession and his position.

Erica silently echoed her friend's sentiment. Until today, she had no idea what to expect of Ian professionally. An investment broker fit his image. He looked the part with his clean-cut appearance and the aura of self-assurance that surrounded him. There was a keen intelligence and warmth in his eyes as he spoke of his business that no doubt soothed a client's concerns or fears about parting with their money.

"It's a job I enjoy," he continued, glancing across the table at Carly and Dan, who listened with interest to his story. "I started investing and socking away money when I was a teenager. And when I was old enough I started playing the stock market. I had a knack for hitting when it was hot and making decent money out of a buck, and it all progressed from there."

There wasn't an ounce of conceit or pretentiousness coating his words, but Erica got the distinct impression that Ian was very wealthy and his business did well. Whether or not he came from money she didn't know, but there had been something in the depth of Ian's gaze when he'd mentioned saving money as a teenager that led her to believe there was more struggle to his success tale. And that was something she understood all too well, since she was *still* struggling to make her mark in broadcasting.

"Are you from Chicago?" she asked, her fingers playing along the cool condensation on her glass.

"I've lived in Illinois all my life, but moved to Chicago when I was seventeen. I've been here ever since."

He made no mention of his family, which Erica found as interesting as her own omission of the mother and sister she'd left behind in California. Had he moved here with or without his family, and where were they now? Curious questions she wondered about but didn't ask—she wasn't ready to delve into more personal territory. With Ian, or herself.

He placed his napkin on his dish and sat back as their waiter cleared their table. His gaze unerringly found Erica's again in the dim lighting. "Chicago is a great city. Full of history and life and plenty of sex appeal."

Erica had never considered Chicago as seductive or alluring before and found his comment intriguing. "You really think Chicago is a sexy city?"

His lashes fell half-mast as a beguiling grin curved his mouth. "I suppose a person's perception of Chicago being a sexy city has a lot to do with who you're spending your nights with."

Erica's heart thumped in her chest as awareness shimmered between the two of them. The meaning behind his words was unmistakable. He was spending his nights with *her,* on the air with the city of Chicago listening as they debated hot and provocative issues....

"He does have a point," Carly chimed in, reflecting Erica's private thoughts. "The two of you on *Heat Waves* have made Chicago a *very* sexy city."

Erica cast Carly a direct look that relayed the silent message for her to *not* pursue the issue at hand. She could almost see the wheels in Carly's mind churning, trying to figure out an angle to capitalize on Ian's comment and put an "on the air" spin to it.

Dan cleared his throat, seemingly in tune to Erica's wish for someone to change the subject. She certainly couldn't depend on her friend to look out for her best interests when Carly was so intent on exploiting the situation in any way she could to help out the station's standing.

"Dessert anyone?" Dan asked.

"Not for me." Erica quickly jumped on the opportunity to put a damper on any intentions Carly might have had. "I'm stuffed." She glanced at her watch, shocked to see that two hours had passed and it was a quarter after nine. "In fact, we'd better leave pretty quick so I don't miss my shift."

Dan nodded in agreement and motioned to the waiter for the bill. Carly propped her elbows on the table, rested her chin on her clasped hands and smiled very charmingly at Ian.

"You know," Carly said, injecting an appropriate amount of persuasion into her voice, "I think it would be great if you came back to the station and reported live about the date."

Erica exhaled hard. She was going to strangle her friend, no doubt about it. "I'm sure Ian has better things to do than spend his evening down at the station."

"Actually, I don't have anything better to do," Ian said. "I was just going to head back home and wait for your show to start. I think it would be fun to discuss our date together in the studio. What do you think, Erica?"

He'd loaded the simple question with an irresistible challenge, which matched the daring light dancing in his eyes. She looked away and breathed slow and deep. She could hear Carly's voice chanting in her mind: *ratings, ratings, ratings.*

But this wasn't just about ratings. Not for her. And especially not since she'd met Ian in the flesh and was more attracted to him than ever. There seemed to be something more personal at stake, and she felt threatened by the powerful emotions he evoked after such a short time. Need and desire surged through her and left her feeling too weak and helpless to resist him.

Having him in the studio with her after their date would be a logical progression to their evening together, she told herself. Her listeners would relish their one-on-one interaction. She'd put her own misgivings aside. For tonight. For an hour. No more.

"All right," she agreed.

Carly's eyes gleamed with excitement as she sent Ian another engaging smile. "And if you could stay late tonight, maybe the two of you could discuss tonight's topic on the air, too."

Which was all about orgasms. *Oy.*

Erica abruptly stood before Carly enlightened Ian on the evening's subject matter. "While you're taking care of the bill, Dan, I think Carly and I will visit the ladies' room." She grasped Carly's sleeve and pulled, giving her friend no other choice but to come along or end up with a tear in her outfit. "We'll meet you out front in a few minutes."

Erica was silent on the way to the rest room. Surprisingly, Carly remained quiet, too, but the surreptitious glances she kept sending Erica's way told Erica that her friend knew what was coming and was awaiting the outburst.

Erica washed her hands and waited for Carly to emerge from her stall. Once she did, Erica got down to business. "What in the hell were you doing out there?"

Carly soaped up her hands and didn't meet Erica's gaze in the mirror. "Just trying to take advantage of a good thing."

Unfortunately, *Erica* felt taken advantage of. "This is *my* show, Carly."

"And I'm the program director, and my job is to make sure all the shows on WTLK are as appealing as possible," she stated simply. After drying her hands on a paper towel, she dug into her purse for her lipstick and applied a slash of red to her mouth. "Imagine the response you're going to get having Ian live in the studio with you. The two of you are going to literally heat up the airwaves—more than ever before."

Erica was feeling set up with Ian and resented being in such a vulnerable position. "Regardless, I don't appreciate you interfering in my private life."

Carly stopped fluffing her hair and lifted a brow at Erica. "Who said anything about your private life, sweetie?" Her expression softened, a knowing glimmer in her eyes. "You like him, don't you? You really, *really* like him, and that's what really has you so on edge, isn't it?"

Yeah, she liked Ian. Too much. There was no denying the plain truth. But it wasn't only their extraordinary attraction that had her shaken and confused and on edge. Going out on a date with him was one thing—taking him back to the station with her was another. It was an act she found as intimate as inviting him back to her apartment.

He was going to invade her private territory. That small, confined space was hers alone and one she'd never shared with *anyone*. It was a sacred place where she felt safe and secure and was able to hide secrets and reactions behind a microphone.

Now he'd see the real Erica behind the radio personality, and there would be no concealing anything from him. Certainly not her response to him, or her expressions that always gave away too much. Would he look at her while she addressed her audience and be able to tell just how little she really knew about orgasms?

At that disturbing thought, Erica averted her gaze and rummaged through her purse for her roll of mints. She popped two into her mouth, too aware of how close she and Ian would be sitting next to each other in her studio.

Carly touched the tips of her fingers against Erica's back in a comforting gesture. "Why can't you just enjoy this wild ride for what it is?"

She applied a slick coat of her cotton-candy lip gloss and sighed. "I don't know what *it* is anymore," she admitted.

"*It* is Ian," Carly informed her. "And he's a gorgeous hunk of a man, and he wants you as much as you want him, so take advantage of that rare chemistry—on the air, and off."

Erica mulled over Carly's suggestion as they headed out of the restaurant to meet up with the guys, still having no idea where this one date would lead her. Having no idea if she had the courage and nerve to pursue an affair with the irrepressibly sexy Ian.

They ran into Barry at the front door and Erica thanked him for his hospitality. As they exited the restaurant, the sultry night air clung to Erica's skin, increasing the restlessness within her.

Dan and Ian waited on the sidewalk, talking companionably. Her date was holding the flowers she left at the table, and this time he handed the bouquet of roses to her. "Can I drive you back to the station?" he asked, obviously assuming nothing.

Wisely, Carly didn't butt in like she'd been doing all night and left this decision up to Erica. She took a huge leap of faith. "Since we're now heading to the same place, sure."

The four of them walked back to the parking lot together, and Ian directed her to a two-door, champagne-colored Lexus coupe. He opened the passenger side for her, and she slid inside. Once he closed the door and she was enveloped in the enticing scent of leather and man, she realized her mistake. She was well and truly all alone with Ian, and they still had one unresolved issue between them.

How would their date end?

4

"MAKE A LEFT HERE at the light, and you can park by the back entrance where the guard is."

Following Erica's directions, Ian pulled into a slot next to Dan's vehicle. Before turning off the ignition, he glanced at the clock glowing on his light display to gauge the time. It was 9:35 p.m. Twenty-five minutes before Erica had to be on the air.

Unbuckling his seat belt, he turned toward his date. He rested his forearm on the back of her seat. Within touching distance, but he refrained from indulging in that luxury for now. The outside streetlight illuminated her profile and added shimmering golden highlights to her silky-looking hair. After how well their evening had gone at the restaurant, she now seemed reserved and quiet—so unlike her bold, sassy, on-the-air persona.

"Did you have a good time tonight?" he asked.

She smiled at him as she absently stroked a rose petal from the bouquet resting in her lap. "Yeah, I did." Her tone was candid and honest.

Relief unraveled the tightness and uncertainty that had gathered in his chest. "I'm glad, because so did I."

Their date had been without pretense. Whether she realized it or not, he'd given her more than he'd offered another woman in eight long years—a glimpse of the down-to-earth man he was beneath the wealthy exterior.

And it had felt great to just be himself and truly enjoy the company of a beautiful, fun woman.

A tapping on Erica's window made her jump in her seat. Pressing a hand to her heart, she glanced to the right and found the guard standing there. Ian rolled the window down a few inches for her.

"You okay, Erica?" the middle-aged man asked gruffly, narrowing his gaze at Ian in a very protective manner.

"I'm fine, thanks, John," Erica assured the guard. "This is Ian Carlisle."

John eyed Ian again. Deciding that Ian wasn't a threat, John gave a nod of acceptance, then went back to his post by the back door of the building.

Ian sealed the window closed again, and Erica released a long, slow breath. "Umm, maybe we should go inside."

"Not just yet," he murmured, and brushed his fingers along the slope of her shoulder where the strap of her silk tank top gave way to smooth, tanned flesh. Much to his pleasure, he discovered her skin was just as soft as it looked.

He felt a shiver course through her and raise goose bumps on her arm. "John might—"

"John isn't going to bother us again," he assured her. "And he can't see us, Erica. The back and side windows are tinted, and we have a few minutes before you need to be inside."

She gave him a sidelong glance, her gaze cautious. "Is there something you wanted to talk about?"

She was nervous, and he understood that. For as much as he wanted her, he wanted to do this right even more. "As a matter of fact, yeah, there is."

Reaching down to her hip, he unbuckled her seat belt,

knowing he was making it easy for her to flee, if that's what she chose to do. She remained seated, but judging by the rapid rise and fall of her breasts and the taut nipples grazing the silk of her top, she was just as affected by their close proximity. The heat gathering inside the car had little to do with the outside weather.

He let his hand linger at her hip, and his thumb lightly caressed the slender indentation of her waist. "So, would you say that this constitutes the end of our date?"

She nodded, and touched her tongue to her upper lip—a nervous gesture, he realized. "Yes."

Her voice was low and husky. Arousing him. Making him want her more than he already did. "How would *you* like the date to end, Erica?"

A kiss or sex? The unspoken question swirled in the air, heightening the sexual tension arching between them.

An unexpected impish grin made an appearance. "Sex in this small car might be kind of difficult," she teased.

"I can think of a dozen different things I could do to you in this small car," he countered easily. "So don't discount the possibility if that's what you want."

Her eyes widened in startled shock. "I was joking, Ian."

He'd known that, but he'd been very serious, willing and able to give her anything she desired. "How about a kiss, then?"

She considered that for a few seconds. "Depends. Are we talking about the same kind of kiss you gave me when we met earlier?"

A chaste brush of his lips across the cheek. It had suited the purpose of a first meeting, but after craving her for a month, he wanted much, much more than that now. "No. That was a 'hello' kiss."

"And this would be…?" she prompted curiously.

"'I had a great time' kiss," he said, lifting his hand to tuck her hair behind her ear, an excuse to keep touching her. "An 'I like you' kiss." His finger traced the shell of her ear and found the soft, sensitive hollow beneath her lobe. "An 'I want you' kiss."

Her eyes grew dark with velvet sensuality and a wanting that matched his own. "Wow, you can say all that with a kiss?" She sounded suitably impressed as well as doubtful.

He rose to the challenge. "Sure can." He leaned forward until his side pressed against the center console. The rest was up to her. "C'mere and I'll show you."

Slowly, she shifted and obeyed his command, meeting him halfway, until their lips were mere inches apart. He caught the scent of mint on her breath and saw the anticipation etching her feminine features.

He threaded his fingers through her loose hair and slipped them around to the back of her head, wondering if she'd left her hair down for him because of his provocative comment from a few nights ago. *There's something incredibly erotic about having a woman's hair wrapped around my hands and being able to hold her where I want her.* Whether she had or not, he savored the silken feel of each strand wrapped around his fingers, caressing his hands.

He lowered his head for their first kiss, and watched her lashes flutter closed. "I had a great time," he whispered, just before his mouth touched hers, downy-soft and fleeting. A kiss as sweet as the cotton-candy flavor slicked across her lips and filling his senses.

His fingers tightened in her hair as he tipped her chin up and angled her head to the side for better access. She sighed, relaxed and followed his lead.

"I like you…" he murmured. Advancing to the next

level of intimacy, he increased the pressure of his mouth until her lips parted for him on their own accord, inviting him inside. As much as he ached to delve deeper, he kept a tight rein on his control, taking this one luxurious step at a time. She had a soft, sensuous mouth made expressly for kissing. He nibbled, suckled and flirted, leisurely exploring tastes and textures for the first time.

A frustrated sound rolled up in her throat, and she scooted closer and placed trembling, tentative fingers against his cheek. Her touch made him burn all the way down to the burgeoning erection straining the fly of his jeans. Giving her a little of what she wanted, he swept his tongue across her lush bottom lip, gradually escalating to the kind of kiss that would be as passionate and intense as their attraction. When she repeated the erotic gesture to him, undeniable need ripped through him.

"I want you," he groaned, and unable to hold back any longer he finally unleashed his restraint. His lips covered hers in a kiss that was as passionate as it was possessive. His tongue stroked deeply, voluptuously, coaxing her to share in the wet heat they generated, revel in the soft flare of fire burning between them. She responded in a way he never could have anticipated, with a rapacious hunger beyond his wildest dreams. She clung to him, greedily returning the kiss and drawing his tongue into her mouth with shameless abandon.

Her enthusiasm thrilled him, and stole his sanity. Heart pumping furiously, he slid a hand downward to cup her rounded breast in his hand, then finessed the ripe, hardened tip through her bra with his thumb and finger. Her supple flesh swelled against his palm, the full, feminine weight a perfect, voluptuous fit. The velvet heat of his tongue stroked hers, deep and explicit, making him ache to taste and lave her elsewhere.

The guttural growl that erupted from him was an instinctive response, primitive and purely male. A warning for him to stop before they went further than either of them intended. Knowing they were damn close to doing those dozen different things in the car that he'd warned her about, he reluctantly dropped his hand from her breast and pulled back and ended the kiss.

She stared at him in utter astonishment, as if she couldn't believe she'd let him take such liberties. As if she couldn't believe she'd been so brazen in return. Her cheeks were flushed with the high color of excitement, and she seemed to struggle for each labored breath she took. But she gave no indication that she regretted the kiss, which gave him hope that there would be many more to enjoy.

He untangled his fingers from her hair and let his thumb skim along her silken jaw before falling away. Her skin was damp, from the humidity that found its way inside the car, and arousal, no doubt. "I take it by the way you kissed me back that you want me just as much?"

"Yeah, I guess I do," she replied huskily, still seemingly dazed by what had just transpired between them. Slowly, she moved back to her side of the car. Her fingers fluttered to her wet lips, and she shook her head in amazement. "Wow, you're a *great* kisser."

She made it sound as though she'd kissed too many toads in her lifetime and had finally found a prince. Could that really be possible?

He couldn't stop the pleased smile that tugged at his lips. "It's not just me, Erica, it's us. We're great *together.*"

She grinned wryly. "There's no disputing that there's plenty of sexual chemistry between us."

"Oh, yeah," he agreed. Explosive, erotic chemistry. His blood still rushed in hot rivulets through his veins, and his lower body was rock hard and clamoring for the kind of release he'd fantasized about since the first time he'd heard her voice on the radio.

And now that he knew what she looked like, now that he'd caressed her soft skin and tasted the incredible sweetness of her mouth, he had no desire to revert back to being just on-the-air acquaintances. She awakened feelings in him that had been buried for years and made him forget about those haunting aspects of his past that had consumed him for too long.

"I want to see you again," he said abruptly.

Her eyes flashed uncertainties in the shadowed interior of the car, and she seemed to withdraw into herself. "Ian, I'm not looking for anything serious or complicated." She glanced down at the flowers in her lap, studying them with too much interest before meeting his gaze again. Her chin rose a notch. "I've been there before, in a serious relationship, that is, and I'm just not ready to go there again. Right now, my career is my first and foremost priority."

He appreciated her honesty, and was curious about that previous relationship she'd mentioned and how it had influenced her decision to remain single. Personal questions tumbled through his mind, but he knew now wasn't the time or place to embark on a serious conversation. Nor was he especially keen on spilling his own past secrets. And how could he ask something of her when he wasn't ready to reciprocate?

He needed more time with her. He wanted to give the undeniable attraction between them a chance to develop into something that went beyond their on-the-air association. This was a once-in-a-lifetime chance to appease the restless longing in his soul. In order to gain more time, he decided to cater to the doubts and the glimmer of vulnerability he detected in the depths of her eyes.

"You know," he began easily, his deep voice reverberating in the interior of the car, "I don't remember asking for anything serious or complicated."

Amusement flitted across her beautiful, classic features, chased by a fair amount of interest. "What are you suggesting? An affair?"

She didn't sound opposed to the idea, and his mind conjured images of the two of them together, their naked bodies tangled amid cool cotton sheets. Her arching beneath him, moaning in pleasure, her slender legs wrapped around his waist. Her sliding above him, straddling his hips and moving rhythmically as she coaxed him to the brink. Them soaring over the edge together in a powerful, shuddering climax.

That wild, seductive vision he dreamed of every night was the culmination of the mental fantasies they'd both participated in during their sizzling, on-air debates.

"If you think about it, we've been having an affair from the first call I made to the station. Maybe not physically," he quickly clarified when her raised brows expressed her disbelief. "But most definitely here, in our minds, which is sometimes the best foreplay there is." He brushed the tips of his fingers against her damp temple for emphasis.

A wicked, teasing smile made an appearance. "So, you want mind sex?"

"I want *you*, Erica. Mind sex and all." He'd established his desire for her with that scintillating embrace they'd just shared. However, he'd like to think that intimate kiss was just a prelude to satiating more provocative and erotic needs. "But for right now, I'd settle for another date. Without chaperones this time.'' He deliberately posed his request as a comment rather than a direct, intimidating question.

She seemed to consider the idea for a moment, then cast a quick glance at her gold-toned wristwatch. ''You know, we really ought to head upstairs before Carly and Dan start to worry about me.''

He accepted her diversion without argument. Considering her sudden reserve regarding them as a couple, he hadn't been expecting an answer. Not yet, anyway. But he would.

He wasn't done with Erica McCree.

INSTEAD OF HER NORMAL quick jaunt up the flights of stairs leading to the radio station, Erica rode the old, slow, creaky elevator with Ian up to the fifth floor. They stepped out of the stuffy lift, and he followed her down the hall to WTLK's offices.

''Is it me after that steamy kiss in the car, or is it hot in here?'' he asked from beside her, his mellow voice infused with a light, teasing quality.

Awareness quivered through Erica, and her pulse quickened at Ian's not-so-subtle reminder of their breathtaking kiss. The man was an irresistible rogue, which was part of his appeal, she had to admit. He was sexy, confident and altogether too tempting. And the combination was a lethal one that hit her dead-center in her sorely neglected libido, which had tingled to life at the first touch of his lips on hers.

She was *still* tingling, and she had no idea how she was going to survive tonight's topic—*orgasms*—without having one of her own from all the sexual tension building within her. She supposed *that* would certainly make for scintillating talk radio.

"I'm thinking it's probably a combination of both," she returned just as sassily. She stopped at the vending machine to purchase herself a bottle of cold water to hopefully douse the burning sensation lingering in her belly.

He had a dollar bill out of his wallet and into the machine before she could dig money out of her purse. "Feeling a little overheated yourself?" he murmured seductively.

"Maybe," she said, unwilling to admit just how turned on she still was and give him that bit of leverage over her. Not when they were minutes away from being on the air together. She feared he'd latch onto that awareness and turn the tables on her in front of her listeners. And she was determined to remain in control of tonight's discussion about their date.

She pushed the button for her water, and the plastic bottle dropped to the bottom slot. She picked it up, turned around and found herself surrounded by two hundred solid pounds of pure male testosterone. Ian casually lifted a broad hand and braced his palm on the vending machine behind her, holding her hostage between firm muscle that was just as strong and unyielding as the metal behind her. And damned if she didn't have the unbridled urge to rip his shirt off and test the resilience of his taut flesh with her fingers, taste the salt on his skin with her tongue, and experience the heady sensation of his bare chest rubbing against her breasts.

He leaned close, his warm breath wafting across her cheek. "You know, if you're as hot as I am, there's more than one way to extinguish the fire." His voice was a husky purr, and as intimate as a lover's caress.

She felt that amorous stroke all the way down her spine and whispering across her thighs—or was that the brush of his legs against hers causing all that wild static electricity? Whatever the cause, the arousing sensation elicited a very female response deep within her.

She shored her sensual defenses against this man, which wasn't an easy task. "Water will do for now."

He grinned wickedly, and her stomach dipped again. "Let me know if you change your mind."

The hint of accepting another date with him was evident in his tone, but just like in the car, he didn't pressure her for a reply and she was grateful. Her hormones were clamoring inside her, screaming at her to tell him *yes*. But despite her body's restless response to Ian, deeper insecurities kept her firmly grounded.

Before she took that giant step with Ian, before she turned one date into two and allowed things between them to become any more intimate than they already had, she had to be certain that she could handle a fun, sexy, uncommitted affair with him. Mind sex. Carnal sex. Any way she looked at it, it would no doubt be *great* sex.

She swallowed hard at the tantalizing thought. In all honesty, she wasn't certain she had the ability to separate physical pleasure from emotional need with Ian, and that's what worried her. He only had to look at her and she melted inside. Her heart rate increased at the sound of his seductive voice. And she ached for him like she'd never ached for another man.

All warning signals she knew she'd be smart to heed.

She'd moved to Chicago to escape a dominating relationship and to start out fresh and new. To make better choices than her mother and sister had. To build her career as a DJ without her goals being sidetracked by a man—especially a gorgeous, virile man like Ian.

She was feeling torn, her desire for Ian clashing with the insecurities she thought she'd left behind in California. The weakness of wanting a man. The fear of getting so caught up in a relationship that it led to dependency and personal destruction.

The big question remained: could she enjoy the time with Ian and walk away in the end still independent and successful with her woman's heart unscathed? She had no reassuring answer.

Inhaling a deep breath and ready to get down to the business end of their date, she slipped around Ian and opened the door that led into the radio station. He followed, and they were greeted with more humid warmth, which brought her mind back to Ian's initial remark about the oppressive temperature in the building.

"I'm really sorry about the heat in here, but there's not a lot we can do about it other than putting extra fans in the outer offices," she said, thinking if she was lucky the heat would cut Ian's visit to the station short and he'd be on his way before she launched into tonight's actual topic of discussion. "The air-conditioning unit is old and temperamental, and after running all day it's usually out of oomph by early evening."

He glanced around at his surroundings as she led him to the back studios. "Is there a reason why it hasn't been fixed or replaced?"

"Money, mostly. And approval from the owner. Can't do it without either."

He frowned, taking in the outdated office furnishings, the gray, dingy walls, and the linoleum floors that were cracked and peeling in places. "Why doesn't the owner make sure his employees have a comfortable working environment?"

"Because *she* doesn't want to have anything to do with the radio station and refuses to spend a penny on renovations." Stopping at a small closet, she put her personal belongings on a shelf. "Marvin, the owner, passed away a few months ago and his widow inherited the station. Suffice to say that the employees' comfort isn't a high priority for Virginia."

His dark brows furrowed in confusion. "Then why is she holding on to the station?"

"She isn't. Not by choice, anyway. She's eager to unload the business and recently put the station on the market," she told him, and took a drink of her water. "Virginia would love to make a mint from the sale, so most of us are wondering if anyone will pay the inflated price she's asking, or if WTLK is facing eventual bankruptcy from her sucking the business dry because no one's interested in purchasing a run-down station."

He braced his hands on his hips as his critical gaze scoured the area. "I don't know, I see lots of potential."

She smiled at his optimism. "Sure, if you're willing to dump a good amount of money into repairs and upgrades."

He tipped his head. "Is the station in that bad of shape?"

It was, in comparison to other local stations that had the kind of money to back up huge promotions and advertising. WTLK wasn't the most luxurious station she'd ever worked for, but the atmosphere was casual and fun, and her co-workers were like family. She hated the thought of all of them going their separate ways.

"WTLK is holding its own, and we've had a few good hits with advertisers lately, which helps." She wasn't about to enlighten Ian to the fact that he was partially responsible for the increase in their on-air advertising. "But there's no telling how the sale of the station will affect our jobs. *If* it even sells."

Not wanting to launch into a discussion about her possible unemployment, she motioned him farther down the hall, to a four-by-four plate-glass window that looked into the small studio where Jay, their early evening DJ, was wrapping up his segment. The other man sent her a wink and a smile.

She waved back. "This booth is where we broadcast all the shows."

Ian nodded, seemingly surprised by what he saw. "I have to admit, it's not quite what I expected. It's very... small."

She shrugged, having long ago grown used to the confined space in which she worked. "I like to think of it as cozy." However, with Ian about to enter the room with her, she was certain cozy would quickly turn to cramped.

Carly sauntered out of an office behind them, swiping a smudge of lipstick from the corner of her mouth, then giving the hem of her racy red dress a quick tug back into place. Dan followed behind, a satisfied smile on his face.

Carly grinned when she caught sight of them. "Nice of the two of you to show up. I was beginning to think I was going to have to go on the air and tell your audience that you hadn't returned from your date yet and let them all wonder a bit longer how the evening ended."

Erica rolled her eyes at her friend's exaggeration. "They'll find out soon enough, and it looks like you were too busy with your own date to worry about *us*."

Carly fluffed her fingers through her mussed hair and cast a sly glance at her beau. "Just giving Dan a little incentive to wait *up* for me tonight, if you know what I mean."

Dan's face actually flushed. Erica laughed while Ian followed their conversation with amusement. Minutes later, Jay came out of the booth as a reel of commercials that would segue into Erica's show played.

"It's all yours, Erica," the other man said, then shook Ian's hand. "It's nice to meet the man behind the voice. You two behave in there."

"Now, what fun is there in that?" Carly quipped. "We want you to spill all the naughty details, and then some." Grabbing Ian's arm, she ushered him into the studio. "Come on, let's get you settled and ready to go."

By the time Carly made room for Ian next to Erica's side so they could share the microphone, she was feeling very *unsettled.* They were sitting so close she could feel the searing heat they generated together, could inhale the arousing, masculine scent of him. She was also in direct line with his smoldering, sensual stare, and was near enough for him to reach out and slide his fingers from her knee, to her thigh, to her hip, and up to her breasts, which had been full and taut and achy since their tryst in the car.

That easily, he was sharing her personal space. That effortlessly, he'd invaded her professional haven. She felt physically shook up, even though he'd hadn't touched her.

In fact, for the next hour as they laughed and joked and discussed their date on the air, he was a consummate gentleman—charming, sociable, and just flirtatious enough to keep their banter balanced with the kind of provocative teasing her listeners expected between them. She assured her audience that Ian was just as sexy as his voice, and Ian told them that their on-air chemistry was indeed just as hot in person. They both admitted that their evening had ended with a mutually pleasurable kiss. When pressured for more details, Ian swore he wasn't the kind of guy who would kiss and tell, and Erica appreciated that bit of chivalry.

The question that was posed over and over again by callers was the same one Erica had yet to answer—would there be a second date? She kept her response vague, noncommittal and ended the segment with the promise that her listeners would be the first to know what transpired between her and Ian, and to tune in the following week to see what happened next.

Ian removed his headset once they were off the air and slanted her a lazy, knowing grin. "That was a shameless hook for your listeners."

She shrugged unapologetically, and her hair fluttered against her neck, damp from the heat and humidity. "There's nothing like a little anticipation to keep listeners on the edge of their seats. It keeps 'em coming back for more." And leaving her relationship with him dangling kept her from committing to anything between *them* until she sorted things through in her mind.

He braced his hands on his thighs and stared at her for a long moment. "What about keeping *me* coming back for more?" he asked, his gaze a deep, intense shade of green. "Don't you think *I* need some kind of incentive to keep spending my nights with you, Erica?"

He wanted an *incentive*. He could have been referring to anything from a second date, to another kiss, to illicit sex. Her mouth went dry at that last thought, and she lifted her water to her lips only to discover the bottle was empty. Damn. She stood, wanting to get a cup of ice from the machine down the hall before it was airtime again and she began her next segment of the show. And maybe, if Ian followed her, he'd go ahead and call it a night and catch the elevator from there.

"You know, I didn't say *no* to another date." As far

as incentives went, even she had to admit it was a pitiful one.

"You didn't exactly say yes, either," he said wryly.

She headed out of the studio with a plastic cup in hand, and he was right behind her. She glanced over her shoulder, affecting a coy, teasing look. "Maybe I'm the type to play hard to get."

He lifted a brow, a dangerous, challenging glimmer reflecting in his striking eyes. "Lucky for you, I'm the type to play along when it's something I want really bad."

And he wanted her. That much he'd made abundantly, physically clear with that delicious kiss he'd planted on her in the car. Which she craved more of. Reaching the machine, she scooped a cupful of ice and popped a cube into her mouth to suck on and cool her feverish desires.

"I'm nothing if not patient and persistent." He leaned against the wall and casually crossed his arms over his chest. While his stance was nonchalant, his body radiated strength and the determination he spoke of. "You should know that about me by now."

She *did* know those traits about him. She was proof that he was a man who set his sights on something and pursued it to the end. Not only as a loyal listener, but as man interested in a woman on a sensual level. She had to admit it was a heady, thrilling sensation being the center of this man's attention and desires, just so long as their attraction didn't escalate beyond what *she* could control.

Carly stuck her head out the door and glanced down the hall toward them. "Three minutes to orgasms," she announced blithely, then disappeared back inside.

Erica cringed at her friend's impertinence, knowing she'd made that particular announcement solely for Ian's benefit. At the rate Carly was going with all the antics she'd pulled that evening, her friend was going to be lucky to live another day.

She glanced back at Ian. A comical look crossed his features, matching the grin pulling at the corners of his mouth.

"Her orgasms or yours?" he asked humorously.

She crunched into the piece of ice. The cold chill bursting in her mouth was a direct, welcoming contrast to the heat pulsing through her body. "She's referring to tonight's topic."

"Sounds...*stimulating,*" he murmured.

Her nipples peaked at his choice of word, which went hand in hand with orgasms. He stood there, waiting quietly, *patiently,* for an invitation to join her for the next segment of the show. To join her for an in-person debate. She thought about discussing such an intimate, erotic subject face-to-face with him. Without pretenses. Without barriers. Without anything but their honest desire for each other laid out in the open between them.

Knowing how potent and sexually irresistible he was, did she even stand a chance against him? *Yes,* if she didn't let him grasp the upper hand during their debate. It was all about keeping *him* unbalanced, she realized. And that meant taking a few calculated personal risks. Letting him share her comfort zone, yet still remaining in control of the situation.

She exhaled a deep, unraveling breath. She needed to do this, to prove to herself that her mother's weakness wasn't her own. That she could enjoy this man—and quite possibly a hot, sexy affair—without the threat of losing her identity and everything she'd worked so hard for since coming to Chicago. That she could handle *Ian* and the pleasure he promised without getting emotionally lost in the process. And what better way to discover if she possessed the ability to hold tight to the reins of control between them than to let him stay for the next segment?

"So, how do *you* feel about orgasms?" she asked before she lost her nerve or changed her mind.

A downright sinful grin curved his full lips. "I've always thought of them as one of life's little pleasures."

"Care to debate that on the air?" she asked impudently.

His eyes blazed with a charged excitement. "You don't have to ask me twice."

5

"TONIGHT I THOUGHT WE'D step outside the boundaries and talk about something forbidden and fun…breathless, mind-blowing orgasms."

Ian sat quietly beside Erica in the booth once again, listening as she tempted and tantalized her audience—as she tempted and tantalized *him*—with her sultry voice and the intriguing intro into tonight's topic.

She glanced his way, a slow, secret smile curving her lips as she paused to let her listeners absorb the impact of her opening statement before she continued. "Ian has graciously decided to stay for tonight's show, so everything you hear this evening between us will be live and uncensored. And after our date earlier, there's no telling what might happen between us. The temperature is sure to rise, among other things."

Judging by the way her gaze dropped briefly to his lap before sweeping upward again, there was no doubt in Ian's mind what "other things" she was referring to. Naughty girl.

He quirked a brow at her sudden brazen display after she'd spent the better part of the evening keeping things between them reserved and low-key, not to mention leaving him dangling on a second date. Something had changed since their conversation out in the hallway. She'd gone from nearly ushering him out of the building after discussing their date on the air to inviting him to debate a very provocative subject on the air. There was a confidence and seductive quality about her that hadn't been evident earlier. And it wasn't just for her listeners' benefit, but for his, he was certain. She was openly flirting and testing her feminine wiles on him.

Not that he minded being the recipient of all that sexy innuendo and attention. Not at all. He found himself fascinated with Erica's sudden metamorphosis, as well as the reasons behind the transformation from cautious woman to a bewitching vixen. For all her outward bravado, there was a bold determination glowing in the depth of her eyes that gave more credence to her sudden change in personality.

She moistened her bottom lip with her tongue, and picked up where she'd left off. "Oral and manual stimulation are no doubt the best ways to climax, but let's go beyond that to specifics, to the very core of the pleasure that accompanies an orgasm." While her words where spoken into the microphone, she addressed him, her gaze locked on his. "What builds you to that breathtaking, explosive release? What do you do for your partner that makes him or her come apart for you? What are your best techniques, and what do you expect in return? The phone lines are open, so let's have fun."

He grinned at Erica, letting her know with that wholly masculine gesture that he most definitely planned to have fun—with the subject matter she'd introduced, and with her. If she was going to be so daring and shameless, then he'd follow her lead and let her take this on-the-air seduction as far as she wanted it to go. Of course they had to behave to some extent considering they weren't completely alone, but there were countless ways to entice without any physical contact at all.

Erica's computer monitor flickered with information

fed in by Carly. Erica pressed a button on the console in front of her and connected one of the phone lines.

"Hi, Richard, you're on the air with *Heat Waves*. Would you like to share your opinion on giving and receiving orgasms and what you like best?"

"Yeah...it sends me over the edge when I bite my partner's nipples, tug real hard, and she claws at my back in that awesome mixture of pleasure and pain," he said, his voice as rough as the visual image his comment projected.

Erica grimaced and pressed her palms to her breasts as if to protect them. Looking at Ian with an appalled expression, she silently mouthed the word *"Ouch."*

He bit back a chuckle, in complete agreement with her. He leaned toward the microphone to add his point of view to Richard's nipple fetish. "I can't say I'm a biter...but I do like to nibble, and suck, and lick. I love the feel of a soft, feminine breast in my hand, and there's something highly erotic about curling my tongue around a taut nipple and tugging *gently.*"

Erica's breathing seemed to deepen, and when her hands finally fell away from her chest he noticed her breasts were full and tight and aroused...just the way he wanted her.

"Hey, different strokes for different folks," Richard said jovially. "I guess I just like my strokes hard and fast and a bit on the kinky side to get that adrenaline rush going, you know?"

Ian knew all about adrenaline rushes...he only had to glance at the woman sitting inches away from him for his heart rate to accelerate and his blood to pulse in his groin. "And I prefer my strokes slow and easy to prolong the pleasure."

Face flushed, Erica thanked Richard and moved on to

the next caller. "Welcome to the show, Cooper. What ultimately brings you to climax?"

"The combination of being enveloped in heat, slick moisture, and tight pressure at the point when I'm first entering a woman sends me straight into orbit."

"Oh, yeah," Ian murmured in male camaraderie.

Erica shot him a curious look. "For you, too?"

"What can I say." He shrugged and grinned recklessly. "That first thrust can be pure, unadulterated ecstasy."

"So you like quickies, then?"

"I didn't say that, and neither did Cooper," he corrected her smoothly. "When a guy is as hard as a rock and wildly turned on, every nerve ending seems to be centered *there*," he said, gesturing to his lap, where his own nerve endings had him in a state of semi-arousal.

"My listeners can't see you, Ian," she said, her eyes dancing with a teasing light. "So try to be more specific with your descriptions. Centered, *where?*" she prompted, displaying more of that impudence of hers.

"At his erection," he stated bluntly. "And the feeling of being wrapped in a woman's tight, snug body is the beginning of great sex, but not necessarily the end. Being a woman, don't you agree that it feels good to be filled and penetrated by that fullness when you're wet and excited and aching deep inside?"

She appeared startled by his candidness, but quickly recovered. "Sure." She sounded too bright, too certain, and when she returned to the phone lines instead of launching into a debate, he wondered if that was her way of avoiding the truth—that she wasn't so certain at all.

Intrigued by the notion, he studied her and all the subtle nuances that contradicted that on-the-air persona he'd known for more than a month. In the flesh, the woman was full of surprises. She had a sexy side he adored, a soft side that pulled at his emotions, and there was a hint of inexperience about her he wanted to cater to and explore.

The problem was, he doubted she'd ever admit to possessing any of those endearing qualities. Or any kind of inexperience.

"Hi, Kristin," she said, greeting the next listener. "What do you do for your partner that makes him come apart for you?"

"I've found that blow jobs are a guaranteed orgasm," she said with a deep-throated laugh. "Men are *so* easy that way, aren't they, Ian?"

Erica lifted an inquiring brow his way, inviting him to respond to the other woman's flirtations—and equally interested to see just how easy *he* was.

He scrubbed a hand along the late-night stubble on his jaw as he took a few extra seconds to think about his answer. He was, after all, a man, and fellatio was something no healthy, red-blooded male refused without a *very* good reason.

"Well...no doubt about it, there's something incredibly exciting about a woman's soft, wet mouth closing around such a vulnerable part of a man's anatomy. But for me, that intimate act is so much more gratifying and intense when its a woman I feel a strong connection to," he said, his low voice vibrating with the slow simmer of desire. Desire for *Erica* to be that woman who performed such an erotic, intimate act.

Tiny beads of perspiration formed on Erica's upper lip as she'd listened to his explanation. She reached for a piece of ice and slipped it into her mouth, tucking it against her cheek. It was warm in the studio, and the temperature continued to escalate with each successive call and response.

After forty minutes of sex talk covering nearly every provocative aspect of orgasms possible, Erica broke for a desperately needed commercial.

In the studio next to theirs, Carly fanned herself with a file folder. "Whew, you two are burning up the airwaves!"

"We don't need any comments from the peanut gallery, thank you very much," Erica muttered, swiping a hand across her damp brow. She stabbed a button on her console, turning off the two-way speaker and tuning out her friend.

"You okay?" Ian asked, concerned with her agitated behavior. She seemed tense and wound up, possibly from all their provocative talk and innuendo. And from the heat in the too small room and the heat sizzling between them.

"I'm great," she said too quickly, too breathlessly. Then a hint of a devious smile canted the corner of her mouth. Dipping her fingers into her cup of ice, she grasped a small melted cube and trailed it down her arched neck to cool off, sighing in sensuous pleasure. "How about you?"

He swallowed hard, his throat as dry as dust. He was suddenly *very* thirsty. Water glistened on her peach-hued skin and rolled down her chest in sparkling, enticing trickles. He followed their path straight into her cleavage, and grew even harder than he already was when he noticed how the cold sliver of ice had affected her nipples. He wanted to sip at the water on her dewy flesh, ached to lap up the moisture with his tongue—all the way to the tight, pearled tips of her breasts.

He raised his eyes back to hers and smiled crookedly.

"My condition should be fairly obvious." He was as stiff as a board, unable to get up without other parts of his anatomy standing at attention, as well.

She eyed his erection unabashedly, contradicting the faint, delicate blush on her cheeks. "A little turned on by tonight's discussion?"

She sounded pleased that she'd managed to bewitch him. There was that glint of determination again. He moved closer, encroaching beyond that invisible, do-not-cross line that had been erected between their chairs.

"A whole lot turned on by *you*," he clarified huskily. "This is what you do to me every night, Erica. No one else."

Her golden-brown eyes darkened and her lashes drooped slumberously. Her lips parted and released a gust of air from her lungs. Want and need chased across her features…leaving behind a flicker of vulnerability that was gone as quickly as it had appeared.

He leaned closer still, his breath feathering across her cheek, his mouth brushing along hers, his tongue touching that soft cleft on her upper lip….

A brisk knock on the glass partition shattered the moment, and Erica jerked back to her side of the microphone, looking shocked that she'd nearly succumbed to him in front of Carly. She dragged a hand through her silky hair and glanced up to find her friend grinning, as well as motioning with one hand to pay attention to her monitor, and counting down the seconds to airtime on the other. Three, two, one…

"You're listening to *Heat Waves* on WTLK," Erica announced, her quick transition back into the show smooth and professional, her voice steady and sure. "We're back on the air with William. What is the most erotic thing your partner has ever done to you to bring you to orgasm?''

''Well…'' William thought about her question for a few seconds, then cleared his throat and said, ''It had to be the time I was taking a shower and my girlfriend joined me. She lathered me up, and gave me what she fondly refers to as a 'wet kiss.' She took one of those full, soft bath sponges and made it slick with soap, then wrapped it around my shaft and squeezed and stroked. Oh, man…just thinking about it is enough to make me climax!''

''What a great way to have a good time with bubbles,'' Erica said, humor lacing her voice.

The evening's topic continued for the next hour and a half, with Ian and Erica engaging in their normal spirited banter and enthusiastic, stimulating debates. The charged sexual tension in the studio increased, nearly crackling in the warm, stagnant air between them.

At fifteen minutes to two in the morning, Erica cued Carly for the final call. ''We have time for one more opinion before we wrap up the show,'' she told her audience, and pressed the last blinking light on the phone. ''Hello, Susan, what's your take on orgasms?''

''Men are easy,'' the other woman said succinctly, and with a thread of disgust. ''A couple of thrusts and grunts and they're done, leaving me far behind and usually unsatisfied. More often than not I take the edge off myself.''

''I hear ya, Susan,'' Erica commiserated. ''Did you know it takes the average man two to three minutes of direct sexual stimulation to orgasm, and it takes the average woman about twenty minutes?''

''That's where foreplay comes in,'' Ian said, adding his two cents to Erica's boring, textbook statistic. ''Which brings us back around to the mind sex we discussed during other shows.'' Which brought the discussion back to *them*. If she was game.

She was, obviously, unable to pass up the subtle dare. "So, are you saying that foreplay and mind sex guarantees an orgasm?"

"There's never any guarantee, but it definitely increases the odds," he drawled in response. Remembering her comment a few nights ago about enjoying a slow seduction, he catered to that fantasy. "All that sexy mind stuff helps get a woman in the mood. So does kissing, and stroking, and touching. It's a matter of building up to that release, and taking the time and care to prime a woman's mind first, then her body. And then, depending on how worked up a woman is, an orgasm can happen quickly. Other times they're meant to be prolonged and savored."

In the booth next to theirs, Carly nodded her enthusiastic agreement to Ian's opinion.

Erica pursed her lips and ignored her friend's response. "Or, like Susan said, they don't happen at all."

"If that's the case, blame it on the Romeo you're with. If a woman is excited enough and in sync with her body and desires, she can have an orgasm fully clothed and from just a kiss."

A skeptical sound escaped Erica's throat. "Women's bodies and responses are different, and not every woman can get *that* worked up over a kiss and with no direct, manual stimulation against her clitoris."

Instead of arguing her point, he changed tactics and hoped it didn't backfire on him. "I take it you've never had an orgasm that way? Fully clothed and from just making out?"

She shrugged indifferently. "I'm sure a lot of women haven't."

"We're not talking about other women, Erica," he said gently, maintaining intense eye contact with her. "We're talking about *you*. Yes, or no?"

She could have lied. Surprisingly, she didn't. "No."

Behind the plate-glass window separating the booths, Carly gaped incredulously, as if she couldn't believe Erica had been deprived of such great foreplay.

He was equally surprised, but Erica's honesty endeared him to her even more. "Ever come close?"

He expected her to fudge the truth, maybe just a little bit. Again, she opted for sincerity with her audience, and with him. "No."

Carly smacked her forehead with her hand and shook her head grievously for her friend's sake.

He grinned wickedly. "Maybe it's time you broadened your horizons and experienced a fully clothed, kiss-induced orgasm."

Carly nodded vigorously and mouthed the words, "Yes, yes, yes!"

Erica shifted in her seat. Crossed one leg over the other. Her thighs flexed as she squeezed them together restlessly. Then she tossed him one of her frivolous smiles. "Maybe I will."

She looked away and wrapped up her segment. "That's it for tonight, everyone. Thank you for joining us, and I hope you enjoyed the show. I'll see you all next week with more scintillating topics to discuss here on *Heat Waves*."

A reel of commercials played, and the early morning DJ stepped into the booth to get ready for his show. Erica politely introduced Ian to Steve on their way out of the studio. Carly stopped them in the hallway, looking her friend up and down as if seeing her for the first time.

"Oh, my God, Erica—"

Erica held up a hand to stop Carly from verbally expressing pity for her pathetic sex life. "I don't want to hear it."

"I just can't believe you've never—"

"Don't say another word," Erica warned, her tone firm.

"Fine," Carly huffed. "I won't say another word about you not experiencing a making-out orgasm," she said impudently. "But after all that talk about kissing and climaxes and such, I'm outta here to finish where Dan and I left off earlier." She waggled her brows and retrieved her purse from the closet, then was out the door and gone.

Erica moved at a slower pace, throwing her cup in the trash and gathering up her belongings, hoping Ian would take the hint and leave on his own. After being grilled by Carly, she had no desire to be interrogated by Ian, too. She'd seen the flicker of shock in his eyes when she'd admitted that she'd never come close to having a fully clothed orgasm, but how many women actually did? And what in the world had possessed her to be so candid with this man and thousands of her listeners and lay her deepest secrets bare?

When he hung around, clearly not going anywhere without her, she decided to be more blunt. "I need to use the rest room. You can go ahead and go, Ian."

He slid his fingers into the front pockets of his jeans, his expression infinitely patient. "I'll wait."

She slung her purse strap over her shoulder as they headed for the station's main door. "It's late, it's been a long night, and you must be exhausted."

"I'm fine," he insisted, sounding very energetic and wide-awake. "Waiting a few extra minutes to walk down with you isn't going to amount to sleep deprivation."

She glanced over her shoulder at him. "The guard will see me to my car. Really."

He tipped his head and grinned, *persistently*. "I don't mind. Really."

"I'm taking the stairs."

Deep laughter escaped him, curling around Erica and eliciting another rush of warmth in forbidden places. As if she needed any more stimulation after four hours of sexy, on-the-air conversation with Ian.

"Sweetheart, my legs are in good shape and I can handle a few flights of stairs."

Sweetheart. She shivered as the endearment touched her much too close to her heart. In a place she'd kept off-limits to men since her disastrous relationship with Paul.

She stopped in the hallway, a few feet away from the women's rest room, and sighed. "Ian—"

He reached out and skimmed his fingers along her cheek and tucked a wispy strand of hair behind her ear, startling her into silence. "Didn't your mother ever teach you not to argue with a date when he's trying to be a gentleman?"

"My mother never dated gentlemen." The comment spilled out of her mouth before she could stop it. She inwardly winced, blaming her slip of the tongue on being tired, confused and thoroughly aroused by this man in front of her. Her body was alive with sensation, and she had a feeling sleep would be a long time coming when she finally crawled into bed.

"What kind of men did your mother date?" he asked with genuine curiosity.

She paused, and found him looking at her with kind eyes. Understanding eyes. And she felt compelled to explain her offhand remark. "My father died when I was six years old, and after that my mother tended to gravitate toward men who were users and took advantage of her insecurities. She's a very needy, clingy kind of woman who believes her life isn't complete without a man in it to take care of her. And the many men who've taken advantage of her weakness were *not* the gentlemanly type.''

She shuddered as old, unpleasant memories swamped her—of growing up watching a parade of guys coming in and out of their house, of resenting her mother for putting her kids second after the newest man in her life. Of spending time in a women's shelter after a boyfriend had taken his anger out on her mother one time too many.

''Sounds like we might have something else in common besides all this hot sexual chemistry between us.'' His words were light and teasing, but the raw emotion in his gaze spoke of something far more painful.

She didn't ask for details, but he shared, anyway. ''My father left my mother when I was one, and she spent her nights partying with guys and doing drugs, and I kind of got shuffled around and was more of a nuisance to her than anything. She died when I was seventeen of an overdose. I pretty much raised myself, as I suspect you did, too.''

There was so much more to his story, she knew, and a part of her ached to delve deeper into his past, to hear that she wasn't the only one who'd struggled to make something of her life after growing up in such a dire situation. But the late hour, and her fatigued mind, wasn't conducive to such an intense conversation.

She smiled, seeing the strong, confident, successful man he was now, despite his disadvantages as a youth. ''Looks like you've come a long way.''

''So have you,'' he said, returning the compliment.

She thought about where she wanted to be in her career, that her success was just beginning to build but had yet to peak. "I have a whole lot further to go."

"And I have no doubt you'll reach your goals."

Without really knowing her, he seemed to know her too well. Yes, she would attain her goals, without following in her mother's footsteps and without allowing herself to be sidetracked by a man or another stifling relationship. While her mother continued to chase after men who were bad for her, it had only taken Erica once to learn her lesson.

She hooked her thumb toward the ladies' room. "I'll be right back if you're still intent on waiting for me."

He settled his shoulder against the wall and smiled. "I am."

She headed into the rest room. As she was washing her hands she found herself searching her features in the bathroom mirror. Remnants of the arousal and excitement Ian had evoked in the studio were still visible. Her skin was pink and damp from the humidity, and her eyes still held a spark of sexual need. A need that coiled deep in her belly and demanded to be appeased.

She ran her brush through her hair and glossed her dry lips, her mind drifting back to her final debate with Ian. The one that had exposed her emotionally to her audience, and to the one man who'd played a big part of her fantasies for the past month. She'd never claimed to be an expert when it came to sex—she just enjoyed the discussions and her listeners' reactions to her provocative topics and liked to make it sound as if she *knew* what she was talking about. So where had all that honesty with Ian come from? And had she risked her credibility on the air by being so open and candid and admitting that she wasn't the orgasmic type?

She frowned at her reflection. Granted, she was incredibly turned on from all that sexy mind stuff Ian had instigated on the air, but it wasn't as though she'd be able to rub her thighs together and magically climax—fully clothed. She was one of those women who needed direct finger stimulation, and lots of it. And the few guys she'd been with had quickly grown impatient with foreplay and moved on to the next level of intercourse, leaving her to handle the delicate matter of her own climax. Like her last caller, she had to hope that many of her female listeners had endured similar experiences and had appreciated her sincerity tonight.

With that thought heavy on her mind, she headed out of the rest room and found Ian right where she'd left him. In silence, he escorted her down the hallway and opened the door to the stairwell for her, which was dimly lit. Side by side, he followed her down the stairs, the quiet punctuated by the sound of her sandals clicking on each metal step.

Finally, he said, "Are you upset with me about tonight's discussion?"

Was the man a mind reader? "Yes. No." She rubbed her temple and sighed, glancing his way. His striking green eyes held a glimmer of worry, and she sought to reassure him. "I'm not upset, just a little frustrated with your pat views on women and orgasms. I might be in the minority, but I think a woman should accept responsibility for her own pleasure."

"And her own orgasms, too?" he asked without missing a beat.

She shrugged as they rounded the corner to the next flight of stairs, her fingers gliding along the cool, metal handrail. She didn't question how comfortable she felt with him, and how easy it was to have these kinds of intimate conversations with a man she'd just met after a month of on-the-air courtship. Nor did she think about just how much of her inexperience she might be revealing. Ian had never judged her before, and she wasn't worried that he'd do so now.

"Since I seem to be the epitome of honesty tonight," she said wryly, "let's just say that it's better for most women to rely on themselves for their own pleasure than ultimately being disappointed or having to fake it."

"It doesn't have to be that way, Erica." His voice was a low, rich murmur of certainty that made her body pulse with renewed awareness. "With the right guy you wouldn't be disappointed, and he wouldn't let you fake it. Not if he could help it."

Ian sounded so confident. Not in a cocky, arrogant sort of way, but in that patient, persistent manner of his. "What if a woman just can't have an orgasm with a man, not even manually?" she tossed out.

The smile that graced his lips was pure, intoxicating male. "Then I'm going to have to assume that he's not giving you the attention you need."

"I'm not talking about *me*," she corrected him too quickly.

"Figure of speech," he interjected smoothly, though there was a certain knowledge in his smoky gaze that seemed to see beyond her protest. "I really do believe that having and enjoying an orgasm is an attitude. You'll only experience as much sexual pleasure as you allow yourself to feel."

His arm brushed hers, a subtle, accidental caress that sent a flurry of sensation straight to her belly. She was feeling too much at the moment, heat and desire and need, but she certainly didn't see all that restless anticipation resulting in a walking orgasm.

She shook her head and argued his point. "You think

a woman can climax with just a kiss and no hands, no fingers and no tongue in intimate places. How unrealistic is that?''

"I think it's *optimistic*," he clarified.

She slanted him a sidelong glance, admiring his strong profile illuminated by the soft, golden light in the stairwell. "You sound so sure of yourself, Mr. Carlisle."

"No, just sure of you, Ms. McCree." An indulgent smile appeared on his lips. "I think I could make you have an orgasm without my hands or fingers touching you at all."

She rolled her eyes dubiously. "Oh, yeah, sure."

He stopped abruptly on the second-floor landing and gently grabbed her arm to stop her, as well. "Since you have so little faith in my ability to excite you and work you up to an orgasm, then why don't we settle the issue here and now?"

The pulse in her throat fluttered. So did the one between her legs. "Because it's late and I have a hot date with the sandman."

"Not a good enough excuse." With very little effort, he backed her up three steps until her spine pressed against the cool, block wall, which was a welcome relief against her feverish skin. He propped his hands flat on the wall on either side of her shoulders, and while he wasn't touching her physically in any way she suddenly felt scorched by the flame in his green eyes.

"What have you got to lose, Erica?" he asked, his voice a low, seductive pitch. "Can you honestly tell me that you aren't turned on by our discussion back in the studio? Can you deny you aren't hot and wet and restless for your own release?"

Again, she couldn't lie or refute his questions. And

even though she couldn't bring herself to voice the word *no,* her omission spoke for itself.

He tipped his head and blinked lazily, contradicting the power and warmth emanating from his large body. "What's the harm in trying a little experiment?"

Nervous laughter sputtered out of her. "I'm not a guinea pig."

"No, you're a woman, thank goodness," he said with amusement that quickly faded into a deep appreciation. "A very beautiful, sexy, desirable woman. And I want to give you something you've never experienced before."

A bout of insecurities swarmed through her. What if she couldn't have that climax he was so certain she'd be able to achieve with him? Would she be able to live with the embarrassment afterward? "Ian, this is ridiculous." She attempted to duck beneath his arm.

He moved his palms lower, effectively trapping her. "No matter what ultimately happens, this is going to be *fun,*" he assured her. "I'll keep my hands right where they are while we're kissing. Worst-case scenario, you'll be kissed senseless, and you'll have proved me wrong and I'll concede defeat—on the air and to your listeners, if that's what you'd like."

That provoked a smile out of her. "I like to gloat," she warned him.

He chuckled deeply. "I can handle it. And you."

She inhaled a breath, bringing her breasts inches away from his chest. Close, but not close enough when she suddenly ached to feel that hard body of his pressed up against hers. "So, what's the best-case scenario?"

A slow, audacious smile sparkled in his eyes and quickly spread across his full lips. "You'll sleep like a baby tonight after I take the edge off of all the sexual tension stringing you tight."

She lifted a teasing brow. "And you think I need *you* for that?"

"I'm beginning to think you don't need a man for anything," he said, too much understanding in his voice and flickering across his expression in the shadowed darkness. "But given the choice, wouldn't you rather experience a real live orgasm with a warm, male body, rather than one all by yourself?"

She heard Carly's voice in her head screaming, *yes, yes, yes!* and made her friend's credo her own. She lifted her chin, unable to pass up the opportunity to indulge in this pleasurable experience, no matter if she didn't reach the big O. "Give it your best shot."

Finally given the permission he sought, he lowered his head and brushed his mouth over hers in a light, warm, barely there kiss. A sweet, persuasive kiss. A kiss that was romantic, and tempting and frustrating for all he withheld. For all that she ached for.

It wasn't supposed to be this way when she'd expected hot and wild from the get-go. Her lips parted on a breathy, needy moan, and still he took his time, seducing her mouth at his own leisure with slow, soft love bites that made her anxious to taste him deep inside. His teeth caught gently on her bottom lip, nibbling and suckling the plump flesh before his tongue stroked along the straight edge of her teeth. She leaned forward, chasing his mouth with her own to deepen the kiss, and he pulled back ever so slightly, maintaining ultimate control of their embrace.

True to his word, he didn't caress or stroke, not with his hands, and not with his body, and she wished he'd never made the promise not to touch her. She burned for the slide of his big hands along her body. She craved the hard, solid weight of him against her breasts, belly and thighs. She wanted to slip her fingers through his thick hair, cup the back of his head, and take their kiss to the next intimate level since he seemed in no hurry to do so himself. Instead she flattened her palms against the wall behind her, determined to behave and not touch in return.

After what seemed like forever, his tongue finally sought hers, and she moaned her gratitude. She started to reach out to grasp his hips, to draw him near, and snatched her hands back when she'd realized what she'd nearly done.

She wouldn't be the first to give in. Curling her fingers into tight fists, she rested her head against the block wall as his lips slid damply, silkily over hers. Then, suddenly, he exerted more pressure against her mouth, manipulating the movement of her head with his lips and chin to instigate a hot, openmouthed, tongue-tangling kiss she couldn't have escaped.

Not that she wanted to. The man was an incredible, consummate kisser, and a connoisseur at erotic foreplay. A master at building taut expectancy. A skilled lover who had no qualms about using every sinful, seductive tactic to his advantage. He kissed her, over and over. Long, deep, breathless kisses. Minutes could have passed, or even an hour. Time lost meaning as pleasure consumed her.

He did things with his mouth and tongue that made her melt and quiver. She imagined that agile tongue stroking and tasting and exploring in other places, just as soft, just as thorough, just as wicked. Lapping along her breasts and flicking across her rigid nipples, gliding down her belly, slipping up the tender insides of her thighs…

The air in the stairwell suddenly seemed as feverish as hot steam. Her skin grew damp, her breathing ragged against his ravishing mouth. Hunger for him, for the all-too-elusive orgasm tingling within her, became a rapacious thing. Building. Throbbing. Pulsing. The heaviness between her thighs and the slick moisture gathering there intensified. She strained toward Ian; he eased away, avoiding any contact other than their mouths.

She nearly wept in frustration. Everything within her was coiled so tight and ready to burst that she was half tempted to touch herself and steal what he was withholding. Her fingers fluttered along the hem of her skirt, skimming her bare skin in a tantalizing, electrifying caress that sizzled its way up to the very heart of her. Refusing to pleasure herself when she wanted Ian to be the one to ease her need, she broke his no-touching rule and reached for him. Finding his belt loops, she gripped them with her fingers and pulled his hips to hers. Taken off guard, he swayed forward. She widened her stance, making room for his muscular thigh between hers, and once she had him there she squeezed tight, refusing to let him go. Her skirt bunched higher, and instinctively she arched into him, sealing their lower bodies. She knew he could probably feel how warm and damp she was through his jeans, and at the moment, she didn't care.

Neither did he, it seemed.

He groaned deep in his throat, his mouth eating at hers in deep, drugging kisses. She felt the hard, impressive length of his erection nudging against her, branding her upper thigh and hip, but his body remained still and tense. She wasn't so disciplined. She rubbed rhythmically against him, letting the pressure gather, reveling in the friction of denim and wet silk sliding erotically along slick, aroused flesh.

Her hands roamed around his sides to his back, then lower, desperate to get closer still. She clenched his buttocks with her fingers, rocked into him again and imagined his powerful body penetrating her, thrusting hard, filling that achy emptiness deep inside her....

Her orgasm hit hard and fast and more intense than any she could ever remember experiencing before. Ian muffled her scream with his kiss as she shuddered and her body flew apart in delicious abandon. She'd never known that an orgasm could be so incredibly *orgasmic*.

Ian wrenched his mouth from hers. *"Yes,"* he hissed in satisfaction, his breath hot and heavy in her ear as she floated back down to earth.

"Erica," he groaned, finally moving one of his hands from the wall and placing it on her quivering thigh. "I *have* to touch you."

Despite his pact not to touch intimately, she couldn't deny him, or herself, the pleasure. Pressing her hand over his much larger one, she dragged his palm upward, beneath her skirt, searing her skin and giving him the permission to do as he desired.

His intense, glittering gaze locked on her face, and her heart pumped fast and furiously. She bit her bottom lip when his fingers feathered across the feminine dampness that drenched her panties. Her breath caught in her throat as he slipped beneath the elastic band and caressed the slick folds of flesh still sensitive from her recent climax. One long finger slowly pushed into her tight channel, then two, and her body clutched at him greedily. His thumb swept over her clitoris, and her knees went weak.

His breathing grew harsh, heavy, the arousing sound echoing in the dim stairway. He shifted against her and rested his forearm at the side of her head, surrounding her with the male scent of him, and an inferno of heat.

"This time I want to watch," he whispered.

This time she let him, savoring the experience and the lush sensations he evoked. Her blood roared through her veins and her entire body trembled as he discovered just the right spot and tempo and wove a magic spell she was helpless to resist. Her eyes rolled back in renewed ecstasy, her lips parted, and she moaned long and low. He took her over the crest, brought her back down gently, and placed the sweetest of kisses on her lips before pulling his hand away and straightening her skirt.

Ian waited patiently for Erica's senses to return and his own blood to cool. Gently, he brushed damp strands of hair away from her cheek just to maintain that intimate connection with her. He'd been with his share of women since Audrey's death eight years ago, but none of those faceless lovers had ever inspired the kind of tenderness that Erica did. With her, he wanted to give without expecting anything in return. And when she blinked up at him, a sated smile on her lips and her eyes hazy with the passion he'd given her, his heart constricted in his chest.

He ran his finger down the slope of her nose and grinned. "You cheated."

Realizing just how shameless she'd been, color rose high in her cheeks, but she didn't look away. "That no-touching rule didn't apply to me," she refuted, a sparkle of sass in her gaze. "You said *you* wouldn't touch, and you didn't, not the first time. And I was fully clothed when I had that orgasm. Doesn't that count?"

He chuckled at her reasoning. "Yeah, I guess it does. So we both proved a point, then. It doesn't matter *how* you achieve an orgasm, as long as you have a good time doing it and it feels good. And judging by your response, you had a good time and it felt good."

"I'll agree to that." A glimmer of worry creased her brows. "Are you going to make *me* admit it on the air?"

He shook his head. "No, this is something I'd like to keep just between us." While he enjoyed bantering with

Erica with her listeners, he saw no reason to share intimate details of their developing relationship.

Gratitude eased across her features, and she dragged a
hand from his chest down to the front fly of his jeans,
where he was still rock hard and throbbing. She cupped
him, squeezed lightly, and he gritted his teeth to keep
from thrusting against her palm.

"What about you?" she asked softly. "What happened
tonight was pretty one-sided, and it doesn't need to be."

"I'll be fine," he lied. Fearing he'd explode in her
hand if she didn't stop stroking him, he gently grasped
her wrist, pulled her touch away and wove his fingers
with hers. "Tonight wasn't about me, it was about you."
And all about showing her she could lose a bit of that
control of hers, and not lose herself in the process.

In silence, he walked her to her car, tucked her safely
into the vehicle and watched her pull out of the parking
lot. He slipped behind the wheel of his Lexus and shifted
to accommodate the fierce erection that had yet to ease.
He released a harsh breath between his teeth, doubting
that his stiff arousal would go away any time soon, not
without a little help.

With the musky scent of Erica's release still clinging
to his fingers, and the vision of her coming apart for him
playing through his mind, he went home and took matters
into his own hands.

6

ERICA SAT DOWN on a wooden bench in the shade, smiling as Tori pushed her daughter, Janet, on one of the swings that was a part of the park's play structure. The young girl squealed in delight as she soared into the air, then caught her breath and demanded, "Higher, Mommy, higher!"

Tori complied, and Erica watched the two of them enjoy the late-morning outing. Erica had promised she'd stop by the shelter that Saturday to visit, and she'd been pleased to find Tori still there, instead of having returned to her abusive husband as Erica had feared she'd do. As Tori had done in the past. Maybe, hopefully, this time would be different for the other woman.

Instead of spending a few hours sitting around the shared residence, Erica had encouraged Tori to bring Janet to the park to play in the warm summer sun. Afterward, Erica planned to treat them to lunch and an ice cream dessert.

After ten minutes of being pushed on the swing Janet decided she wanted to explore the wooden jungle gym, complete with bridges, slides and even a fortress. Tori lowered her to the ground, and Janet ran happily through the sandbox to the elaborate structure, climbed a rope ladder and found a friend to play with when she reached the platform. Tori made her way back to the bench and sat beside Erica, both of them keeping an eye on the little girl and her whereabouts at all times.

"So, are you going to tell me how your date with Ian *really* ended last night?" Tori asked, anticipation lacing her soft voice.

Erica smiled and glanced briefly at the young woman who'd become a friend over the past few months. She just wished different circumstances had brought them together. Though Tori was wearing sunglasses, the bruise on her cheek was still visible, now a pale yellow shade instead of the bright purple and blue it had been last week. The split on her bottom lip had healed, and overall Tori seemed in good spirits and rested, despite the ordeal she'd endured.

"The date ended just as we said on the air," she told Tori, returning her gaze to Janet as she trudged across a wooden bridge with her new little friend tagging behind. "With a kiss."

And two of the best orgasms of her life. Her heart beat faster at the mere thought of what had transpired in the stairwell—a physical surrender beyond anything she ever could have imagined. She wanted to tell herself their tryst was all about satiating lust and Ian proving a point, but neither did Ian ask her to reciprocate the pleasure, nor did he gloat when he had every reason to. Not only was the man as sexy as sin, he was incredibly sensitive and caring, and that was a dangerous combination to her emotional well-being.

After completely turning her mind and body to mush with those climaxes, Ian had walked her to her car, kissed her softly on the lips and whispered "Have sweet dreams" in her ear before she'd driven away. Her dreams had been anything but wholesome and peaceful. They'd been hot, wanton and wicked, with Ian playing a starring role in her midnight fantasies and her waking up aching for the kind of seductive release he'd given her.

She greedily wanted more of those delicious, addicting orgasms. She wanted *Ian*, and an affair was beginning to sound better and better to her independent way of thinking. They could enjoy their attraction *off the air*, and participate in mutual pleasure without the threat of emotional demands messing with her mind. She'd already told him that she wasn't looking for anything complicated or serious, and he'd seemed to accept her terms.

It sounded like an easy solution, as long as she didn't find herself losing control of the situation, and her emotions. She already liked and respected Ian, and that deeply buried and vulnerable part of her feared he'd be an easy man to fall for if she allowed herself to get caught up in this sexy liaison of theirs. Which she wouldn't do. Maintaining ultimate control and calling the shots with Ian was the key. She hadn't spent the past three years building her confidence and a life of her own only to let a man steal it all away or waylay her personal goals.

"Are you going out with Ian again?" Tori asked curiously.

Erica grinned slyly. "Hmm, that seems to be the million-dollar question with my listeners, doesn't it?" she teased. "You're going to have to wait and see what happens, just like everyone else."

Including herself. She'd held Ian off on accepting a second date, and he'd been an exemplary gentleman about her uncertainty—even when he could have coerced an unequivocal *yes* out of her last night when she'd been on the brink of her first or second orgasm. He'd held such power in his hands, and never once tried to take advantage of it, or her.

"Well, I hope there is a second date," Tori said, her

gaze trained on her daughter, whose bursts of girlish laughter brought a smile to her mother's lips. "Listening to the both of you on the air...well, it's like the two of you belong together. It gives me hope that maybe finding a guy like Ian for myself might be possible."

Erica heard the quiver of longing in Tori's voice, and something else—hope?—that caught her attention. Not sure what the other woman was getting at, she reached out and gently laid her hand on her arm. "Tori, what do you mean by that?"

Tori wrung her hands together in her lap. "I'm leaving my husband, Rick," she stated.

Erica sucked in a startled breath, knowing how difficult that decision had to have been for Tori—walking away from the only security she'd ever known, even if that false sense of stability had come at a very steep physical price for her.

"Are you sure?" she whispered, almost too afraid to hope that Tori was truly serious about ending things with her volatile husband.

Chin held high, Tori nodded emphatically. "Yes, I'm sure."

The determination and grit Tori displayed made Erica want to jump up and cheer for the young woman's courage. Erica was so relieved to see the change in Tori.

"I swear I'm not going back this time," Tori said fiercely, her gaze on her daughter. "I can't. Not after the way he beat me up and threatened to go after Janet, too." Her voice broke, and it took her a moment to regain her composure. "I took out a restraining order against Rick. I don't want him anywhere near me or Janet."

Tori's defensive actions were a huge step in the right direction, and Erica could only pray that Tori remained strong and didn't let herself be swayed by any pleas for forgiveness and empty promises from her temperamental husband. Paul had attempted the same tactic when Erica had broken off their relationship, and it had been difficult not to allow her emotions to be swayed. To remain strong and confident enough to start a new life on her own. But in the long run, it had been the best decision she'd ever made for herself.

"I'd be lying if I didn't say that I wasn't scared," Tori admitted, seeking out Erica's gaze. "I'm petrified of being alone. I have Janet's welfare to think of, and I have no idea how to support us."

All legitimate concerns, Erica knew, and all she could do was offer support and reassurance. "You let the counselors at the shelter worry about that, okay?" She gently rubbed her back in soothing circles. "Take things one day at a time, and just know that you made the right decision for you and Janet."

Without the negative influence of her husband overshadowing her every step, Tori was free to make the right choices for her and her daughter. Now that she'd found the strength to end an unhealthy, stifling marriage, the rest would hopefully work itself out for Tori, just as it had for Erica.

"NOW THAT I FINALLY HAVE you alone and to myself, what's this I hear about you becoming a nightly talk-show guest on WTLK?"

Ian reclined in the cushioned chair out on the Winslows' patio after enjoying the family's weekly ritual of Sunday brunch, followed by an early evening round of golf with the men. He glanced across the outdoor table to Gayle Pierce, David and Eve's only living child. Gayle was not only a trusted friend, but she was as close to a sister as he'd ever get. When Audrey had been killed in the car accident only months before she and Ian were to marry, together Gayle and Ian had mourned her death, then bonded over the mutual loss. Gayle knew the guilt he lived with, even though no one in the Winslow family blamed him for the unforeseen tragedy that had claimed Audrey's life. It was his own heart and soul that had accepted responsibility and lived with the pain and grief of that devastating night.

Gayle was as beautiful, sweet and refined as her sister had been, and she knew him better than he understood himself sometimes. And like any good friend, she exerted a more direct, straightforward attitude with him that he'd always appreciated. It kept the lines of communication open between them, and gave them the freedom to be honest with each other without fear of being judged or hurting each other's feelings. It was a special relationship he cherished since he had no siblings of his own.

Gayle cast a quick sweeping glance toward the house where her mother and father had disappeared moments before but would return shortly. Out in the large, landscaped yard, Gayle's husband, Adam, tossed a football to their son, Greg, and their four-year-old daughter, Shelly, sat on the patio steps playing with the doll Ian had given to her for her birthday a few weeks ago. Ian loved the sense of family surrounding him, especially after having grown up without that security and closeness the Winslows so easily shared.

Gayle drummed her fingernails impatiently on top of the glass surface of the table. "If you don't fess up, and quick, you're going to be explaining your sexy little secret to the entire family."

He chuckled and clasped his hands over his stomach. "I don't care who knows," he said honestly. He'd never meant to keep his association with Erica a secret. Then again, he never could have anticipated how one spontaneous call to debate a provocative issue on the air with Erica would escalate into something so hot and intense off the air a month later. "But how did *you* hear about it?" He was curious to know.

"I was having lunch with a girlfriend yesterday, and Marissa was going on about you and the late-night DJ on WTLK, and how the two of you were literally heating up the airwaves. I was sure she was mistaken because I would have *known* if you were spending your evenings flirting with a radio talk-show host, because you would have told me." She sent him an affectionately disgruntled look that he'd kept her in the dark about his after-hours activities. "And then Marissa mentioned that you and the woman on the show were going out on a date and discussing the details on the air afterward, so of course Adam and I listened last night to see if it was really *you*."

He grinned. "Surprise."

"Surprise, my butt!" She lowered her voice when Shelly glanced their way at her mother's outburst. She leaned forward, a sly smile curving her lips. "Ian, you're leading a double life! You're an investment broker by day, and women's sexiest fantasy come to life by night."

"Women's sexiest fantasy?" He winced at Gayle's outrageous description of him as some kind of sex symbol to the female gender. "Being a call-in guest on *Heat Waves* wasn't something I was trying to hide from you or anyone else."

She eyed him dubiously. "Well you certainly didn't share it with the family, either," she grumbled.

"It started out as one call, Gayle," he explained. "One debate that was supposed to be a fun distraction. And it sort of escalated from there. I honestly didn't expect things to go as far as they have."

"How could you *not?*" She shook her head incredulously, causing her soft auburn hair to shimmer around her shoulders. "I only listened to the show once, but it was enough for both me and Adam to realize that the chemistry between the two of you is something to be pursued." Resting her elbow on the table, she propped her chin in her hand, her expression eager. "Erica kept her listeners in suspense at the end of the show, but you can spill the beans with me, Ian. Are you going out with her again?"

He worked his jaw, stalling for a minute before he answered. If it was up to him, yes, they'd go out again and again. As many times as she'd allow, as many days as there were in a week. He just wasn't certain of Erica and what *she* wanted. She'd made it more than clear that she wasn't looking for a serious relationship, that her career was her first-and-foremost priority. Yet, he wasn't positive that an affair would be enough for him when there was so much about Erica that intrigued him. There were so many fascinating dimensions to her personality he wanted to explore.

He'd been tempted to call her this weekend after their date, but made the decision to hold off, not wanting to overwhelm or pressure her. In a very short amount of time he'd come to learn that she was a woman who needed her space, and he respected that, even as he longed to fill that space with his presence.

He needed to tread cautiously with Erica, and maybe that meant letting her set the pace and direction in this budding relationship…and follow wherever she might be willing to take him, and see where it all led.

"I don't know about another date," he said quietly. "It depends on Erica."

"What's there to 'depend' on?" She pursed her lips. "Do you like her?"

He didn't hesitate. "Yeah, I do."

She grinned. "Then go for it."

Easy for her to say, he thought, and sighed. "It's not as simple as *going for it,* Gayle."

She stared at him for a long, uncomfortable moment. "Is this about…Audrey? Because I know you've used her death as the biggest excuse not to let another woman get close—"

"No, this isn't about Audrey." Not this time. It was about him and Erica and him wanting things from her, with her, that he'd spent the past eight years avoiding with any woman. She had him tangled up in a huge knot of need that seemed to pull tighter and become more urgent the more time he spent with her. She made him laugh, she filled hollow places in him that had been empty for too long, and she gave him something to look forward to each night.

He was beginning to crave much, much more than a few hours with her, shared with thousands of other listeners.

"When you're ready, I know we'd all love to meet her, Ian." Gayle's voice pulled him back to the present. "Mom and Dad only wish the best for you, and don't expect you to be faithful to Audrey's memory forever. Life goes on, and so should yours."

Her approval, her kind and understanding words, meant more to him than he realized. "Thanks, Gayle."

The glass slider leading from the house opened, and Eve stepped outside dressed in a silky shorts outfit, followed by her husband, David. The older man clapped Ian affectionately on the back. "You ready for a round of golf, son?"

Son. He'd always felt like David's son. The honor would have been his by marriage to his daughter, Audrey, but he'd instead gained the older man's trust and respect in other ways. In return, the Winslows had offered him family ties, the kind of traditional values he'd grown up without, and a secure place in their lives.

He'd lived with the guilt of Audrey's death for eight long years, and he was ready to take Gayle's words to heart: *Life goes on, and so should yours.* It was time to let go of the past and start building a future. One that involved more than long days at work and nights spent alone.

One that possibly included Erica.

ERICA JOGGED UP the five flights of stairs to the radio station, welcoming the slow burn in her thighs and hoping to work off the extra-large order of french fries she'd eaten for lunch—just before Carly had called to request her presence for a 7:00 p.m. meeting that evening. The excitement in Carly's voice had been unmistakable, and while her friend had refused to tell Erica the reason for the impromptu meeting, Erica figured it had something to do with the possible sale of the station.

Anticipation swirled in her belly as she headed down the fifth-floor hallway. Judging by Carly's enthusiasm, it *had* to be good news. If someone was interested in the station, then he or she had to be considering keeping the format and programming as it was. And that meant job security for her and everyone else at WTLK, rather than dreaded unemployment.

She opened the door to Dan's office, expecting to find the room filled with the station's staff, and stopped abruptly when her gaze found Carly and Dan...and Ian sitting in one of the chairs in front of her boss's desk.

"Ian," she blurted in surprise.

"Hello, Erica," he replied, low and deep.

He must have come from work. Instead of the casual jeans he'd opted for on Friday night, today he wore navy slacks and a white dress shirt with an abstract silk tie, and the sleeves were rolled back to reveal his strong, muscular forearms. A matching jacket was draped over the side of his chair. His hair was mussed, as if he'd repeatedly run his hands through the thick strands throughout the day. She had the strong urge to do the same, to test the warmth and texture between her fingers.

Awareness unfurled within her as his eyes turned a smoky shade of green and the corner of his mouth lifted in one of those seductive, private smiles that turned her inside out with wanting. Just that easily she was lost in the moment, lost in *him* and the erotic, provocative memories of his coaxing kisses and fingers stroking her in feminine places until she'd come apart for him in the most rapturous way. Her heart pounded in her chest and her entire body flooded with a trickling warmth that had nothing to do with the day's heat and humidity, and was a direct result of being near Ian.

She inhaled slow and deep. She hadn't seen or talked to him since he'd left her in the parking lot early Saturday morning after their stairwell embrace. She'd kept herself busy over the weekend and hadn't allowed herself to get too caught up in thoughts of Ian, but her response to seeing him again wouldn't let her lie. She'd missed him. Missed being with him and talking to him and feeling that light, carefree mix of infatuation and desire he evoked.

Oh, boy.

"Close the door, Erica," Carly said cheerfully, effectively yanking her from her thoughts and fantasies of Ian.

"You're letting all the cool air we've got out of the office."

Erica did as Carly requested, though Carly's version of "cool" had to be in the mid-seventies. The fans in the room were on high, recycling the air and offering a modicum of relief from the more stagnant climate in the hallway. But as soon as the door clicked shut behind Erica, she suddenly felt stifled and trapped, as if she were being set up. And she didn't like the sensation one bit.

Erica's shock at seeing Ian ebbed to caution. Suspecting that Carly had some kind of elaborate scheme up her sleeve that involved her and the gorgeous man in front of her, she pinned her friend with a mildly accusing look. "Obviously this isn't a *staff* meeting," she said dryly.

Carly blinked with feigned innocence. "I never said it was."

Of course she hadn't, banking on the hope that Erica would make that assumption. And she had. "A very clever ploy on your part," she muttered beneath her breath. If Carly had gone to such lengths to keep her real reasons for the meeting with Ian a secret, Erica was willing to bet she wasn't going to like what her friend had concocted on her behalf.

"Erica…" Dan began in a placating tone, seemingly sensing her agitation. "We thought it best if you heard our idea in person and not over the phone."

"Well, I'm here," she said, resignation in her voice as she settled herself into the chair next to Ian's. "Let's hear what you have to say."

Carly grabbed a glossy women's magazine from a stack of papers in front of Dan and rounded the desk, her face wreathed with the same excitement Erica had heard on the phone. Carly perched herself on the desk in front of Erica and Ian, though Carly's attention was mainly directed at Erica.

"Do you remember the discussion we had at dinner Friday night, about Chicago being a sexy city?" Carly asked.

Erica thought back to that evening, recalling how Ian believed the city held lots of sex appeal, depending on who he was spending his nights with. Uncertain where Carly was headed with her line of questioning, she answered in a very careful tone. "Yes, I remember."

Her friend grinned, her eyes flaring with a giddy light. "Well, I was thumbing through this magazine over the weekend and came across an article about sexy city nights in Chicago. How appropriate is that? You have *got* to check this out!" Carly opened the periodical to an earmarked page, then thrust it toward her to take a look at it.

Very tentatively, Erica accepted the popular magazine geared toward today's modern woman and perused the feature titled "Sexy City Nights in Fiery Chicago." Along with the article was a two-page spread of color photographs taken of couples near and around city landmarks—some poses fun and playful, others undeniably inspiring and provocative.

Intrigued despite her best efforts to remain disinterested, Erica took in a picture of a man and woman in a heated embrace near the Buckingham Fountain in Grant Park at night, backlit by the spectacular light display with water spraying a fine mist around them. On the opposite page, lovers shared a hot dog at Wrigley Field, with the caption below them referring to a "home run." Another photo featured a couple out on a yacht anchored in Chicago harbor with a view of the city and skylines. Their bodies were shadowed, but the pale shimmer from the full moon reflected off of smooth, bare skin, and rippling muscles along a very masculine posterior.

Erica swallowed to ease the sudden dryness in her throat, her gaze shifting to yet another sultry image, this one in the darkened back seat of a limo with a scantily clad woman doing something very erotic on the man's lap. Both of them appeared to be in the throes of passion and enjoying the illicit, private moment. The kind of illicit, private moment she and Ian had shared in the stairwell.

A throbbing started low and deep, matching the unsteady rhythm of her heart. Her and Ian's tryst would have fit in perfectly with the collection of photos, the two of them depicting another sexy city night in fiery Chicago. The mere thought caused a pleasurable ripple to cascade down her spine and gather between her damp thighs.

Ian leaned close to her chair, his arm brushing hers as he reached out and pointed to a snapshot of a couple in a cart at the very top of the Ferris wheel at Navy Pier. "Hmm, that one looks like fun, wouldn't you say?" he murmured near her ear.

With the lights of the harbor twinkling in the background and the pair shrouded in the darkness of night, they were creating their own version of the mile-high club. The woman's parted, glossy lips were making their way down the man's bare torso, while her fingers worked the snap of his jeans to release the burgeoning erection straining against denim. There was no mistaking what she intended to do, and there was no denying he wanted it just as much.

Erica's stomach dipped, and her face heated when she imagined doing those lusty things with Ian. Maintaining her composure, she sent him a sassy look. "I hope for the guy's sake there aren't any jarring stops on the ride."

Ian winced at her implication, but he was grinning rakishly, tempting her with his bedroom eyes, making her restless for something as equally forbidden as what the photos portrayed.

"Isn't that a fabulous feature?" Carly asked, clearly expecting Erica to be just as thrilled as she was with her find.

Erica fanned the magazine shut and tossed it onto the surface of the desk, wishing she could dismiss those scintillating pictures from her mind just as easily. "And this article concerns us how?" she prompted, not certain she really wanted to know.

Carly exchanged a quick, encouraging look with Dan, who gave her a nod to continue. "When I first read the article and saw the pictures, I told Dan we ought to try out all those sexy places ourselves, and that's when it dawned on me what a great campaign this would be for you and Ian."

"Campaign?" Her *and* Ian? Erica frowned, feeling the beginning of a headache coming on. "What do you mean?"

Carly's entire body seemed to hum with energy and exuberance. "After the success of your Friday night date with Ian, and with your listeners clamoring for more of the two of you, I thought you could do your own version of sexy city nights in Chicago and make it a weekly part of your show. The two of you could hit one of these night spots, then report back on the air like you did for your last date. We've already filled Ian in on the details, and he's agreed to do the series of dates—"

"No." Her response was an automatic defense mechanism. It was one thing having Ian as a nightly call-in guest and tantalizing her listeners with their one date, and another thing entirely to make him such an integral part of *her* show. "That's not what *Heat Waves* is about."

"*Heat Waves* is about anything sexy, hip or provocative," Carly refuted. "This would be all three."

And it would mean going out with Ian. Every week. Which wouldn't be such a bad thing if their date didn't have anything to do with the success of her show. And therein lay her biggest complaint, that her show and Ian were becoming much too intertwined for her peace of mind.

Dan added his opinion to the matter. "Friday night's show created such a huge buzz and this is just another way to capitalize on the hype. It's all about marketing your show and the station and taking advantage of whatever press and publicity we can."

Any extra coverage for *Heat Waves* or WTLK was something Erica couldn't argue with. And both Dan and Carly knew that.

A spontaneous, gregarious grin brightened Carly's expression. "We've even looked into having bus and billboard ads done up with the picture of the two of you together with the slogan And You Thought The Heat Ended With The Fire emblazoned across the top of the ad." She looked pleased with her creative, catchy phrase. "What do you think?"

Stunned by just how far Carly planned to take this campaign of hers, Erica shook her head incredulously. "We can't afford to do billboard ads!"

"We can't afford *not* to," Dan said, speaking strictly from a marketing angle. "I worked out a budget, and if this draws in the big-name advertisers the way we project it will, it'll put us in a better position for the sale of the station."

Erica's mind whirled and her chest tightened with resentment. She felt ambushed and cornered by the two people she trusted. She knew Dan and Carly truly had her best interests at heart, and the show's ratings in mind, but that success came with a price—one that was connected directly to Ian and felt very personal.

"Would you mind if Erica and I discussed this alone for a few minutes?"

Ian's deep voice startled her. She'd been so caught up in her own anxiety and jumbled thoughts, and he'd been so quiet during her discussion with Carly and Dan that she'd nearly forgotten that he was in the room. Now it seemed he wanted to state his opinion on Carly's idea— privately.

"Take all the time you need," Dan said as he came around his desk and gently but firmly grasped Carly by the arm. "We'll be in the lunchroom when you're done." He ushered Carly out of his office, shutting the door behind them.

A huge sigh unraveled out of Erica, and she smoothed her hair behind both of her ears before glancing Ian's way. He sat there in that patient way of his, his eyes a strange mixture of kindness, caring and sensuality. "How do you *really* feel about all this?"

An adorable smile creased his mouth. A mouth capable of giving her such wondrous pleasure. A mouth she ached to feel on hers again...and other places, too. She was becoming a shameless hussy when it came to Ian.

He stretched his arm across the back of their chairs, letting his fingertips slip through the ends of her hair and feather along her neck. "You honestly have to ask that question after Friday night's date?"

Her sensual reaction to his touch spoke for Ian, and herself. She trembled from the inside out, wanting him with a fierceness that was foreign to her, but was becoming increasingly familiar when it came to him. "No, I guess not," she conceded.

Confused by all that had happened in such a short span of time, she stood and walked to the windows overlooking the street below and the evening traffic wending its way through the city. "This whole thing with you and me and the show is getting so out of hand," she muttered.

"What is your biggest objection, Erica?"

He might as well have asked her "What is your biggest fear?" The two went hand in hand and stirred so many levels of emotions in her. Resistance to change. Desire for Ian. Panic that she wouldn't be able to separate this deep craving she'd developed for Ian from the aspirations she'd clung to for the past three years.

She wrapped her arms around her middle and wondered how everything had become so complicated when her life and ambitions had seemed so stable and clear cut two months ago. Before Ian had entered her life and made her feel things she'd managed to do without for all of her adult years. He made her want him—sexually and emotionally—and the combination was one she had no idea how to handle.

What was her biggest objection? He deserved an answer. Turning back around, she faced him, and her insecurities. She'd learned from an early age to confront her weaknesses head-on and not to give in to them, and this situation with Ian would be no different. "Everything with the show is starting to revolve around me *and* you."

He regarded her through eyes that were at once serious and bemused. "And that's a bad thing?"

Personally, no. Professionally, yes. "The hype, the interest…it's something I never anticipated," she said, compelled to be straightforward and honest with him.

"Not this quickly, anyway. I've spent the past three years struggling to make my own mark as a DJ here in Chicago, and because of you I've become an overnight success and a household name."

His smile held a wealth of understanding. "You wanted to make it on your own."

"Of course I did, and I still do. And that's part of the reason why I'm so hesitant about jumping into this sexy city night campaign with you." Moving across the room, she settled her bottom on the edge of the desk a few feet from Ian. She sat in front of one of the oscillating fans and caught an intermittent breeze that fluttered through her hair and along her warm skin. "When I left California, I had certain aspirations in mind and I've worked hard to achieve them. I'm single, independent, and I don't have to answer to anyone but myself. But one of my biggest goals when I arrived in Chicago was to succeed in this dog-eat-dog world of broadcasting. On my own."

"I think you were on your way to being successful, even before I started calling in," he assured her. Tipping his head, he scrutinized her deeper than she would have liked. "Do you mind my asking what made you leave California?"

She'd effectively dodged that question when they'd gone to dinner Friday night, but she wasn't going to evade it now when she was spilling so many truths. And if it gave him a clearer understanding of *her,* then all the better.

"I grew up in California. My mother and sister still live there." Her dysfunctional family was a whole other issue, and one she had no desire to delve into. "I was dating a guy named Paul, and things turned serious between us fairly quickly and I ended up moving in with him because he insisted it made things easier for both of us. Everything was fine for a while, and then he gradually changed. He didn't like what I did for a living, the late nights and working with male DJs. He started limiting what I could and couldn't do, what friends I could see, and for a while I went along with his demands because I was so lost in the relationship I couldn't see how much he was controlling my life and even my decisions."

Ian absently rubbed his thumb along his jaw as he listened attentively. "Something obviously made you see the light."

She nodded, curling her fingers around the square edge of the desk. "A new guy at the station who didn't know I was in a serious relationship made a pass at me. Paul found out about the incident from one of his friends who worked at the station and he went berserk. He demanded that I quit my job, and I almost did because that's what *he* wanted."

But on the drive to terminate her employment, she'd realized if she followed through on Paul's orders she'd be succumbing to her mother's greatest weakness…she'd be giving a man power and influence over her life and emotions, as she'd sworn she'd never do.

She shuddered at how close she'd come to getting sucked into that same vicious cycle. "I knew if Paul got his way, it would be as good as me handing over my independence and freedom to him on a silver platter. So, I refused to turn in my resignation, and Paul countered by issuing me an ultimatum. Him or my job."

She laughed, but the sound held no humor. "That ultimatum was a huge wake-up call for me and made me see just how controlling Paul was, and that the relationship was heading toward something far more destructive if I didn't get out of it then and there. A few days later I did quit my job, but I did it for *myself*. And then I packed my belongings, picked a city where I felt there would be ample opportunities for me to pursue a career as a DJ, and drove to Chicago.''

She stretched her legs out in front of her, and the cool material of his trousers brushed her bare calf. There had been absolutely nothing sexual about the accidental caress, yet she couldn't stop the slow, building awareness strumming through her.

''It's important that I make it on my own merit, Ian,'' she continued, needing him to accept those aspirations. ''For so many reasons. And especially now that the station is on the market. If WTLK doesn't sell, or someone decides to change the program or bring in their own personalities, I want to be able to audition at another station and get a job without everyone asking about you or expecting you to be part of the package. Can you understand that?''

''Yeah, I can.'' He leaned forward in his chair and braced his arms on his thighs, his gaze never leaving hers. ''So, where does this leave us and the sexy city nights campaign?''

''I don't know.'' She had no ready answers, just doubts and uncertainties that kept rearing their ugly heads. ''You've been a part of my show for the past month as a call-in listener, and even I can't deny that you've made *Heat Waves* hotter and sexier and more exciting, but where and how will all this end?''

Something flickered in his eyes, that persistence of his clashing with a deeper hesitation. ''Do you want it to end here and now?''

He was leaving the decision up to her. Offering her the opportunity to end their on-the-air relationship with one simple word from her. *Yes.* A huge knot formed in her chest at his selfless act, so unlike anything she'd ever known from any man. Ian was willing to give her back her nights as a solo DJ and step out of her spotlight. But being put in the position of giving him up or sharing her nights with him—both on the air and dating—she knew she wasn't ready to let him go. She wasn't ready to relinquish the chance to experience everything he had to offer. The passion. The seduction. The best orgasms her body had ever had the pleasure of receiving.

Like a woman starved for ultimate fulfillment, she craved more. She wanted Ian Carlisle. And she knew the desire was mutual. Her listeners were eager to share in the sensual relationship blossoming between her and Ian, so why not enjoy the wild ride until all their hot sexual chemistry fizzled out? And if their weekly dates helped boost her ratings, all the better.

Pushing aside deeper emotional fears, she made her decision based purely on the arousing, feminine needs this man kindled in the deepest part of her. "No, I don't want us to end. Not yet."

Relief eased the tension bunching across Ian's shoulders and set his heart to racing. He'd been prepared to accept her answer, even if it meant putting an end to their on-the-air association. Thank God she'd agreed to give them more time.

Feeling as though she'd granted him silent permission to touch her in the way he'd been aching to since first seeing her walk in that door, he stood up and closed the scant distance that had been separating them. After listening to her bare a part of her soul to him, he decided to take a different approach with Erica and focus on something less threatening, something she felt as though she had rules and boundaries for. Their attraction. An affair.

With his knee he nudged her slender legs apart, stretching them wide as he moved in between and pinned her against his lean hips and taut thighs. Their position was inherently sexual, a classic erotic fantasy of making love on a desk. Despite her shorts and his slacks separating them, he instantly grew hard. The soft gasp that escaped her throat told him she felt his erection. Her hands settled on his waist, and the subtle, instinctive rocking of her hips and the way her lashes fell half-mast let him know that she'd welcome his thickening shaft deep inside of her, given the chance.

Given the chance, that's exactly where he wanted to be.

He pushed all ten of his fingers through Erica's hair, wrapping his fingers around the silken strands and tipping her face up to his. "If we're going to do this sexy city nights campaign, then let's take it to the extreme and have fun with it and each other. Ride the crest and enjoy the affair for as long as it lasts. What do you say?"

He'd obviously said the right words to sway her, because agreement sparked in her beautiful brown eyes, glittering with golden excitement. "I say *yes.*"

He smiled and lowered his head, sealing their deal with a long, deep kiss that she returned with equal ardor and unfettered enthusiasm. His lips on hers stripped away any lingering inhibitions she might have had. Eventually, he softened the caress of his mouth against hers and murmured, "First official sexy city night date, this Saturday night."

She tugged gently at his bottom lip with her teeth, then soothed the love bite with the stroke of her tongue. "Okay," she said agreeably.

Another hot, drugging kiss, and then he pulled back, his gaze scanning her face, flushed with arousal. "I'll pick the place."

"All right." A seductive smile curved her mouth, and a wave of desire surged to his groin, making him impossibly thicker, harder—to the point that he felt as though he was about to bust the seam in the crotch of his slacks.

He nuzzled her neck, tasting her with his tongue all the way up to the sensitive spot just below her ear. "Wear something slinky, sexy and *accessible,*" he whispered hotly.

Groaning, she clasped his buttocks in her hands and stroked his erection against her mound. "Unlike these *inaccessible* shorts?" Frustration laced her voice.

He chuckled, the sound low and strained. "Nothing is *that* inaccessible."

She squirmed to get even closer, and pouted when her attempts didn't give her the satisfaction she obviously craved. "I beg to differ."

He lifted a brow. "Do I hear a challenge in your voice?"

A brazen smile curved her swollen lips. "Yeah, I believe you do."

She wanted an orgasm. Here and now. He wasn't sure if she was serious or teasing, and called her bluff. "We could get caught."

Her thighs clenched tighter around his hips, inviting the illicit, forbidden tryst. "I'm willing to take that risk," she said huskily.

He'd created a sexual monster, and she was all his. "Greedy witch."

Stroking her flattened hands up his spine, she aligned her body with his and rubbed her breasts against his chest. "It's all your fault."

He accepted full blame and responsibility for her newfound sensuality, liking the fact that he'd been the one to introduce her to the pleasures of orgasms. The woman was an incredibly soft touch, so responsive, and he knew it would be so easy to give her what she wanted.

And so he did. Here and now. His mouth closed over hers, pulling her into a tongue-tangling kiss that was nothing short of wicked. His hands coasted down her sides to her hips, tipping her pelvis up to better receive his slow, rhythmic thrusts in a simulated act of sex. She wrapped her arms around his neck, arched her back and raised her knees high around his waist for deeper penetration, more pressure, greater friction.

Her breathing deepened, and she moved in sensual, tempting counterpoint to his long, slow strokes. Heat blazed through his bloodstream, and he gritted his teeth against the primal urge to let go of his restraint. Each caress became more frantic, more needy, sweeping him up into the moment and leaving coherent thought behind. He imagined sinking into her tight, damp heat, feeling her swell around him and tremble with the first signs of her climax.

And then she *was* trembling, and moaning, and clutching at him like a wild thing spinning out of control. He grasped her bottom, slid his large hands down to the back of her smooth, bare thighs and pumped harder, faster. He felt her shudder as she climaxed, and swallowed her soft cries with his mouth. This time, he couldn't hold back. The pleasure was too intense and explosive. Tearing his lips from hers, he swore vividly and came right along with her in a mindless rush of molten heat and liquid fire.

Heart beating furiously, and mortified at his lack of control when he'd never lost his restraint like that before, he lifted his head and found Erica grinning at him, her expression sated and her gaze curious. "Ian?"

The question in her tone was unmistakable, and he felt his skin warm. "Don't say a word," he growled in embarrassment. "It's bad enough that I'm going to have to walk out of here with my jacket folded strategically in front of my lap to insure I keep my dignity intact, I don't need you making any sassy wisecracks, too."

She pressed her damp palm to his cheek. The gesture was so tender and gentle it made his heart turn over in his chest. "Actually, I think it's kinda sweet, and very sexy." She kissed him softly on the lips, then looked at him again. "Now I think I know the true meaning of a fully clothed orgasm."

And she'd obviously enjoyed herself. Immensely, if the satisfied look on her face was any indication. "Enough of being fully clothed. The next time I give you an orgasm, you're going to be completely naked."

Her eyes widened in mock fear and she feigned a shiver. "Ooh, is that a threat?" she teased.

He grinned wickedly. "Nope, it's a promise I intend to keep."

7

"TAKE THESE, PUT THEM in your purse, and use them in good health."

Erica stared at the half-dozen or more small square packets Carly had pressed into her open palm. The eclectic assortment of prophylactics included colored, scented, lubricated, ribbed, extra-large and even flavored—orange, banana and cherry. While Erica was grateful for Carly's foresight, she found herself overwhelmed by the choices she held in her hand.

With a wry grin canting her lips, she met her friend's bright-eyed gaze. "You stopped by my apartment to give me *condoms?*"

"Hey, what are friends for?" Carly shrugged impertinently as she sauntered past Erica into her small living room, which connected to the kitchen and tiny breakfast alcove. "You're the one with the hot date tonight with Ian, and I figured since I'm not getting any at the moment, you might as well."

Shaking her head in bemusement at Carly's way of thinking, Erica closed the door after her friend and glanced at the clock on the kitchen wall. She had a half hour before Ian arrived to pick her up for dinner at a restaurant he'd selected for their first official sexy city night "date."

"All I can say is that Dan must be worth the wait."

"Yeah, he is." Carly's expression softened with a

mixture of adoration and satisfaction. "We've done everything short of actual intercourse, and I have to tell you, my love life has never been so hot!"

"Mine, too," Erica admitted.

Carly gasped, her eyes widening in astonishment. "You and Ian have already done the deed?"

A rush of heat stained Erica's cheeks. Looking away, she opened the small black purse on her dinette table and stuffed the packets inside for safekeeping. "No, but like you and Dan, the foreplay has been great." Verbal, mental and physical foreplay.

It had been almost a week since she and Ian had agreed to do the sexy city nights campaign...a week of pure seduction and erotic mind sex as he continued to call in to the show and they debated provocative issues on the air. One night had even ended in lusty phone sex when Ian had called her after she'd arrived home from work and they'd launched into a private discussion about fulfilling fantasies. He'd verbally fulfilled her secret desires that night, and left her aching for more.

Sighing at the pleasurable memory, she picked up her gold hoop earrings lying beside her purse and used the brass-framed mirror hanging next to the door to help guide them into her lobes. The air-conditioning unit situated below the decorative mirror was on medium, and the rush of cool air felt refreshing on her warm, bare skin, but also caused her nipples to pucker tight against the thin, stretch silk of her dress.

She wasn't surprised. The littlest, most mundane things seemed to trigger a sensual, needy response from her lately. Even buying peaches, cherries and cucumbers at the store that afternoon had turned into an arousing experience for her! She constantly felt turned-on and sexual in a way that made her very conscious of her body, and all too aware of the fact that she and Ian had yet to consummate their affair.

The last five days had passed in a whirlwind of activity that had left little time for her and Ian to spend *alone*, without interruptions or being surrounded by other people. While Ian's day hours at work conflicted with her nighttime schedule, they'd managed to meet in between for the photo shoot Carly had set up to get the billboard ads done, which had started going up around the city and were already generating a very enthusiastic response. They'd even squeezed in two live appearances—one at a local bookstore, and another at a coffeehouse—to promote the campaign and WTLK. All in all, the advertising was proving to be a huge success.

The time she and Ian had spent together during the week had been fun and relaxing, and the sexual tension and chemistry between them was as sizzling hot as ever. Any private time they'd managed to grab Ian had used to *his* advantage, weaving an alluring, seductive spell with his insatiable kisses and slow, breathless caresses that built the waves of anticipation toward a more physical, carnal joining. After enduring so much of Ian's arousing foreplay—on and off the air—she was as primed as a woman could be, and tonight she planned to be the one to end the torment for both of them and take their relationship to its logical conclusion.

Carly slid into one of the two chairs at the table and sent her a chastising look. "From that naughty look on your face, it appears you've been holding out on me with Ian."

Erica laughed and shook herself from her intimate thoughts. "Actually, Ian's the one holding out on *me*," she said meaningfully. Retrieving her new cinnamon-flavored lip gloss from her purse, she applied a coat of the shimmery red glaze to her lips. "I swear we've yet to do the wild thing, but like you, I can't really complain." She felt thoroughly romanced and pursued, and it was truly a wonderful, unique feeling. One she planned to enjoy while it lasted.

Carly grinned. "With a little persuasion on your part, you'll get lucky tonight…if that's what you want."

Oh, yeah, she wanted Ian, very badly. But she couldn't deny that along with the anticipation and excitement of taking that giant leap to sleeping with him came a huge dose of anxiety.

"I'm nervous," she confessed, meeting Carly's gaze in the mirror. "It's been a long time since I…well, since I've been with anyone that way." Since she'd allowed a man so intimately close. And for all her sexy talk on *Heat Waves,* she didn't want Ian to be disappointed if she wasn't everything he expected her to be in bed.

Carly dismissed her concerns with a wave of her hand. "Sweetie, considering how the two of you literally sizzle when you're together with your clothes *on,* I'm betting you set the sheets on fire when you get naked. And trust me when I say that going without sex for a long time tends to add kerosene to the flame once it's ignited. Your biggest worry should be that you both don't incinerate."

Erica laughed at her friend's outrageous comment, which helped to ease some of the tension and insecurities swarming within her. "Okay, I'll take your word for it."

Carly's gaze skimmed down the length of her, taking in her outfit. "By the way, that's a fabulous dress. One that screams 'take me.'"

"That's certainly reassuring." Erica tucked her lip gloss into her purse and glanced back at the mirror. She was far enough away to get a full-length view of herself. Per Ian's request, she was wearing something slinky, sexy and *accessible,* and she was hopeful that he'd like what he saw. The little black dress she'd bought was held up by thin straps and made of a stretch silk fabric that contoured to her slender figure, from her braless breasts down to just above the knee where her legs, encased in smoky hued thigh-high stockings, extended. She wore strappy high heels that completed the ensemble and boosted her height a few inches.

All in all, she was *very* accessible.

Carly scrutinized her a bit longer. "I hope you're wearing something sexy beneath that dress."

Erica fluffed her hair one more time, giving it a soft, tousled kind of look. "That's for me to know, and *Ian* to find out."

"Let's hope he does." Grinning, Carly stood. "Well, I've done my duty by delivering those condoms, it's up to you to put them to good use."

Recalling the variety Carly had given her, she smirked in return. "The hard part is going to be choosing which one to use first."

Carly sashayed toward the door. "The strawberry ones smell great, and the ribbed ones are kinda fun—" She opened the door, gasped, and spun back around with a hand pressed to her heart. "Ohmigod, your Prince Charming is here and he's picking you up in a limo! This guy is definitely a keeper, Erica."

Erica didn't want to think about the fact that she *wouldn't* be keeping Ian for her very own. Not permanently, anyway. She swallowed the unexpected lump of discontent that rose in her throat and peered over her friend's shoulder to get a glimpse for herself. Sure enough, an elegant black stretch limousine was parked at the curb—*all the better for her to seduce him in,* a little voice in her mind whispered.

Ian was making his way up the sidewalk to her apartment, dressed in black slacks and a long-sleeved black-and-gray printed shirt. Despite the heat and humidity that was still evident at six-thirty in the evening, he looked refreshed and energetic, and sophisticated and wealthy enough to clash with her modest neighborhood. It was a contrast she didn't want to analyze too closely, but it wasn't the first time she'd wondered about his lifestyle, especially when hers seemed so meager in comparison.

He saw her and smiled, and that's all it took for her pulse to leap with thrilling excitement, and every other thought in her head to take flight and disappear. The man was sinfully gorgeous, breathtakingly sexy, and for now, tonight especially, he was all hers and she wouldn't have to share him with anyone.

"WOW, THE VIEW UP HERE is incredible!"

Ian sat back in his chair in the private dining area at Everest, one Chicago's finest French restaurants. He smiled at Erica's genuine enthusiasm as she gazed in awe at the cityscape from the posh dining room located on the fortieth floor of the Chicago Stock Exchange.

She was the one who was incredible, he thought, taking in her natural, fair beauty backdropped by the sun setting in the distance and the simple but elegant decor of the restaurant. Her lips were parted in admiration of the scenery, and he caught the faint shimmer of red still evident on her bottom lip. He'd kissed off most of the candied gloss on the limousine ride over—a sweet "hello" kiss that had intensified into a seductive "I want you" kiss that had ended much too soon for either of them. She'd tasted like cinnamon and fire, and the hot flavor, coupled with her uninhibited response to him, had started a slow burn of desire that still flowed through his veins.

And then there was that sexy black dress she was wearing, which revealed a whole lot of bare skin for him to touch and caress, which he'd taken advantage of during their kiss. He'd discovered that she wasn't wearing a bra when his hand had wandered to her breast, and knowing she was half-naked beneath that clingy outfit kept him in a state of semi-arousal.

Oh, yeah, she was incredible, and gorgeous, and sensually exciting. Yet her outward strength and confidence was underscored with a vulnerability he'd glimpsed when she'd shared her past relationship with him last week. There were so many facets to Erica's personality, more than he ever could have anticipated, and each layer fascinated him like no other woman ever had.

Shifting in his seat, he took another drink of his champagne just as their tuxedo-clad waiter delivered the first course of hors d'oeuvres.

Once the server left their table, Erica dipped her spoon into her cauliflower fondant and took her first taste. She closed her eyes and moaned in ecstasy as she savored the rich taste. "Oh, Ian," she sighed as her lashes drifted open again and she smiled with unabashed pleasure. "This is absolutely heavenly."

He smoothed his linen napkin on his lap and sampled his own appetizer, and found it just as delicious as Erica claimed hers to be. "I wasn't sure if you liked French cuisine, so I took a chance."

"I'll admit, when it comes to French cuisine my taste buds are limited to French fries, French toast, and French apple pie," she joked, and ate another spoonful of her fondant. "I think you've spoiled me for the real thing."

He chuckled, amused and completely beguiled by her

and her appreciation of fine food. He'd wanted to take her someplace memorable, special and quiet, where they wouldn't be mobbed by people who recognized their faces as the radio personalities on the billboard ads around the city. "Anytime you have a hankering for French cuisine you just let me know."

She slanted him a curious look as she dabbed her napkin across her mouth. "Which brings me around to a question I've been dying to ask since I realized we'd be eating dinner at one of Chicago's finest and most elegant restaurants. How were you able to get reservations here so last-minute, and a window seat in the private dining area, no less?"

"It pays to know the right people." He winked at her.

She set her spoon on her bowl and quirked a blond brow his way. "And just *who* do you know that has that much clout?"

"David Winslow, who's good friends with the manager here." Ian had brought many clients here for business dinners due to David's connection, but never a woman he'd dated. Erica was the first.

She blinked lazily as she took a sip of the bubbly champagne in her fluted glass. "Winslow..." she repeated the name, her head cocked to the side. "Isn't that the name of the investment firm where you work?"

"Yes," he said with a nod. "Winslow Financial Investment."

"And David is the owner?" she asked.

Their waiter stopped by their table again, this time clearing away their appetizer plates and replacing them with a bowl of beef consommé, then topped off their champagne. Ian waited until their server moved on to another table before answering Erica's question.

"David Winslow is the retired owner of the firm,

though he's remained a silent partner in the company. He made me partner and CEO and handed over the business to my care when he retired years ago, and I've been at the helm ever since.''

Erica broke open a piece of warm bread and slathered it with butter. ''No one in his family was interested in the investment business?''

Picking up his spoon, he stirred it through the savory broth, inhaling the sweet, nutty scent. ''David had two daughters, and neither one followed in their father's footsteps, not that he expected either of them to.''

''*Had* two daughters?'' she questioned, catching his word choice.

''His oldest daughter, Gayle, is married and a stay-at-home mom. The Winslow's youngest daughter, Audrey, died eight years ago.'' He paused for a heartbeat, then decided to share a part of his past with her. ''I was engaged to her.''

''Oh.'' Surprise reflected in Erica's tone. ''I'm sorry.''

''Me, too,'' he said quietly.

Compassion filled Erica's soft brown eyes as she met and held his gaze. ''You still miss her?''

That wasn't the reason why he'd apologized. Memories of Audrey still entered his mind at times, but it had been a while since those recollections were accompanied with that aching, empty loss that had consumed him the first few years after she'd died.

He tried to explain in a way that she'd understand. ''I meant that I was sorry, too, for her death, and the circumstances surrounding it.''

She sipped another spoonful of her consommé, then asked, ''Do you mind my asking what happened?''

''No, I don't mind.'' He'd never discussed the accident with anyone other than someone in the Winslow family, but he felt compelled to share those details with Erica now. "We were coming home after having dinner together, and I was driving through an intersection. The light was green, but another car ran the red light coming the opposite way and rammed into the passenger side of the car at about forty miles per hour. The impact killed Audrey instantly. One minute she was laughing at something I was saying, and in the next she was gone."

"Oh, Ian," she whispered consolingly. "That's awful."

The whole experience now seemed like a distant dream, but the emotions attached to that night were still present, constricting his chest for all the "if only" scenarios he'd played through his mind over the years. If only they'd never gone out that night. If only they'd left the restaurant five minutes later. If only they'd taken another route home. There were a hundred regrets, but none changed the fact that Audrey had died and he'd walked away from the accident with only a few scratches and bruises.

Finished with his soup, he leaned back and went on. "It was especially hard for me because I felt responsible for Audrey. Not necessarily for her death, but to take care of her and keep her safe. David and Eve trusted me, and I felt as though I let them down, though they've never blamed me for her death."

Erica looked appalled that he could think such a thing. "Of course they wouldn't. You couldn't have anticipated what happened that night. No one could have."

"I know that, but guilt has a way of eating at a person." He smiled a bit sadly. "I've always felt that I owed the Winslows so much because of everything they've done for me, and yet I'm the one responsible, even indirectly, for their daughter's death."

The waiter interrupted their conversation as he smoothly and efficiently served them their main course—sautéed veal chop and mushrooms for Erica, and wild sea bass for him. Once the server was assured that they had everything they needed, he left them alone again.

Erica sliced into her tender veal chop, thinking about the private, personal story Ian had shared with her. He talked of the Winslows as an integral part of his life, but they obviously weren't his direct family. She recalled the discussion they'd had that night at the station about his father leaving his mother when he'd been a toddler, his mother's addiction to drugs, and Ian pretty much raising himself—before and after his mother's overdose. Somewhere along the way, the Winslows had become important enough to Ian for him to believe he owed them somehow.

She was curious enough to ask the reason why, to know more about the man he'd become after living a life of poverty. "Why do you feel you owe the Winslows?"

"Because they accepted me so completely, and they became the family I never had," he said without giving the question any lengthy thought.

While his answer was simply stated, Erica detected a wealth of emotion attached to the comment. His debt to the Winslows was based on gratitude and resulted from being given the unconditional acceptance he'd obviously never received from his own mother. A deep-rooted part of her understood that craving for acceptance, which was something she'd struggled to find for herself, a sense of belonging she still felt as though she was searching for. She had her independence and freedom, but she'd yet to find total contentment. She'd always believed that ultimate fulfillment would come with success, so she was taken off guard by the pang of envy she felt toward Ian and his tight, familial relationship with the Winslows.

He took a bite of his sea bass, and continued to explain. "I was twenty when I met Audrey at the University of Chicago. We started dating, and when I met her parents for the first time I swear I'd never been so nervous in all my life." He smiled across the table at Erica, his handsome face alight with fond memories of that momentous occasion. "But for all my fears that I wasn't good enough to date their daughter, they were warm and welcoming and gracious, despite the huge difference in our backgrounds. And when David Winslow discovered that I was majoring in economics and had a knack for playing the stock market and making wise investments, well, that pretty much cinched our relationship."

Erica laughed, the effects of the champagne and easy conversation making her feel relaxed and mellow. "I could imagine. He saw a future son-in-law to take over his investment firm."

"Yeah, I suppose he did." There was no conceit in his voice, just more appreciation. "When I graduated from college, I asked Audrey to marry me, she said yes, and her father's way of approving of the marriage was to offer me a job at his firm. And for the first time in my life I seemed to have it all. A great job that I loved, stability and family ties. I had grand visions of settling down with Audrey, raising a family of my own, and giving my kids everything I grew up without. I still want that someday."

She finished her meal as his last comment swirled through her mind, making her consider her own future goals, which didn't include settling down and starting a family of her own. Not anytime soon, anyway. After her unpleasant ordeal with Paul, the whole idea of entangling herself in a committed relationship, marriage especially, still struck a certain amount of trepidation in her. While she'd made the vow to depend on no man for her own personal happiness as her mother and sister had spent their lives doing, Erica feared that she'd be expected to give up everything she'd worked so hard to attain to be a wife, and a mother.

Once they were done with their main courses, Ian refilled their glasses with champagne, emptying the bottle as their waiter cleared their plates. "After Audrey died, I poured myself into my work, taking on big corporations and Chicago's elite as clients and spending twelve or more hours a day at the office. Work became my life, and before I knew it, I had more money than I knew what to do with." He shook his head in genuine amazement of the fact. "And then a few years ago David retired, and he offered me the position of CEO and partner."

She dabbled her fork in the apple beignet their server had delivered during their conversation. "You've obviously earned David's respect." She took a bite of the deep-fried dessert, and the warm, sugary pastry nearly melted in Erica's mouth.

"I'd like to think that I have." He dragged a piece of beignet through the raspberry sauce on his plate. "But the past few years I've been so single-minded and my days and nights have revolved around work, and financial portfolios, and my clients' needs. I didn't really know what was missing from my life until that night I turned on the radio and heard you on *Heat Waves*."

His voice, a low, lazy rumble of sound, caused her nerve endings to tingle with sensual awareness. She welcomed the shift between them, from serious to sexy and playful. "And what did you discover was missing?"

"Fun. The constant urge to be with a woman because I truly enjoyed her company." His gaze dropped to her lips, then slowly traveled over her bare shoulders, to the skimpy bodice of her dress, making her wish it was his hands on her instead. Finally, he lifted his eyes back to hers. "*Real,* hot sexual chemistry," he murmured intimately. "The kind that keeps me up late at night and fills me with anticipation during the day."

The kind that you and I generate together. She read the unspoken words in his eyes, and her heart skipped a beat. Desire pooled in her belly, and lower. "I know exactly what you mean."

He leaned his forearms on the table, his eyes darkening to a bold, earthy shade of green—direct and all male. "So, what are we going to do about all this anticipation, sweetheart?"

A subtle challenge. A sexy dare. She wanted him to have fun. She wanted him to forget his painful past. She wanted to seduce him and be seduced—in wicked, erotic ways. She thought of all those condoms in her purse, and couldn't dismiss the aching, burning need to make love to him that had consumed her for far too long. She inhaled deeply, prepared to make her intentions known.

"We agreed to take our affair to the extreme and have a good time with each other for as long as it lasts," she said with a sultry smile. "I think tonight's the perfect time to make good on that promise."

"DO YOU THINK WE HAVE sufficient material to report back Monday night about our first sexy city night date?" Ian asked Erica once they were sequestered in the back of the limousine again. "You can tell your listeners how I wined and dined you, and just how romantic a place Everest is for dinner."

"You definitely get a ten for your choice of restaurant, but our date isn't over yet." She glanced at her watch, then slanted him a very seductive look that jump-started his libido. "It's only nine-thirty, and you know what a night owl I am, considering my hours at the station. We've got the rest of the night ahead of us and the possibilities are endless."

After her comment at the restaurant about making good on the promise of their affair, her insinuation was unmistakable. But still, Ian assumed nothing. He'd wait for her to make that first move toward a more intimate relationship and follow her lead.

He stretched his arm across the back of the leather seat and feathered the tips of his fingers along her bare shoulder. "What would you like to do now? We could head over to the Navy Pier and take a night cruise on the *Odyssey.*"

"I'd like to keep you all to myself, I think." She moistened her bottom lip with her tongue and slid across the foot of space separating them, until her breasts brushed the side of his chest. "Could you tell the chauffeur to just drive, and maybe make it a bit more private back here?"

"Sure." He'd do *anything* for her, he realized. He'd grant her simplest request or greatest desire. And right now, it was apparent that she had the latter on her mind. Giving in to Erica's request, he asked the driver to head down the scenic highway of Lake Shore Drive until he told him otherwise. Then Ian pressed the button that secured the partition between the driver and guests, cocooning them in the cool, spacious compartment, illuminated by the soft, buttery glow of the dim overhead light.

He settled back against the seat and smiled at Erica. "Your every wish is my command."

"That's good to hear." Gracefully, she moved over him, bracketing her hands against the back of the seat on either side of his head.

Surprised by the brazen move, he automatically spread his legs to accommodate her, and she positioned herself in front of him, resting both of her knees between his widened thighs. She'd yet to touch any part of his body, but he felt singed from head to toe.

He found himself eye level with her pert, full breasts, and her tight, hard nipples straining against the thin fabric of her dress. She dipped her head closer, and her thick, silky hair tumbled forward, spilling over her shoulders, beckoning to his fingers. He caught a light, floral, feminine fragrance, and the combined effects caused an immediate tightening in his groin. He swallowed hard and kept his hands splayed flat on his taut thighs.

"You know, per *your* wish, I'm not quite as accessible as I could be," she said, her voice low and throaty, her lips so close to his he could almost taste their hot cinnamon flavor. She tipped her head, the shadowed lighting playing across the guileless expression on her face. "Do you think you could, um, remove my panties, please?"

Her polite tone, combined with her courteous request for a very provocative, highly arousing deed rendered him momentarily speechless. It was the last thing he'd expected her to ask, and he gave her extra credit for the shock value of her outrageous invitation.

He rested his hands on the curve of her waist, belatedly realizing his mistake in touching her and making that connection that ripped through him like a bolt of electricity. He met her gaze, seeing the temptation glittering in her deep brown eyes.

A playful grin eased up the corners of his mouth. "If this is a shameless ploy for me to give you another orgasm, I meant what I said about you being completely naked. Unless you're willing to let me strip you naked here and now, which it would be my pleasure to do."

"No, the dress stays on." Her breathing deepened, and her lashes fell half-mast. "This is all for you. I just want to make myself as accessible as possible...for later."

Her excuse was meant to be pure torment, he knew. "And drive me crazy in the process," he growled.

Her soft, teasing laughter filled the intimate space around them. "You're on to me, Mr. Carlisle," she murmured silkily. "It would be nice to turn the tables on you for a change. Is it working?"

For all her outward display of confidence, he caught a faint tremor of uncertainty in her voice. He catered to those doubts, wanting to make sure she knew just how much she held him enthralled. "Yeah, it's working." He was completely and totally under her spell—a slave to her every whim.

"Then do it," she dared.

Unable to resist her, and wanting to give as much pleasure as he gained, he placed his hands on the sides of her stocking-clad legs and slowly, gradually, skimmed his palms upward along her thighs. He captured her gaze with his, holding her hostage with that heated stare as his hands slipped beneath the hem of her dress. Coasting higher still, he discovered the lacy band of the thigh-high stockings she wore, which gave way to a two-inch patch of soft, warm skin before he found the elastic band of her high-cut panties.

By the time he hooked his thumbs beneath the strip of silk hugging her slender hips and began the thrilling process of dragging the wispy scrap of material down her thighs, he was just as caught up in Erica's seduction as she seemed to be. Her breath caught erotically, and she bit her bottom lip against a wistful moan when he feathered his fingers along her flesh in a leisurely exploration—everywhere but where he knew she ached for his caress the most. Lashes fluttering closed, she tipped her head back and arched her body toward him, yet stopped shy of making that ultimate contact, teasing him and exciting him with her wanton behavior.

Waves of need gripped him, and his pulse beat wildly in his throat. Her panties caught around her knees, which were still perched on the edge of the seat. "Lift up, sweetheart," he said, and she obeyed, straightening her legs so he could push them down to her ankles and help her step out of them.

He stuffed the souvenir into his pants pocket, and she sighed hotly, damply, against his cheek. "Oh, wow, that was *close*."

Strangled laughter escaped him as he caught her meaning—that she'd nearly climaxed fully clothed yet again. Hell, he was damn close himself, *again*. "You really are a soft touch, Ms. McCree." Beneath that I'm-in-control facade she wore like armor, she was a woman who was learning all the wondrous pleasures her body had to offer. And he was reaping the benefits.

"Only with you," she admitted, and settled herself astride his lap, sliding forward so that her knees pressed against his hips. Knowing he'd go off like a rocket if she pressed any closer, he grabbed her waist and stopped her before she could execute that downward movement that would join them way too explicitly.

She smiled knowingly, and he couldn't resist looking down at their position. Her skirt was bunched high on her thighs, revealing the lacy tops of her stockings and about an inch of bare, smooth flesh. The thought of her wearing nothing beneath her dress spurred illicit images of unzipping his slacks, unleashing his fierce erection and sinking deep inside her welcoming warmth and letting her ride him to completion. It would be so incredibly easy to do just that, but he wanted her naked in a bed, *his bed,* the first time they made love and he joined their bodies. Not a quickie romp that would probably end with the first blazing stroke, considering how turned-on he was.

He shuddered, banished those forbidden thoughts to the far recesses of his mind for now, and held on to his restraint with everything inside him. Despite his vow not to touch her intimately, she had him curious where and how far she intended to take this sexy interlude of hers. She didn't take long to enlighten him.

She began unbuttoning his shirt, her cool fingers trailing along the heated skin she gradually revealed. "How do you feel about reenacting some of those photos that we saw in the magazine that depicted sexy city nights in Chicago?"

"What did you have in mind?" Stupid question, considering she was attempting to strip *him* naked.

A naughty twinkle appeared in her eyes. "A cross between the limo ride and the Ferris wheel."

He recalled the first picture in the limousine, of a woman straddling a man and the two indulging in kisses, caresses and seduction. Then the latter photo of a woman intending to pleasure her man with her hands and mouth.

Saying no was impossible. "I think I could be persuaded."

She proceeded to do just that, enticing him with a silky, hot, tongue-tangling kiss while finishing her task of unbuttoning his shirt, all the way down to the waistband of his pants. She tugged the tails free, spread the sides open and pushed it off his shoulders until the material caught around his biceps. She splayed her hands on his broad chest, and stared in fascination as she skimmed her delicate fingers down his lean torso to his flat belly. Every muscle in his body flexed in response to her exquisite, reverent exploration.

She lifted her gaze back up to his, her irises dark and needy and oh-so-sexy. "Pull down the straps of my dress, Ian," she whispered on a ragged breath.

His blood pumped hot and fierce. Like a man in the throes of an erotic dream, he obeyed her order. Grasping the thin straps holding up the top, he slowly pulled them down her arms, until the stretchy fabric gave way and her high, firm breasts swayed free. She moaned as the cool air caressed her newly exposed skin, and he stared in awe at the glorious bounty before him. Hunger for her gripped him, and his mouth watered for a taste. She was all soft swells and pale curves, her aureoles a deep, dark pink tipped with tight nipples begging to be pleasured by him.

With a finger tucked beneath his chin, she raised his gaze back to hers, her smile decadent and teasing. "No biting," she said, her comment reminiscent of last week's on-the-air conversation with the caller who'd gotten off on biting his partner's nipples, and Ian's response to the man's odd fetish. "But you may nibble, suck and lick, and curl your tongue around my nipple and tug *gently*."

Those were his words exactly, at the time meant to arouse her. Now, he was the one inflamed. A muscle near his jaw ticked from restraint. "Is that what you want?" He needed her to be absolutely sure.

She leaned forward, brushing the peaked crests along his lips. "Oh, yeah," she murmured.

He opened his mouth, laved her with his tongue from

the underside of her breast all the way to her beaded nipple, and felt a shiver course through her. She shut her eyes on an unraveling moan and clutched his shoulders, urging him to continue, to deepen the contact and take all of her.

He wanted to savor, claim and possess. He did all three. His palms cupped her, kneaded her, learning what she liked best, what made her sigh wistfully, how a light touch caused her to whimper, and how a firm caress made her restless and tremble in anticipation.

She wriggled anxiously on his lap, and delved her fingers into the hair at the nape of his neck. "Ian...*please.*" She thrust her breasts closer and locked her legs tighter against his hips.

Finally, he drew her into his mouth, feasting on the sweet taste of her. He swirled his tongue around the plump fullness, and grazed the puckered tip with the edge of his teeth. He nipped playfully, sensuously, first one breast and then the other, then soothed the gentle bites with a long, leisurely stroke of his soft, wet tongue, driving her steadily into that realm of pleasure where nothing existed but sensation and hot, feverish need.

He felt it, too—the build-up, the hunger, the wildness. Her hips undulated, seeking pressure and the hard ridge of his erection to ease her distress. Intensity pulsed and burned between them, nearly flaring out of control. She sought his mouth, and he kissed her, deep and soulful. Running his hands up her naked back, he hugged her close, crushing her breasts against his chest, feeling the fire of that ultimate contact and the rapid beating of both of their hearts.

Dragging his mouth from hers, he tucked her head against his neck, sucking air into his lungs in an attempt to calm his raging hormones, his rampant lust, and the sharp, aching desire pulsing in his groin. He didn't think he could withstand any more foreplay without exploding, but Erica had other ideas.

She nibbled on the lobe of his ear and tugged the sensitive flesh with her teeth to get his attention. And then she whispered huskily in his ear, "Wrap your fingers in my hair, Ian, and guide me where you want me. Show me what you want and what you like."

He squeezed his eyes shut and groaned. She was making all his fantasies come true, taking their on-the-air debates and recalling everything he'd said he liked and wanted to do sexually and making them all reality.

Enthralled and too far gone to stop, he buried both hands in her silken hair and started with a kiss, because he just couldn't seem to get enough of the taste and texture of her mouth. From there he guided her damp, parted lips along his jaw, down his throat, and gradually lower to his chest. Her tongue flicked across his rigid nipple, and she nibbled and sucked and licked the same way he'd done to her. It felt *incredible*.

She scooted off his lap and settled to her knees on the floor between his spread legs, her breasts grazing the insides of his thighs on the way down. With his fingers still tangled in her thick mane, she blazed a trail of sizzling kisses along his torso, and he groaned when she dipped the soft, wet tip of her tongue into his navel. When she shimmied lower and pressed her open mouth against the hard length of him straining painfully against his slacks, he instinctively bucked upward and hissed *"yes"* before he could restrain his enthusiasm.

And then it was too late to retract his acquiescence, and he wasn't altogether sure he wanted to when he was suddenly feeling very greedy and she was busy unbuckling his thin leather belt, undoing the button on his pants, carefully but eagerly unzipping the fly. Without hesitation, she tugged the waistband of his briefs down and freed his hard, thick erection…then stared at him with a combination of guile, admiration and hunger that made him swell to enormous proportions.

She wrapped her slender fingers around his throbbing sex and squeezed and stroked, discovering the ripe and ready heat of him, the satin-and-steel texture. A drop of moisture beaded on the tip of his penis, and she tentatively tasted his essence with her tongue—a long, slow, lazy lap that made his whole entire body tremble.

That was merely the beginning. She experimented with her lips, her fingers, teasing and tormenting him with languid caresses, discovering the sensitive ridge just beneath the swollen, velvety tip with her thumb, measuring his length and breadth with her palm and fingers until he was certain he'd go mad.

"Erica," he rasped, surprised he'd managed to utter even that one word when his vocal chords were strangled with a multitude of emotions—tenderness, caring and raw sexual craving.

It was enough for her to look up at him, her eyes soft with arousal, her smile pure sin, and he knew he was in big trouble. "I'm betting I can make you have an orgasm with a kiss," she said impudently, reversing the roles of their stairwell tryst and making *him* the captive this time—intent on evening the score between them.

Before he could do or say anything, her parted lips took his engorged shaft in an unbelievably deep, wet, erotic kiss. He watched in a red haze of desire as she suckled him in a way that made him wild for release, wild for *her*. He clutched fistfuls of her hair, gently urged her to a faster rhythm, and with a low growl of need he took what she offered—a forbidden pleasure of her own making.

His breathing grew harsh as his climax rushed up at him. Sensations, as exquisite as they were intense, rippled through him, tightening the muscles in his belly, his thighs. He uttered a warning and tried to pull her away, but she ignored his attempts. The silky, heated depths of her mouth stole his restraint, and then it was too late to do anything but ride the wave of release as it crashed over him. With a low, harsh groan, he gave himself over to her generous, giving gift and selfless ministrations.

Minutes later, she settled in beside him again and whispered, "Take me back to your place and make love to me."

8

IAN'S SIXTEENTH-FLOOR penthouse was like nothing Erica had ever seen or had the opportunity to experience in her lifetime. Spacious, elegant and decorated with expensive, richly textured furnishings, his home held every luxury a person could ever want or wish for. Including a breathtaking, million-dollar view of Grant Park and Chicago Harbor from the floor-to-ceiling windows in his living room.

The men she'd dated had never come close to Ian's wealth and sophistication, and she was impressed with his success. And despite the independent, feminist attitude she had when it came to men, she couldn't deny that a part of her liked being swept off her feet and being romanced by Ian. But for as much as she enjoyed Ian's ability to make her feel special and cherished, she couldn't allow herself to get used to his lavish attention and pampering, because their affair was as temporary as the sexy city nights campaign they were involved in.

She continued to gaze at the exquisite scenery as she waited for Ian to return from the back part of the penthouse, where he'd disappeared minutes after they'd arrived at his place. He'd excused himself, told her to make herself comfortable while he changed, yet she hadn't been able to sit for more than thirty seconds on his luxurious suede couch before jumping up and pacing to the window.

She crossed her arms over her sensitive breasts and chewed on her thumbnail. Despite what happened in the limo and her bold request for Ian to bring her back to his place, she was glad for the brief reprieve. She was nervous all over again—this next step wasn't just about pleasuring Ian as it had been in the limo, but an intimate act that would strip bare her body and soul.

No matter that she talked the sexy talk on her show, she'd never been the promiscuous type and she didn't take sex lightly. An affair with Ian wouldn't equate to frivolous sex as she'd once believed. Instead, having gotten to know him on an intimate, personal level, and truly liking the man he was, she feared making love with him would encompass something far more emotional than a satisfying romp in bed. The kind of feelings she'd steadfastly avoided, yet Ian had an effortless way of bringing to the surface with his mere presence, his touch, a glance.

One of the lamps behind her clicked off, leaving the light from the marbled entryway as the only source of illumination in the house. She turned around and found Ian wearing a pair of gray cotton sweat shorts, and nothing else, which drew her gaze to all the bare parts of his athletically toned body. And there was plenty about him to admire, as she'd learned earlier.

Reining in her fascination, she smiled. "You really have done well for yourself," she complimented, indicating with a wave of her hand the valuable artwork on the wall, the costly furnishings, and the home in which he lived.

He shrugged modestly. "They're just things, Erica."

Things that equaled success, she thought, all too aware of the fact that she'd yet to reach that level of accomplishment in her own career, that sense of satisfaction of making it big and on her own. She was close, closer than she'd ever been before—thanks to Ian.

He spread his arms wide. "What you're looking at right now is the *real* Ian."

She looked her fill once more of the down-to-earth, unpretentious man standing before her—his broad chest, flat belly, muscular thighs. And if she wasn't mistaken, he was semi-aroused beneath those thin cotton shorts he wore. "I do have to say that the real Ian is very appealing."

An amused smile curved his lips. "I'm glad you think so."

A familiar shiver of awareness coursed down the length of her spine as he slowly approached her from across the room.

He stopped a few feet away from her and glanced around the room, seemingly taking in everything through her eyes. "I'll admit it's nice to be able to buy anything I might want, but these objects and this house aren't what's important to me." His warm gaze returned to hers. "I could be just as happy in a small house in the suburbs or even a modest apartment. I'm just very fortunate that I have a good job and that I've made wise investments and choices with my money and the people in my life."

Unlike her, who'd made unwise choices, especially when it came to men. And even though she acknowledged that Ian was nothing like Paul in so many ways, she knew from their earlier conversation about Audrey that he was a natural born caretaker, a man who believed in traditional values, including protecting and caring for those closest to him. The kind of man she swore she didn't want or need in her life.

He tipped his head, studying her too intently. "Having second thoughts about tonight and us?" he asked.

He was so in tune to her, and she found it unnerving that he instinctively understood what she was thinking and feeling. She knew he'd respect her decision if she changed her mind, but she wanted this night with Ian, and she wasn't giving it up for anything. Not even for a case of nerves. She wanted tantalizing, sexy memories to take away with her, to keep her warm at night and to replace all the old memories.

Making that conscious decision, she acted on it. Reaching out, she skimmed the tips of her fingers over the smooth, warm surface of his chest, reveling in the flex of muscle beneath her hand. "Is there such a thing as a premature orgasm for a woman?" she asked coyly, and when he lifted a brow in confusion, she explained. "After what happened in the limousine and considering how turned on I still am, I don't think I'm going to last very long once you strip me bare."

Heat simmered in his gaze, making his eyes glitter like rare emeralds. "It's going to be a *very* long night, and since I haven't even begun to do all the things I want to do to your body, I'm thinking we ought to take the edge off your first orgasm so you don't come prematurely, since that seems to be your concern." His voice was low and teasing, his grin filled with humor, but his intentions were serious, she realized, when he gently turned her around to face the window again. His long, blunt fingers toyed with the straps on her dress. "This way, we'll be starting out even in the orgasm department before we get to the bedroom."

Her heart beat rapidly in her chest, and desire flowed to every feminine nerve ending. With the lights off, she could see her reflection superimposed on the darkened glass, could feel the heat emanating from Ian standing behind her. "But I'm not naked," she said in breathless anticipation, reminding him of the stipulation *he'd* set.

"You're not wearing any panties or a bra." Pulling the top of her dress down, he released her full, aching breasts. He fondled the plump flesh in his large hands and raked her sensitive nipples with his thumbs. "I'd say that's close enough for now."

Biting back a moan, she arched more fully into his touch. "You're cheating?" she rasped.

"If you'll remember correctly, I made up that rule about being completely naked the next time I give you an orgasm," he murmured huskily, then smoothed his palms leisurely downward to the hem of her dress. She closed her eyes and sighed as he inched the stretchy material up, until it bunched around her hips and she could feel the cool air in the room kiss her feverish, exposed skin and the moist curls between her thighs. "And because I made up the rule, it's my prerogative to cheat, sweetheart."

She trembled, feeling that coiling tightness begin in her stomach and radiate outward, and wondered if she'd have an orgasm without him touching her at all. It was a novel thought, but at the moment she was so aroused she knew it was very possible.

She attempted to turn toward him, but before she could execute the move he wrapped an arm around her waist, splayed a hand on her belly and drew her flush against his chest. His inflamed body scorched her, from her shoulders all the way down to her thighs. His erection pressed insistently against her bottom through his shorts, and she quivered at the thought of him removing that thin barrier and taking her just as they were.

But Ian had pure, seductive foreplay in mind. "I want *you* to watch this time, Erica." He nudged her legs apart with his knee, opening and preparing her for his caress. "Look in the window in front of us," he said, his words effectively drawing her gaze to the lush, wanton display that was her, and the large hand he pressed high on her thigh that was sliding toward the heat and heart of her. "Watch me touching you and your response to my touch."

Entranced by the eroticism and decadence of the act, she watched, and moaned in unadulterated ecstasy as his long fingers separated the dewy folds of her femininity and stroked the slick, swollen nub of flesh hidden there. Her head dropped back against his shoulder, and she gripped his thighs for support. Her hips jerked forward, encouraging his questing fingers, desperate for more pressure, more friction, more depth. Gradually he gave her all three, making her pant shamelessly and eliciting a liquid rush of desire that made *him* groan, long and loud.

"God, you're so wet, so hot," he said, his voice a low rumble of sound that vibrated against her back while his lips and tongue found the soft hollow under her ear. "Let it go and come for me, Erica."

That easily she did, welcoming the deep, intense, rippling contractions buffeting her body. With a high-pitched cry and his name on her lips, she let him know that he thrilled her like no other. Her knees buckled when it was over, and she was grateful for his hold on her or else she would have dropped to the floor.

He removed his fingers and nuzzled the side of her neck. "There, now we can move this to the bedroom, without any worry that you'll come prematurely."

Hearing the satisfaction in his tone, she laughed lightly. "Umm, I'm definitely more relaxed and less tense."

"Good, because I'm not done having my way with

you.'' He scooped her up into his strong embrace, and she gasped in surprise and latched her arms around his neck as he started out of the living room.

''Wait, my purse,'' she said, and he bent low so she could grab it off the couch. She smiled sheepishly at him as he continued down a long hallway. ''I brought condoms.''

''Lots of them, I hope.'' He carried her through double French doors into his enormous master bedroom, which also had floor-to-ceiling windows and the same stunning view as the living room.

She took in the huge, high four-poster bed in dark mahogany, illuminated by the soft lamplight on the nightstand. ''Yep, and different textures, flavors, scents and sizes.''

He placed her gently on the middle of the mattress, but remained standing by the side of the bed. ''Sounds like we're going to be very busy tonight.'' He pulled off her shoes and let both drop to the carpeted floor. ''Pick one for me.''

While she blindly reached into her purse beside her on the bed and retrieved the first packet her fingers came into contact with, Ian skimmed his palms up one leg and grasped the lacy band of her stocking. He removed the piece of lingerie, then the other, making Erica burn and ache anew, which she found amazing considering the incredible orgasm she'd just had. Finally, he dragged her dress over her hips, down her long limbs, and tossed the material somewhere behind him.

''Aah, naked at last.'' He looked his fill, his appreciative gaze licking across her skin in a hot, velvet caress that found and devoured every feminine, intimate swell and curve.

''Except for you.'' Feeling at a distinct disadvantage,

she sat up and slipped her hands into the waistband of his shorts and pushed the material down, until it fell to his ankles and he stepped out of them. He was fully aroused, long and hard and pulsing with virile life. Her womb clenched in anticipation of finally feeling all that aggressive male length deep inside her, stretching her, filling her to completion....

He reached out to pluck the condom from her hand, and she moved it out of his reach. "Let me," she whispered, wanting to do to him what she'd never done for another man. Another first she wanted to experience with him. She tore open the package, and a rich, fruity scent filled the air.

Ian sniffed, then cocked his head curiously. "Is that...*bananas* I smell?"

Erica laughed softly. "Yeah, it is." Removing the condom, she slowly, playfully sheathed him in the snug, fragrant latex, then bent low and swirled her tongue along the plump tip. "And you taste just as good."

A low, harsh groan escaped him, and he tangled his fingers in her hair to stop her sensual assault. Easing her back on the bed, he moved beside her, capturing her mouth in a slow, delicious kiss that made her restless and built a greater urgency to join with him. But he seemed in no hurry to end all their provocative foreplay. Her fingers twisted in his hair as his lips moved on, scattering moist, lingering kisses over her jaw, along her throat, her breasts and belly.

And then he shifted, pressing her knees apart with his broad shoulders so he could settle in between. He slid close, hooking her legs over his biceps as he went, spreading her wide and pinning her hips to the mattress so she couldn't move. He dipped his dark head, and his hot, damp breath brushed along the most intimate part of her.

Startled to find herself in a position that gave Ian total control and left her completely vulnerable to him and his whims, she pushed at his shoulders, holding him at bay. "Ian?" her voice trembled with uncertainties. She'd never felt so exposed, and she was taken off guard by all the new and illicit sensations she was experiencing.

Gently, he grasped her hands, and weaving their fingers tightly together he locked her arms at her sides, rendering her immobile. He placed a delicate bite on the inside of her thigh that made her gasp, then soothed the sting with his tongue.

"I *have* to taste you," he groaned desperately.

He said the words as if he'd die if he didn't, and she couldn't refuse him because she was beginning to feel the same way...hungry for his mouth on her, wild for the caress of his tongue, desperate for yet another release.

He wasted no time with teasing preliminaries. Pressing his open mouth against her, he glided his tongue upward in a deep, full-bodied stroke as slow and hot and erotic as a French kiss. Her entire body shuddered as he licked and suckled her as if she were the sweetest nectar he'd ever tasted. His tongue swirled, flicked, *ravished,* then thrust deep, but not deep enough when she felt so empty inside.

She tried to tug her hands free to pull him closer, but he held tight. She moaned and thrashed and heard herself beg. Heat and desire flared bright. Pleasure glowed and beckoned. Her thighs quivered from being restrained, and the sharp, spiraling need expanded within her as he continued his ruthless quest to savor, to feast, to send her over the edge.

And then she tumbled mindlessly and all she could do

was cry out and arch her body, and let the explosive contractions consume her. Once the aftershocks receded, he reared up and released her hands, then lifted her left leg and crisscrossed it over his opposite thigh, bending her knee back toward her to give him greater access. Limp and boneless, she let him do as he pleased, completely trusting him with her body. He rubbed the tip of his swollen penis against her slick flesh, and with a flex of his hips he buried himself to the hilt.

He groaned in pleasure, and her breath hitched at the force and pressure and depth of his invasion, then released on a ragged moan. And then he moved over her completely, gathering her close and tilting her hips up to meet his slow thrust as he braced one arm near her head so that his fingers tangled in her hair, and rested his other palm over her breast.

Though she felt him pulse and throb where they joined, he grew still, and stared searchingly into her eyes. "Are you okay?"

Her heart turned over in her chest when she realized he was holding back for her, making sure she was comfortable and that he wasn't hurting her. While this man claimed to be traditional at the very core, she discovered that Ian was unpredictable in the bedroom, and an expert, innovative lover that took her to new heights. The sexual position he'd maneuvered her into was not only erotic and exciting, it allowed him the tightest fit and deepest penetration, all the way to her soul, it seemed.

A surge of unexpected tenderness welled up in her. With trembling fingers, she lightly traced his jaw and dragged her thumb across his full bottom lip, still wet from her. "I like this position," she told him with a smile. "A lot."

"We're a perfect fit," he said, and a part of her wondered if he was talking about more than just the inter-locking of their bodies.

And then the thought drifted out of her mind as he began to move—strong, powerful thrusts that ignited the same raging fire within her that she saw flickering in his dark, sensual eyes. His breathing grew harsh, his jaw clenched from restraint. But she didn't want him holding back for her; she wanted his wild, uninhibited surrender.

Coasting her flattened palms down the taut muscles bisecting his back, she clenched his buttocks in her hands. Rocking against him rhythmically, she urged him further, higher, harder. The friction they created was exquisite, a slow building wave of pleasure that consumed them both and sent her careening over the precipice first. With a low, guttural growl, he closed his eyes, tossed his head back and gave into his own shattering release.

Once he caught his breath, he lowered his head and kissed her, slowly, deeply, tenderly, conveying exactly how he felt with that show of intimacy. How much he desired her. How much he cared. And despite all that had come before, he made her tremble all over again, made her want the impossible, made her need more than was wise.

And for tonight, she knew she'd greedily take every-thing he had to offer.

ERICA GRADUALLY WOKE the following morning with a long, slow, languorous stretch, a sleepy yawn, and a con-tented smile on her lips. She'd never meant to stay the entire night, but Ian had been *very* persuasive, and she hadn't been able to resist his tempting means of coercion.

Rolling to her side, she let her lashes drift open…and was disappointed to discover she was all alone in Ian's huge bed. Especially since she wanted him yet again—

even after a night of the most incredible lovemaking she'd ever had the pleasure of experiencing.

There were four empty condom wrappers somewhere, attesting to their night of wickedness, lust and the mutual desire they'd slaked. Her belly grew warm with recollections of how eager and insatiable she'd been, an enthusiastic partner to anything and everything Ian had in mind. He'd taken her in fun and playful ways, and in more erotic, uninhibited positions that might have shocked her at first, but had ultimately thrilled her. The man was an adept, generous, earthy lover—one who now knew her body more intimately than any other man in her past. And he'd been just as willing to let her have her way with him. Their lovemaking had been equal measures of give and take, and it was a novelty and freedom she'd enjoyed.

With a sigh, she reached out and touched the pillow beside hers and inhaled the musky, arousing scent of sex permeating the air, the sheets, her skin. Unexpected emotions rose to the surface, demanding her attention, demanding that she acknowledge the truth she'd done her best to ignore last night—that Ian had branded her in more ways than just physically.

Despite how she might want to neatly categorize their night together as a mutually gratifying encounter, she couldn't deny that there had been an emotional intimacy between them that had superceded satisfying physical needs. Now that she was alone, now that the sensual glow had faded a bit and she could analyze the situation more objectionably, she knew they'd indulged in more than just sex. Each and every time they'd made love he'd filled her body with the very essence of his, and somehow, someway, during the night he'd touched that part of her heart she swore she wouldn't risk again. He'd most definitely rocked her very soul the few times she'd caught him looking at her with such fierce tenderness, and a longing that echoed deep inside her.

A longing that had no business being a part of their affair.

She squeezed her eyes shut and clutched the sheet tighter to her breasts. Emotional involvement with Ian wasn't supposed to happen, not when she didn't have the time and room in her focused life for a serious relationship—especially with a man intent on being such a huge part of her life.

She heard a muted sound coming from the opposite end of the house, and guessed that Ian was up and about, probably making himself coffee or breakfast. The clock on the nightstand revealed that it was 9:20 a.m., and she needed to leave shortly. It was Sunday and she'd promised to visit Tori at the shelter, to check in with her and see how her week had gone. And since Tori was expecting her, there was no way she'd let the other woman down—not even to spend the day with Ian.

Dragging herself from the warm, rumpled bed, she investigated the adjoining bathroom and found it nearly as big as her bedroom in her apartment. She stepped into the spacious, glass-enclosed shower stall, turned the tap on to hot, and moved beneath the pulsating spray. She washed her body until it was pink and glowing, then shampooed her hair and dried off with a dry fluffy towel that Ian must have left out for her. Figuring that they'd swapped enough germs last night to justify using his toothbrush, she used it to clean her teeth and ran his comb though her wet hair.

Back in his bedroom, she peeked into his closet and took the liberty of choosing a worn, comfortable-looking chambray shirt to wear instead of the skimpy dress that was now folded neatly over the chair by the door. The man was obviously a neat-nick. As she buttoned the thigh-length shirt, she glanced around for her panties, but couldn't find them, or the slacks he'd stuffed them into last night. She did spy the extra packets of condoms on the nightstand and snagged one and slipped it into her breast pocket—just in case the mood struck.

She grinned wryly as she padded quietly down the hall to the kitchen, wondering when she'd turned into such a sex fiend—a wanton woman who couldn't seem to get enough orgasms, who constantly craved Ian's hands on her body, his mouth on her flesh and the exquisite heat of him stroking deep, deep inside her. The answer came too easily. It was Ian's fault for addicting her to all the wondrous pleasures of lovemaking.

She entered the bright room decorated in dark blue, white and shiny chrome, and found Ian sitting at the table, drinking a cup of coffee and engrossed in a section of the Sunday paper. He was wearing a pair of faded jeans, no shirt or shoes, and his damp hair curled around the nape of his neck. There was a certain intimacy about the situation that caused a fleeting pang of longing in Erica's midsection.

Dismissing the frivolous emotion, she crossed the room toward the fresh pot of coffee on the counter beckoning to her. "Good morning," she murmured.

"Hey, sleepyhead," he greeted, folding down a corner of the paper to look at her. A warm, private smile curved his lips. "Nice of you to finally join me."

The man was way too refreshed and cheerful when she had not yet had her first cup of coffee to jump-start her day. "I take it you're a morning person."

"Yep," he said, and set his paper aside. "I'm usually up at six faithfully, though I do have to admit that I stayed in bed this morning a little longer, just watching you sleep.''

She ducked her head as she felt an unaccustomed blush stain her cheeks. There was that tenderness again, and just imagining him taking such avid pleasure in watching her sleep in his bed made her entire body tingle.

"I debated whether or not to wake you up, but figured you were exhausted after last night.'' The insinuation in his deep, sensual voice was unmistakable. As was the male satisfaction. "Considering how late you slept in, I'm guessing you needed the rest.''

He'd left a mug out for her, and she added cream and sugar in the cup. "Actually, with the hours I keep at the station and how late I get home, I'm not normally a morning person at all.''

"We'll have to work on that.'' Standing, he brought his mug to the counter, placed a warm, flirtatious kiss on the side of her neck, then nuzzled near her ear. "I think being a morning person all depends on *how* you wake up.''

She grinned and slanted him a sassy look. "Then it sounds to me like you left the bed too early.'' She wouldn't have minded waking up to Ian beside her, over her, inside her....

He poured hot coffee into her mug, then refilled his and sweetened the brew with cream and sugar, too. "And here I was, trying to be a gentleman.''

She winked at him. "Next time, don't try so hard.''

He chuckled. "Next time I won't.'' He settled a hip against the counter, his gaze taking in her attire as he took a sip of his coffee. "By the way, nice outfit.''

She shifted on her feet, suddenly feeling very presumptuous wearing his clothing and uncertain of her decision to do so, though he didn't seem the least bit bothered. "I hope you don't mind that I borrowed a shirt. I didn't feel like putting my dress back on—"

Ian placed a finger over Erica's lips to silence her, seeing the insecurities that had flashed in her eyes. "I don't mind and you don't have to explain," he said, then let his arm fall back to his side. "You look good in my shirt, but you look even better wearing nothing at all."

She rolled her eyes, then picked up her mug for a drink. "You sure know how to flatter a woman."

"It's the truth." Another realization struck him. Not only did she have a way of filling out his shirts, she looked great in his kitchen in the morning, and she fit perfectly into his house, his life. He kept those thoughts to himself, knowing she'd bolt if he so much as hinted at anything serious between them—despite the fact that the emotions that passed between them last night had elevated their relationship beyond a superficial affair.

"You have a beautiful body and it's a shame that you have to cover it up at all," he continued instead, keeping the moment light and teasing. He stroked his knuckles down her smooth cheek, loving the soft feel of her skin. "Maybe I'll tie you to my bed naked and keep you there forever, purely for my sole enjoyment and pleasure. And yours, too," he added playfully.

The corner of her mouth lifted in a sultry smile. "Umm, sounds decadent, but you're gonna have to save that particular fantasy for another night."

He was glad to hear that there would be another night, and that she was up for more of the sexy, seductive kind of games they'd played last night. He wasn't sure what to expect of Erica this morning, given that independent streak of hers, and that's why he'd given her time alone in the bedroom, to wake up and assess the situation without him crowding her thoughts or influencing her in any way. While he knew he wanted more from Erica than a temporary affair, she was slower in coming around. Considering what he knew of her past, he understood. And he was trying like hell to be careful not to move too fast, or pressure her, or make demands that would send her bolting before she truly gave them a chance. That she was still here and sharing a cup of coffee with him was a huge concession on her part. Especially after all the "I really should goes" he'd talked her out of last night.

"Would you like some breakfast?" he asked, stalling for as much time with her as he could.

She shook her head. "I'm not a big breakfast eater." She saluted him with her mug. "Caffeine is my most important meal of the day."

"Looks like you have some bad eating habits we need to work on." He sent her a look of mock disapproval as he went to the refrigerator and pulled out sliced and chilled cantaloupe for himself. "How about a bowl of cereal, or fruit? Or I can make you some eggs or pancakes—"

"No, really, it's okay." Her gaze drifted to the clock on the wall, then back to him as he filled a bowl with the fruit. "Besides, I have to leave in about an hour."

His stomach constricted with disappointment, but he didn't let it show. "Oh? How come?" he asked casually. He'd been hoping she'd join him for Sunday lunch at the Winslows'. "You got a hot date with someone else?" he teased.

She wrapped her hands around the warm ceramic mug as she lifted the edge to her lips and took a sip. "Yes, a date," she confirmed, and something near the vicinity of Ian's heart faltered until she followed that up with, "but not even close to being as hot as you were last night."

Relief poured through him, and he had to restrain himself from taking her in his arms and kissing her senseless. "Who's the lucky...person?" He didn't want to assume her "date" was a guy, though the mere thought made him feel extremely territorial.

She hesitated, chewing on her bottom lip, and he couldn't help but wonder what was going on with her. He waited patiently for her answer, remembering his motto of No Pressure. Besides, he had no claim to her, other than her luscious body. Yet. He was still working on the rest of her, and that meant trusting her completely and giving her space if she felt she needed it.

He took his bowl of fruit to the table and sat down. "Erica, honey, if you don't want to tell me, that's fine." The lie nearly killed him.

Another five seconds ticked by before she finally said in a soft tone of voice, "No, actually, I do want to tell you." She joined him at the table, setting her coffee cup on the surface, then met his gaze head-on. "I'm going to the Camenson Women's Shelter downtown."

Confusion assailed him, before he was hit with a wave of concern when he realized that the Camenson Women's Shelter took in abused and battered women. He lowered the piece of cantaloupe he'd speared on his fork that had nearly reached his mouth and searched her face, looking for signs of distress. "Is everything okay, Erica?"

Her eyes widened when she realized he was thinking the worst. "Oh, not for *me*," she clarified quickly. "I'm going to meet with one of the women who's been staying there. Her name is Tori, and she has an adorable little five-year-old girl named Janet who is also under the protection of the shelter. I promised Tori I'd come by today, and I don't want to stand her up or cancel."

He nodded in understanding. Intrigued with this private side of Erica, but not at all surprised by her generosity in helping other people, he asked, "Do you go there often?"

"Usually once a week, for about the past eight or nine months now," she said, looking into the depths of her coffee cup. "I met one of the counselors from the organization at a WTLK appearance, and she told me that they're always looking for volunteers to help out at the shelter, even if it's for emotional support. So, I went there one day and have been visiting ever since."

He ate a bite of the succulent fruit, suspecting there was more depth to Erica's story than she was letting on. He took a guess that made his belly cramp with the possibility, but he had to ask. He had to know. "Did Paul abuse you?"

She raised her eyes back to him, seemingly unsurprised by his question. "No, not physically. He never hit me... not the way a boyfriend abused my mother," she revealed.

He digested that bit of information, and recalled a disturbing comment Erica had made to him that night at the station: *My mother never dated gentlemen.* Her mother had obviously been involved in a relationship with an abusive man. Erica had witnessed it and it had seemingly made a huge impact on her.

He speared another piece of cantaloupe and lifted it to Erica's lips to take. "Is what happened to your mother part of the reason why you've become so involved with the women at the shelter?"

She nodded and automatically took the piece of fruit and ate it. "When I was thirteen, my mother hooked up with a guy who made her all the kinds of promises she wanted to hear—of taking care of her, supporting her and even marrying her. She believed it all, and even moved us into Todd's apartment. But from what I remember all he did was use her as his personal maid," she said in disgust. "He'd sit in front of the TV most of the time and drink beer, and she'd wait on him hand and foot— and got verbally degraded for her efforts. But she never seemed to care because she had his attention and Todd was taking care of her. And the more he humiliated her, the harder she'd try to please him, to the point that my sister Daphne and I were forgotten most of the time. Which was just as well since I spent most of my time in my room or at a friend's house because I couldn't stand the guy."

She drew a deep breath and exhaled slowly, her lips stretched into a grim line. "Then he started hitting her. At first it was a slap, which he'd immediately apologize for and swore it would never happen again. But of course it did, and each time his attacks would escalate and become more brutal. One time he shoved her against the wall so hard she hit her head and the force of it knocked her unconscious."

He stared at Erica incredulously, unable to believe that any woman would put up with repeated assaults. "And your mother still stayed with him after that?"

"Yeah, she did." She traced the rim of her coffee cup with the tip of her index finger. "At that point, she'd lost one husband and had been divorced twice, and I think she was desperate to make the relationship work, no matter that the guy was a jerk. My mother was so insecure that she couldn't see past the fact that she had a man in her life, no matter how bad he was for her."

He nudged her lips open with another bite of cantaloupe, and she absently accepted his offering, then caught a dribble of juice from the corner of her mouth with her tongue.

"So, what happened with this guy?" he asked, resisting the urge to lap up the sweetness with his own tongue and taste her deep inside.

"When he started threatening me and my sister my mother finally started getting nervous. I came home from school one day and was on my way to my room when he made a rude comment to me that I ignored. He jumped up from the couch, stalked after me and grabbed my arm so tight he left a bruise."

Ian watched a shudder ripple through her and felt a surge of fury rise within him for what she'd endured. He remained quiet, listening, wanting to know how everything had played out.

She tucked a wisp of hair behind her ear, her dark brown eyes meeting his as her chin lifted a defiant fraction. "I remember feeling so frightened and scared, but I told him he was a jerk and that I wish he'd get the hell out of our lives. My mother was in the kitchen and came out to see what was going on, and I think seeing me as the recipient of Todd's violence finally made her realize just how bad things had gotten. She stepped between us and told him to let me go. And he did, only to take the brunt of his anger out on her."

A pained look etched her expression. "He beat her up so badly, gave her a black eye, then stormed out, which he normally did. Knowing he wouldn't return until late that night, I begged my mother to leave while he was gone. At first she said no, that we had nowhere to go, and I told her I'd go anywhere so long as he wasn't there. My mother had no idea what to do. So I looked through the phone book until I found a local women's shelter, then started packing us up. As soon as my sister came home, we were out of there."

Ian was amazed and awed at her internal strength, even at such a young age. He saw that fortitude even now, and realized how her mother's dependency on men, along with her own experience with Paul, had instigated that deep determination to make it on her own. It also made her very wary of trusting her own feelings when it came to men and relationships. Even when it came to them.

"We stayed at the shelter for about a week," she continued, "and I remember thinking that all the women and kids there had suffered some form of abuse. And it was really sad to me that we'd ended up in such a place when my memories of my real father before he died were of a kind and gentle man." She shook her head with regret. "My mother had every opportunity to turn her life around, to take control of her life and future, but she just couldn't get past that need to rely on a man. Even after we left the shelter and moved into a place of our own, she went back to her old ways with men, though to my knowledge she hasn't been in another abusive relationship, thank goodness."

He silently echoed her sentiments and fed her another cube of melon. "Where are your mother and sister now?"

"The last time I spoke with my mom she was engaged to husband number five. He sounds like a nice-enough guy. Maybe it'll last, maybe it won't. I've quit holding out hope that she'll marry for true happiness." She sighed and rolled her shoulders. "As for my sister, she married a wealthy older man who couldn't have children and needed a young hostess. But materialistically Daphne has everything she could ever ask for. I can't say I'd make the same kind of sacrifice."

Ian silently mulled over her comment. He didn't think marriage should be a sacrifice at all, and agreed that if either party had to give up anything that was important to them then the union wasn't meant to be. Yet he got the distinct impression that Erica believed that matrimony meant relinquishing freedom and choices and individual interests. She'd obviously never known any differently.

She cast him a benevolent smile. "I honestly never intended to get involved with the Camenson shelter and the women staying there, not to the extent that I have, but after one visit I saw my own mother in so many of the women who were there, and I just wanted to make a difference in their lives," she said, her voice infused with warmth and caring. "I felt a special connection to these women, and wanted to give them support and understanding."

He held up another slice of cantaloupe to her mouth. "I think what you're doing is very admirable."

"Thank you," she said softly, and chewed and swallowed the bite he gave her. "I think somewhere along the way I've adopted Tori and her daughter. This is Tori's third time to the shelter in the past six months. I think she's serious about leaving her husband this time. But she's scared about starting over and finding a job to support herself and her daughter. I want to make sure I'm there for her, as often as possible, to give her as much support as I can and build her confidence."

His chest swelled with pride for her. "You're incredible, Erica. You know that?"

She shrugged off his compliment, then stared at him, her gaze holding a hesitant glimmer of hope, and something else he couldn't quite decipher. "You know... would you like to go with me to the women's shelter today? It would really boost the women's spirits to meet you in person since they all listen to the show. And I know that Tori would love meeting you."

What she was asking was a huge step for her, he knew. Whether she realized it or not, she was letting him into a sacred and private part of her life. It was the first tangible shift in their relationship to something more meaningful and he wasn't about to blow this chance to establish a deeper, more emotional intimacy between them. Even if it meant canceling his standing Sunday lunch with the Winslows.

"Yeah, I'd like that," he told her before she changed her mind. Picking up the last cube of fruit with his fingers, he lifted it to her lips.

She nibbled on the juicy wedge all the way down to the tips of his fingers, which she then sucked clean. "You're very sneaky," she said, her voice tinged with husky nuances. "It just dawned on me what you were doing with that cantaloupe while I was busy talking. You were feeding me breakfast."

He shrugged unapologetically. "I wanted to make sure you ate something." Before she could think of his remark in terms of him taking care of her, he said, "C'mere and sit on my lap so I can have *you* for breakfast."

She stood and took his empty bowl and their mugs to the sink, then returned, settling herself across his thighs. His groin tightened in anticipation, and he lifted his lips to hers. He kissed her softly at first, and once he gained entrance to the welcoming depths of her mouth and tasted the heat of desire and sweet nectar on her tongue, he turned ravenous. His fingers unbuttoned the front placket of her shirt, then pushed the material aside so he could lave her full, ripe breasts crowned with tight nipples.

He heard a crinkling sound from the shirt pocket and stopped for a moment to remove the foil condom packet. He grinned with lazy amusement at Erica. "What's this?"

Grasping his shoulders, she twisted toward him and rubbed her breasts across his bare chest, making his breath hitch in his throat and her grin with satisfaction. "That is your chance to make up for leaving me alone in bed this morning."

He chuckled, and shifting them both, he stood and lifted her up to sit on the table in front of him, more than willing to atone for his earlier decision to let her sleep when it was becoming obvious she would have enjoyed waking up to a more real-life sexual dream. He kissed her again, hard and deep, and pushed her back with his upper body until her shoulders pressed against the hard surface of the table. With her fingers tangled in his hair and her eyes heavy-lidded with need, he began a leisurely trek downward, breathing damp fire on her neck and throat, filling his mouth with her breasts, grazing her stiff nipples with his teeth, dragging his wet tongue lower, until the buttons on the shirt she wore hindered his progress. His fingers slipped and fumbled with the catch and release, frustrating him. Growing impatient, he lifted up and ripped the sides open all the way, sending buttons flying across the room and momentarily startling Erica with the force of his desire.

He groaned in male appreciation when he discovered that she wasn't wearing any panties, and groaned more raggedly when she parted her thighs for him and offered him a tantalizing view of her glistening, swollen female flesh. He pulled in much needed oxygen into his lungs, and the aroused scent of her made his nostrils flare and his blood surge through his veins.

Her chest rose and fell rapidly, and her skin flushed with excitement. "Touch me, Ian," she whispered invitingly.

He wanted that more than anything…to caress her body, to touch her heart, her very soul. If she'd just let him.

Splaying a hand on her flat belly, he dipped a finger into her navel, then dragged the heel of his palm downward, over her mound until his thumb delved through her moist, dark-blond curls and found that intrinsic, feminine part of her that pulsed as wildly as he did. She was already wet and ready, primed for his possession...and that's exactly what he wanted to do. Possess and brand every part of her.

His restraint shattered, crashing through him in a frenzied fever pitch of hunger he felt helpless to resist. Wrenching open the fastening of his jeans, he shoved the denim down around his thighs and sheathed his fierce erection with the ribbed condom...all the while enduring Erica's hands stroking across chest, and her lips and teeth and tongue doing wicked, seductive things to his nipples. Finally protected, he pushed her back down, guided himself to her entrance and watched as her tight body enveloped the hard, straining length of his penis until he was all the way home. Mesmerized by the erotic sight of him gliding in and out of her, he slowed his thrusts, withdrawing and joining again in unhurried, languid increments.

Erica writhed her hips restlessly and locked her legs against his flanks to pull him closer. "Ian," she moaned in frustration. "I want faster...harder...*deeper*."

He leaned over her, bracing his hands on the table on either side of her head where her hair was spread out in silky, tousled disarray, and looked into her dark brown eyes. "You're a bossy thing this morning," he murmured teasingly, and placed a light kiss on her parted lips. "Maybe you'd like to set the pace?"

She twined her arms around his neck and grinned brazenly. "Maybe I would," she dared.

"Then hang on." She obeyed his order, wrapping her

arms and legs securely around him. Scooping her off the table, he took a step back and sat down on the chair behind him, switching their positions so that it was Erica straddling his lap and he was fused deep inside her. Erica who was in complete control of their pleasure. Erica who held him captive with her body. And judging by the sultry heat in her eyes, she liked having that leverage.

Sliding his hands down her spine, he brought their bodies flush from chest, to bellies, to thighs. Grasping her hips and rocking her closer, he drifted his mouth across hers. "Ride me, Erica," he whispered urgently. "As fast and hard and deep as you'd like."

Eyes glowing with passion, a come-hither smile on her lips, she did exactly that, taking her pleasure and giving back so much more until all that restless energy between them finally erupted in a hot, scalding whirlwind of sensation. There was no holding back for either of them... not the intensity of their climax or the powerful emotions that swelled and buffeted between them.

Then and there, Ian knew he was deeply, irrevocably in love with Erica McCree.

9

Janelle Denison

"DO TELL, HOW WAS your weekend?"

Finished putting away her purse and personal belongings in the closet at the station for her shift, Erica turned to find Carly leaning against the door frame leading into Dan's office, arms crossed over her breasts. Her expression was expectant, and her eyes brimmed with curiosity.

Erica smiled mischievously. "Like the rest of my listeners, you're going to have to wait to hear the details of our sexy city night date on my show—" she glanced at her watch "—in about twenty minutes."

"Argh! No fair," her friend complained with a pout. A few seconds later, a sly grin replaced her sulking expression. "Just tell me this…did those condoms come in handy?"

Erica's entire body flashed hot, and it had nothing to do with the stifling air in the room, and everything to do with all the different, provocative ways they'd used those prophylactics. "Yes," she admitted. "They did come in handy, thank you very much."

"You lucky, lucky girl." Carly sighed enviously. "I supplied the condoms, so of course that makes me privy to details."

Erica rolled her eyes as she brushed by Carly on her way out to the hallway to get herself a snack from the vending machine before her shift started. Naturally, Carly followed, determined to get the nitty-gritty information, and Erica realized in that moment she wasn't willing to dish out the specifics of her physical relationship—to her good friend, or her audience. What had transpired between her and Ian this weekend in the bedroom—and out of it—wasn't something she wanted to taint by sharing with thousands of listeners. Oh, sure, she could *insinuate* what had happened, but this was one time she might leave them all guessing and wondering.

She hadn't seen or talked to Ian since yesterday evening when he'd dropped her off at her apartment after they'd spent the day with Tori and Janet. Quite honestly, and much to her surprise, she'd missed him today. She was anxious to hear his deep, rich voice, and a part of her resented that she had to share tonight's conversation with the city of Chicago when she wanted him all to herself.

As for Carly, she'd give her friend just enough to whet her appetite and stir her interest. Pushing through the door, she glanced over her shoulder and grinned. "Let's just say that Ian has me addicted to sex." No doubt about it, she was addicted to *him,* if the light, floating, giddy feeling she'd been experiencing all day was any indication.

"Oh, wow!" Carly exclaimed in excitement, and clasped her hands to her chest. "Did you spend the whole night with him?"

"Yeah, I did." Digging into the front pocket of her shorts, Erica retrieved two dollar bills and inserted one into the snack machine, then changed the direction of their conversation to a less intimate topic. "And yesterday he went to the women's shelter with me. I took some promo stuff to sign and hand out, and the women there had a ball meeting him. It really bolstered their spirits. Of course he charmed them all." She punched a button for cheese crackers, and the package fell to the bottom slot for her to grab.

"Hmm, what's not to love about Ian?" Carly asked dreamily, seemingly infatuated with him, too, despite her devotion to Dan.

Love. The word, in context to Ian, startled Erica. Especially since she was battling with her own emotions when it came to him and where he fit in the scheme of things beyond her radio show. She had no solid, concrete answer.

She cared for Ian, respected him, even, and enjoyed their conversations and the easy way she could talk to him, seemingly about anything. And there was no denying she wanted him. But beyond the incredible, mind-blowing sex they'd indulged in, she'd also shared a very intrinsic part of herself with him yesterday in telling him about her painful past, and by inviting him to the shelter.

Not so surprisingly, he'd fit right in at the shelter. He'd been sensitive, compassionate and genuine when the situation called for it, as well as funny and engaging during lighthearted moments. He'd even talked to Tori about her decision to leave her husband, and tried to assuage the woman's fear of supporting herself on her own. And while Erica wouldn't go so far as to label what she felt for Ian as *love,* the emotions and longing taking up residence in her superceded anything she'd ever experienced for another man.

As Erica munched on her crackers, she told Carly about Ian's suggestion to take Tori and Janet to Navy Pier for the afternoon and how much fun they'd had together. The four of them had a blast on the Shoreline Shuttle that cruised its way to the Shedd Aquarium, which was something even Erica had never done before. They rode the Ferris wheel and carousel and visited the

Children's Museum—a high-tech playground with inter-active exhibits for youngsters. And that's when Erica dis-covered that Ian was a big kid at heart and loved children. He'd played with Janet in the Waterways and Inventing Lab, and followed her through the Treehouse Trails while she and Tori sat and watched the two of them enjoy the various attractions.

The way that Janet bonded to Ian, as if she craved the kind of male attention she'd never received from her own father, gave Erica hope that Janet wasn't permanently scarred from her father's abusive tendencies. Ian had showered the little girl with attention, and by the time the evening ended after an early dinner it was obvious that Janet adored him. Erica had been overwhelmed with joy when Janet wrapped her tiny arms around Ian's neck and hugged him tight, then asked him to come back soon to see her. Ian assured the little girl he would…and knowing Ian was a man of his word, Erica had no doubt that he'd make good on his promise.

Carly appeared totally enthralled and captivated with her story, and Ian. "The guy is a real prince, I'm telling you," she said adamantly. "Don't let this one slip through your fingers."

Done with her snack, Erica turned toward the soda vending machine to purchase a bottle of water. Opting to take a more realistic approach to her friend's comment, she said, "He may be a prince, but all romantic fairy tales eventually come to an end."

Carly pursed her lips determinedly. "And some end happily ever after, if you give them the chance."

More confusion wove through Erica, but her opinion remained firmly grounded. Water in hand, she twisted off the cap. "I just want to enjoy the time with Ian for as long as it lasts. I really like him—a whole lot, in fact—

but I can't say I'm ready to give up my freedom to settle down with just one person."

A frown furrowed Carly's brows. "Who said you had to give up anything at all?"

But in Erica's experience, relationships meant sacrifice. And that scared Erica. She feared she'd get so wrapped up in a relationship that she'd lose sight of her independence, her identity, without even realizing the loss until it was too late. But she didn't expect Carly to understand her insecurities and she didn't have the time or inclination to launch into an explanation.

"Never mind." She shook her head, dismissing their conversation and effectively sidestepping Carly's interrogation. "So, how was *your* weekend?"

"Not quite as eventful as yours," she said enviously, and propped a shoulder against the vending machine. "But I do have a secret to share."

Erica swallowed the mouthful of cool water she'd gulped, intrigued despite herself. "Oh?"

Carly glanced around, making sure that they were alone, then lowered her voice conspiratorially. "It's not official yet, so don't say anything to the other DJs, but there's a young group of upstarts interested in buying the station and changing the programming to a heavy metal format."

Erica's stomach turned over and churned at the suddenly very real possibility of having to start her career all over again, just when she was beginning to rise to the top. "Tell me you're not serious."

"Unfortunately, I am." Carly dragged her fingers through her hair, appearing just as discouraged by the news. "There hasn't been a firm offer yet, though. From what Dan told me, Virginia is being difficult and haggling over what she believes is a fair price, and the buyers don't want to pay what she's asking. Yet.''

Erica took another drink of water, hoping to calm her upset stomach. "No big surprise there, considering how run-down the place and equipment are.''

Carly nodded in agreement. "All we can do is hope the buyers back off.''

"What does it matter?'' Erica asked, heading back inside the inner offices. "It's inevitable that something will happen to the station one way or another. Either WTLK gets bought out, or we go bankrupt, though I hate to see either happen when things are going so well.''

"I hear ya,'' Carly commiserated. "Oh, by the way, I set up a personal appearance for you and Ian Saturday afternoon at Wrigley Field. Dan got a hold of two tickets on the mezzanine level for the Cubs game against the Los Angeles Dodgers, and we thought it would be great if WTLK set up a booth beforehand and you and Ian met with fans. In fact, Dan suggested that we make this your second sexy city night date to get the most out of the publicity and on-the-air promotion during the week. What do you think?''

Erica stopped at the plate-glass window looking into the broadcasting studio, watching as Jay wrapped up his show. She had to admit that the idea held appeal. Then again, just spending time with Ian, on any terms, tempted and enticed her. "Sounds like fun.''

"Great,'' Carly said, enthusiasm infusing her voice. "I'll let Dan know it's a go, and I'll get moving on advertising the appearance this week.''

Five minutes later Erica was on the air addressing her listeners, and Carly was in the booth next to hers with Ian waiting on the phone to discuss their date on the air.

"Hello, Chicago. This is Erica McCree, and you're

listening to *Heat Waves* on WTLK. We had a scorcher of a weekend, didn't we? Or maybe that was just my date with Ian that had me so hot and bothered,'' she teased huskily. "I haven't spoken to Ian all day, and I know you're all anxious to hear how our first sexy city night date went, so I won't keep you in suspense any longer."

She pressed the button for line one, connecting Ian to the show. "Hi, Ian. How are you tonight?"

"Better now that I'm on the air with you." His voice was low and intimate, coaxing erotic memories of how they'd spent their weekend together. And more tender recollections of how much fun they'd had at Navy Pier yesterday. "I think today was one of the longest days of my life. I've been counting down the minutes until I'd be on the air with you."

Something within Erica softened, a part of her heart that was growing increasingly defenseless when it came to Ian. "Okay, ladies, if you haven't figured it out by now, Ian is one of the most romantic, sexy, charming men around. And now, I'll give you a summary of our date, which was fabulous and absolutely perfect, by the way." She wanted to be sure that Ian knew what a wonderful time she'd had with him, if he didn't already know it. Hot, sizzling chemistry aside, they'd connected in so many ways other than physically, giving their relationship a depth she'd never anticipated. An emotional depth that was making her question her own beliefs and her outlook on the future.

She shared with her listeners how Ian had surprised her by picking her up in a limousine, and went on to describe their private, enchanting dinner at Everest overlooking the city. She described their after-dinner limo ride along scenic Lake Shore Drive, but omitted the more intimate activities that had occurred in the back seat.

She smiled at Carly as her best friend gave her a I-know-there's-more-to-this-date-than-you're-letting-on kind of look. Erica merely shrugged, not admitting to anything but superficial details. "I do have to say that Ian has exceptional taste in restaurants, and I was completely wined and dined and swept off my feet. He really knows how to treat a woman and make her feel special. Now we'll open up the phone lines and take questions from listeners."

All the lines lit up and blinked wildly, and Erica glanced at her computer monitor to check the name of the first caller. "Thanks for listening to *Heat Waves,* Pete, and for following our sexy city nights campaign. What would you like to ask?"

"This question is for Ian," Pete replied. "I'm sure I'm not the only guy out here wondering this but…what turned you on the most about Erica during your date?"

Erica winced and shifted in her seat, knowing it was a hazard of her job as a radio personality that male admirers would fantasize about the woman behind the voice and wonder what she was really like. She remained quiet, just as curious as the rest of her audience as to Ian's reply.

"Everything about Erica excites me," he said, making her pulse pick up its tempo. "But if I had to narrow down my choices, I'd have to say it was the sexy black dress she wore, and her hot, cinnamon-flavored lip gloss that turned me on the most. I think I admitted on the air a while back that I'm attracted to a woman's mouth, and Erica has, by far, the most sensual lips I've ever had the pleasure of kissing."

Erica shivered deliciously at his compliment and tried to ignore the spiraling hunger and need building within her. Especially since she knew she'd be going home to a cold, lonely bed in the early hours of morning after her shift ended.

Stifling a discontented sigh, she introduced another caller, this time a woman, and waited for the next question.

"How did the date end?" Deborah asked eagerly.

Erica jumped in before Ian could answer. "With a kiss...or two, or three." She injected humor into her tone, and before the woman could request specifics, she hit line three. "Welcome to the show, James. What question is on your mind tonight?"

"Did Ian get lucky?"

"As lucky as a man can get," Ian replied smoothly, his response subtly sexy, but vague enough to protect their privacy, which she appreciated.

"Erica, you said on a previous show that a slow seduction turns you on," the next listener said. "How do you rate Ian in terms of your personal fantasy?"

Erica was amazed that the woman remembered her comment about wanting a slow seduction, but was pleased that her topics and remarks had made a lasting impact with her audience. "Let's just say that he's a master at mind sex and foreplay," she said seductively. "And he made sure I was completely satisfied."

"And vice versa," Ian added, his tone equally flirtatious.

Swallowing light laughter, and wishing he were there with her in person so she could see one of his warm, private smiles, she moved on to the next caller. "Do you have a question for us, Candace?"

"What's up for your next sexy city night date?"

Erica glanced toward Carly, who gave her a thumbs-up sign to let her know that Ian had agreed to the outing. "Ian is taking me to a Cubs game this Saturday at Wrigley Field. For those of you who might be attending the game, we'll have a booth set up beforehand to meet and greet listeners. We'll also be giving away free promotional items, so be sure to stop by and say hello.''

"Who are the Cubs playing against?" Ian asked.

"The L.A. Dodgers, and since they're from my home state of California, I'm afraid I'm going to have to root for the underdog this time.''

Ian chuckled, the deep, rich sound resonating through the airwaves. "Should make for an interesting game. We'll be rivals, since I'll be cheering for the Cubs.''

She skimmed her tongue along her bottom lip and touched the perspiration gathering at the top swells of her breasts. "I take it you're up for a friendly wager in terms of the game?''

"Umm, most definitely," he murmured, a tantalizing insinuation lacing his masculine tone. "I'm hoping for a lot of home runs.''

SATURDAY AFTERNOON couldn't come quickly enough for Ian. After spending the entire week without seeing Erica because of their busy, conflicting schedules, he was anxious to be with her…to watch her eyes light up when he talked to her, to hear her laughter over something silly they said or did, and to finally be within touching distance.

He'd started their day together by greeting her with a long, deep, passionate "hello" kiss when he'd picked her up at her apartment that afternoon. The kiss left them breathless and eager for a more physical joining. There had been no doubt that they both would have taken that embrace straight into the bedroom if it hadn't been for the fact that they had their scheduled appearance to attend. Ian considered suggesting a quickie to slake their immediate needs and hunger, but opted to build the sexual anticipation for later, instead.

Arriving at Wrigley Field, they held court in the small booth WTLK had set up outside the entrance to the stadium, and from the moment they made their presence known they were absolutely swamped with fans and listeners who wanted their autographs or a picture taken with the two of them. Others clamored for the bumper stickers, T-shirts and other promotional items they were handing out.

The people they met were enthusiastic and supportive. Most of them were avid listeners of *Heat Waves* and were thrilled to meet them both. And while last week's dinner engagement had been private and intimate, this date was sexy, playful fun for everyone to enjoy and be a part of.

Forty-five minutes into their appearance Erica excused herself and stepped away from the crowd for a moment. Her face was flushed from the heat and humidity, and her lips lacked their normal pink, glossy luster. Ian continued signing autographs and passing out trinkets while keeping an eye on Erica, just to make sure she was okay. He watched as she took a long drink from her bottled water and knew he was in big trouble when he found even that simple action stimulating and arousing.

Her lashes drifted shut as she drank, and the way she tipped her head back made her breasts more prominent. She wore a denim miniskirt and cotton tank top overlaid with a sheer, loose blouse, and the way the stretchy material contoured seamlessly to her firm, full breasts led him to believe she was braless.

He gritted his teeth when he realized he wasn't the only guy to notice the sensual display. He was eternally grateful when their obligation to the show's fans was over fifteen minutes later so he didn't have to share Erica with anyone else for the rest of the night. Once they left the booth and a crew took over to break down the stand, Ian ushered Erica to the refreshment bar. They ordered hot dogs, peanuts and sodas, then settled into their private seats on the mezzanine level to wait for the game to begin.

Erica swiped a hand across her damp brow, then dug into her purse for a barrette. "Wow, that was certainly hectic!" Smiling despite being overwhelmed by fans for the past hour, she gathered up the ends of her hair, twisted the strands into a loose knot and secured the mass on top of her head with the clip.

She'd exposed the slender column of her neck, moist with a thin sheen of perspiration, and he resisted the urge to caress that soft flesh with his fingertips and see that glimmer of arousal leap to life in her eyes. Another few hours and he'd have her alone and all to himself.

He returned her grin and handed her the large diet soda she'd ordered. "That's what happens when you become a celebrity."

"I'm far from being a celebrity," she said modestly, and accepted the hot dog she'd piled high with a little bit of everything from the condiment stand. "But it is nice to see the station get the recognition it deserves. Too bad it probably won't make much difference in terms of Virginia keeping the station."

He cast her a curious glance. "What's up with that, anyway?"

She bit into her hot dog, chewed and swallowed. "Just between you and me, it looks like the station might get bought out by a group interested in a heavy-metal format." Her lips twisted with frustration and worry. "And if that happens, every one of us who now works for WTLK will be out a job."

"What are you going to do if the sale goes through?"

"I honestly don't know." She sighed, and when she met his gaze there was no denying the distress in the depth of her dark brown eyes. "Start sending out résumés, no doubt. I hate to see all the hard work from this campaign be for nothing, especially when we're starting to see an increase in ratings. We've even got big-name advertisers finally sitting up and taking notice of WTLK, and Virginia is just going to sell us off to the highest bidder, just to make a few bucks."

She ate another bite of her hot dog and took a long drink of her soda. "I hate to even consider unemployment right now, but a part of me knows it's inevitable, one way or another. At least I'll have the success of our campaign to put on my résumé. And I've been thinking…if I can't find a comparable position here in Chicago, then I might see what's available somewhere else, like Indianapolis."

Ian nearly choked on the portion of hotdog he'd been swallowing. *Indiana?* She was considering moving hundreds of miles away and starting over in a different state? His belly cramped with a slow-building panic, along with the urge to blurt out his feelings for her, which he *knew* she wasn't ready to hear. "I'm sure if anything happens to WTLK you won't have a hard time finding something here in Chicago."

"Thanks for your vote of confidence," she said with an indulgent smile, "but as I've learned in life, there are no guarantees, and no matter how much I might not like the thought of relocating, I have to keep an open mind and consider all my options."

Ian stared at Erica, seeing that strength and determination that made her the independent woman she was. No matter what, she would make it on her own. She'd proved that many times, and at the moment he was feeling helpless and fearful of ultimately losing her. And there wasn't a damn thing he could do about her decision to leave, if that's what it came down to. He could only hope that what they had together counted for something and made her rethink her plans when the time came for her to reevaluate her life and goals.

"Enough about my woes," Erica said lightly, and wiped her mouth, then her fingers on a paper napkin. "I heard some very interesting news I've been wanting to talk to you about."

"Oh?" he asked, fairly certain he knew what she wanted to discuss. "And what did you hear?"

"I stopped by the shelter this morning, and Tori told me that you interviewed her yesterday for a job, and hired her."

"I did." He shrugged, not wanting to make a big deal out of his actions and the choice he'd made. "I needed a receptionist for the office, and I automatically thought of Tori. I know she was nervous about getting a job because she didn't have any experience, and I thought this would be a good start for her. She'll be answering the phone and doing light administrative tasks. I know she'll do great once she gets the hang of it."

Erica nodded in agreement. "And not only did you start her off on quite a high pay scale with full benefits, way above the norm for a receptionist," she pointed out needlessly, "she also mentioned that you gave her a substantial advance for her to find a decent apartment for her and Janet, with enough money left over to buy furnishings."

He stretched his arm along the back of her chair and rubbed his thumb along the bare nape of her neck. "It's not a big deal, Erica."

"Maybe not to you, but it is to her," she said, sounding very pleased that he'd thought of Tori for the employment opportunity. "I don't think I've ever seen her so happy and confident."

Erica's gaze softened with adoration, and though he loved seeing that affection directed solely at him, gaining her approval hadn't been the reason why he'd hired Tori at his investment firm. His reasons went much, much deeper than that, to his own struggle to find a place where he fit in. He remembered how the Winslows had offered him such unconditional acceptance at a time in his life when he'd needed it the most. He liked to think he'd returned the favor in helping Tori.

She glanced out to the field, where the teams were still warming up before the game started. On the lower levels, people were finding their seats and buying refreshments from the vendors strolling through the stands.

After a few silent moments passed, she turned back to him and asked, "Why didn't you tell me about hiring Tori?"

"I was going to." He grinned lazily. "If you haven't noticed, this is really the first stretch of time we've had alone since we arrived." And honestly, he hadn't been sure how Erica would take the news, considering her staunch views on being an independent woman. Obviously, he'd done well with Tori, and she approved.

Unexpectedly, she leaned across the plastic armrest and placed a warm, lingering kiss on his cheek. "Thank you," she whispered.

He tilted his head. "For what?"

Her fingers touched his jaw reverently. "For giving Tori the chance she needed to build her self-esteem. For giving her the opportunity to prove that she can make it on her own and support herself and doesn't need her abusive husband to take care of her.''

"Everybody needs someone to believe in them, Erica." He spoke from his own personal experience, and knew beneath that stubborn, headstrong facade of Erica's she needed someone who supported her emotionally, too—whether she realized it or not. "I see so much potential with Tori, and I know she's going to fit in well at the firm. I don't know if this makes sense, but I just wanted to do something for someone else, in much the same way the Winslows helped me when I was starting out.''

"I understand," she said, her gaze and tender expression backing up her simple but powerful words. "You're very lucky to have the Winslows in your life.''

He heard the wistful catch in her voice, and wondered if she'd heard it, too, or if she didn't even realize what she longed for. "Yeah, I am." He made a split-second decision, one that would yet again shift the dynamics of their relationship. "You know, I'm having Sunday lunch with the Winslows tomorrow afternoon, and I know they'd enjoy meeting you—''

She was shaking her head in denial before he even finished. "Ian...I don't know." Insecurities infused her voice. "I mean, you and Audrey and the Winslows...''

He understood her concern but wouldn't accept it as an excuse. "Audrey is gone, Erica," he said gently but firmly. "There's nothing I or anyone else can do to change that. You're here and now for me, and I know that the Winslows are wondering who the sassy mystery woman is that I'm debating with on the air every night.'' He followed that up with a persuasive grin.

Still, she hesitated, her concern and uncertainty evident in the absent way she chewed on her thumbnail and her unwillingness to give him a verbal commitment to the very personal date.

"Last weekend you shared a part of your life with me," he said. "Now, it's my turn to share with you."

That request seemed to penetrate her defenses, and she released a pent-up breath. "You make it very difficult for me to argue with you, Mr. Carlisle."

He chuckled. "I take it that means yes?"

"Yes, that means yes." She pinched him playfully in his side, letting him know that the choice was truly her own, not instigated by guilt or a sense of fairness she felt she might owe him.

Grabbing her wrist, he brought her hand to his mouth, pressing his lips to her fingertips. "You know, we never did nail down the specifics of our wager on the game."

Her lashes fell half-mast and her mouth curved into a beguiling smile. "Since your focus seems to be on making a lot of home runs, the team with the highest score wins, obviously. And since a home run in terms of sex is going all the way, let's say the winner calls the shots later—any way they want it."

"You're on," he murmured, welcoming the heat of anticipation that flowed through his veins and settled in southern regions. No matter how he analyzed the bet, whether he claimed personal victory with his team or lost the wager, he'd still come out a winner.

"I DEMAND A REMATCH," Erica grumbled, not for the first time since the game ended with a six to seven score in the Cubs' favor. "I swear Dave Hansen slid into home base *before* the catcher touched him with the ball. That umpire had to have been blind not to have seen that he was safe!"

"Don't be a poor loser, Erica," he said consolingly,

having listened to her complain the entire drive to her place about the injustice of her team losing. That third and final out for the Dodgers at the top of the tenth inning had cost them the game. The Cubs had triumphed by one run, and that's all Ian needed to win the bet. Despite her fun-loving quibbles and claims that his team cheated, they'd both concurred it had been a close, exciting game.

"The ump called the play an out," he said, "and I happen to agree."

"Of course you would." They headed up the walkway leading to her apartment, and she dug her keys out of her purse. "And you don't have to look so smug about the fact that the ump is biased toward your team."

He chuckled at her outlandish accusation, one of many he'd had to endure the past hour. "It's my right as the winner to be anything I want. And just as soon as we get inside your apartment I get to call the shots, any way I want." He was already hard and aching with wanting her, and anxious to get them both naked.

She sent him a look of mock surrender. "Then I guess I have no choice but to accept defeat and be a slave to your every desire."

He grinned wickedly. "Nope, no choice at all."

Unlocking the door, she entered, and he trailed behind, closing and securing the bolt behind them. It was warm inside her apartment after being unoccupied all day. She tossed her purse and keys onto the couch and walked over to an air-conditioning unit protruding from the wall. She turned the knob to high and a gust of cool air blasted her midsection. Catching his reflection in the brass-framed mirror mounted over the unit, she sighed in relief, unbuttoned the sheer blouse she wore over her tank top and let it fall to the floor.

A tempting smile teased her mouth as she inched her

denim skirt high on her thighs to cool off, then pulled the stretchy material of her tank top to just beneath her breasts so the cold air hit her belly. Her nipples puckered into tight peaks, and he could see their dusky rose outline through the thin fabric.

She closed her eyes, and with loose tendrils of hair wisping around her face and her lips parted enticingly, she tipped her head back in a pose straight from a centerfold magazine. "Aah, that…feels…*so good*."

His blood heated, gripping him with a need so strong he knew this first time after a week apart would be a wild, frenzied joining. And while he was enjoying her provocative show, this seduction was supposed to be his by virtue of winning their wager, and he meant to make sure she knew that.

Tearing off his own shirt, he tossed it aside and came up behind her. Grasping her wrists, he lifted her hands and placed her flattened palms on the wall in front of them, forcing her to lean into the air conditioner and arch her back so that her bottom was on a perfect level with his hips and the bulge straining behind the fly of his jeans.

The position also left her no choice but to watch their images in the mirror, and his eyes burned and glittered like chips of green coal when they met hers. "Keep your hands on the wall…at all times," he ordered in a low, raspy tone.

Nuzzling the side of her neck with soft, suctioning kisses, he skimmed his hands down her raised arms to the hem of her tank top, which he pushed up around her chest so that her full breasts were bared. Then, he bunched her skirt up around her waist and shoved her panties down. The wispy scrap of pink silk caught and tangled around her knees and he left them there.

A moan slipped from her throat and she shifted restlessly against him as the now frigid air blew across her nipples, intimately kissed the damp curls between her thighs and chilled her exposed flesh.

He aligned the front of his body along the back of hers and moved his mouth up to her ear. Holding her hips in his hands, he slowly gyrated his hard length against her sweetly curved, naked bottom. "I've wanted you all week," he murmured hotly, eagerly, sharing one of his most illicit fantasies with her. "Every night when we talked on the air, I'd get off the phone and close my eyes and continue listening to your voice. I'd pretend you were in bed with me, that it was your hands on my aroused body, your tongue replacing the stroke of my thumb over the rigid tip of my cock, your tight body replacing my fist…."

Her breathing deepened, and she dampened her lips with her tongue. "Ian…"

He ignored her silent plea and unbuckled his belt, then unzipped the front placket of his jeans, *finally* releasing his burgeoning erection, which pulsed and throbbed despite the direct gust of cold air on his body. "Tell me you did the same thing when you got home at night," he coaxed in her ear. "Did you take me to bed with you, Erica?"

Her entire body shuddered, and her hands curled into fists against the wall. "Yes," she whispered.

He feathered his fingers over her stiff nipples, then plucked the distended tips, the play of his hands a burning contrast against her icy flesh. "Did you feel my mouth on your breasts, my teeth tugging on your nipples, and the stroke of my tongue between your thighs?"

"Yes." She nearly wept.

Pulling his wallet from his back pocket, he withdrew

one of the condoms he'd stashed there, dropped his bill-fold to the floor and sheathed his pulsing sex. In less than a minute he was back. "Tell me, Erica…did your fingers slip deep inside your body like I longed to do every night? As I'm aching to do right this very instant?" His touch coasted down her quivering belly and dipped low, finding her wet and ready and drenched with passion.

Her knees buckled and he caught her around the waist, holding her tight against him. *"Yes,"* she admitted on a strangled groan, and widened her stance and tilted her hips, seeking to be filled.

Accepting her invitation and unable to wait any longer, he drove into her, plunging deep and to the hilt. She sucked in a breath, and he exhaled hard as his hips pumped instinctively until the rhythm of his penetrating strokes matched the frantic beat of his heart. Capturing one breast in his hand, he slipped the other between her thighs to finesse the swollen nub of flesh there. He turned his head and opened his mouth against her neck, and was overcome with the primitive urge to brand her. Finding the tender skin between shoulder and the nape of her neck, he bit, sharp enough to make her gasp and rear back, and hard enough to leave his mark on her.

And that's all it took for that wildness to ignite and flare out of control along with an essential hunger that spiraled from the depth of his soul. The muscles in his back and buttocks flexed with each powerful, upward thrust. He heard Erica's panting breath and looked in the mirror and witnessed the glaze of desire in her eyes. Saw the flush of ecstasy transforming her expression as searing pleasure crested. Felt the internal contractions sweep through her and clutch at him as she climaxed and cried his name as the force of her release ripped through her.

He followed right behind with his own fierce, explosive orgasm that left him completely wasted.

Seconds later he was still holding her, their bodies still joined, their skin damp with perspiration where he pressed against her from behind, despite the cool air blowing steadily from the air conditioner. "How about a cool shower?" he suggested.

"Umm, that sounds good," she said, though she seemed content to remain right where she was.

He met her gaze in the mirror and grinned sinfully. "Just be warned, this was just the beginning, and I'm not done with you."

She reached back and touched her fingertips to his jaw, a drowsy, seductive smile making an appearance. "I certainly hope not, she murmured. "You've got a whole week to make up for."

TYING OFF THE BELT of her cotton robe, and grateful for the few minutes reprieve Ian had given her after their shower, Erica rubbed condensation from her bathroom mirror until she could see her reflection. Eyes a soft shade of brown stared back at her. Her skin was pink from the glow of delicious, satisfying lovemaking and from the cool shower she'd shared with Ian that had rapidly turned into a hot, steamy, erotic romp.

She felt sensually pampered and completely aware of erogenous zones she'd never knew existed. It was a wondrous feeling, one she never wanted to end. Reaching into a drawer for a comb to run through her freshly washed hair, she caught sight of the faint crescent shape of Ian's teeth marks on her neck and shivered in remembrance. The man was an incredibly physical, earthy lover, and even though they'd already made love twice, she was already anticipating what Ian had in store for the rest of the night. She was game for anything, knowing that she'd enjoy the encounter just as much as he.

She ran the comb through the damp strands of her hair, wondering what she was going to do once their time together was over and this constant craving she had for him didn't go away. Her need for him was beginning to overwhelm and frighten her, which she didn't need with all the other upheaval being dumped on her with the station and possible unemployment.

Not wanting to think about the possibility of leaving Ian, and determined to enjoy whatever time they spent together *now,* she headed back into her bedroom and found him over by the bookcase in the corner, the towel he'd dried off with knotted low on his hips. She winced when she realized he was perusing the section with her collection of sexual manuals and volumes on every kind of erotic, sensual topic imaginable.

Her heart thumped self-consciously in her chest, and she forced her feet to move forward while scrambling for an excuse for all those manuals other than the truth—that she'd never experienced really good sex, had never truly known what she'd been missing, until he'd introduced her to the various sensual pleasures of making love. She'd learned more from him during their sexy debates and being with him than any textbook ever could have taught her.

He glanced toward her with an open book in his hand, a slow smile unfurling. "Quite a library you have here."

She closed the distance between them. No lies. No excuses. There was no reason for either after everything else they'd shared. "Would you believe I use them to come up with hot, sexy topics for the show?"

He lifted a dark brow. "Really?"

She drew a deep breath, exhaled slowly. "I'm not the

sex expert I come across as on *Heat Waves*," she admitted.

"No?" Mock disbelief laced his tone.

She frowned. "You're making fun of me."

"Yeah, I'm teasing you." He winked at her, and she automatically forgave him. "Actually, you sound pretty convincing on the air, but that night when we were discussing orgasms in the stairwell was a dead giveaway that you weren't the vixen you wanted everyone to think you were."

She ducked her head in embarrassment. "Well, I'd appreciate it if you didn't mention the sex manuals to anyone, especially my listeners."

Tucking a finger beneath her chin, he raised her gaze back to his. "My lips are sealed," he promised, his eyes glimmering with sincerity. "Besides, you won't be needing these books anymore."

She strolled to the bed and sat down on the edge of the mattress, not certain what he meant. "No?"

"Nope." He looked all confidence, all male. "Now you've got me and I'll teach you anything and everything you need to know about sex."

She laughed lightly. "Oh, and aren't you the know-it-all?"

"Any complaints so far?" he challenged, approaching her, the book he'd been looking at still clutched in his hand.

She saw the intent in his gaze, and heat and quivering excitement blossomed within her. "No, no complaints."

"I didn't think so." He grinned cockily, then opened the *Kama Sutra* to a two-page spread of color photographs of lovers engaged in different sexual acts. "There's a few positions in this book that look interesting. And since I only have a few hours to take advantage of the wager I won, I want to make sure I get my time's worth.''

She scooted back on the bed. ''Oh, yeah?''

''Yep.'' He tugged the towel around his hips loose, let it drop to the carpet and joined her. ''Starting with this one,'' he said, pointing to a photo of a woman sitting astride a man who was kneeling on the bed, his thighs spread to afford a deeper penetration into his partner. ''I want you on top like that.''

Already, he was completely aroused and ready for her, and it was a heady sensation to know she affected him that powerfully. He pushed the open book aside and stripped off her robe, then easily maneuvered her into that provocative position, and she gave herself over to him and his insatiable desires, knowing the pleasure would be completely mutual.

They tried many new positions, some lusty and adventurous, and others so impossible and silly that they'd laughed over the twisted, awkward positions they'd gotten themselves into. But during it all, she felt the closeness between them grow, felt the trust between them become so intertwined with her body and soul.

After all their attempts and a few orgasms for her, they ended up face-to-face, embraced in an intimate missionary position with her calves draped over the back of his thighs and him buried deep inside her. Fun and games aside, he made love to her slowly this time. And with each heavy glide of his body into hers he filled her so wholly, moved her so intensely and made her feel cherished, yet so incredibly vulnerable, too.

He framed her face in his hands, and their gazes locked as tightly as their bodies. And there in his caring green eyes she saw raw honesty, a wealth of promises and a tenderness she'd never before known.

Then, in the barest of whispers he told her, "I love you."

She trembled and found herself tumbling, drowning, and tried to claw her way back to the surface. He must have seen or sensed her alarm, because he immediately attempted to soothe her fears.

"You don't need to say anything in return, Erica," he murmured in the velvet darkness surrounding them. "I don't expect anything in return. The timing felt right and I just wanted you to know."

But it was too late. His declaration changed so much. It shifted the tenor of their lovemaking, the gentleness of his long, slow kisses, and the emotional intensity of her climax. Tears gathered in her eyes in the aftermath of her release.

But most of all, his love unlocked a part of her heart that had remained closed off for far too long.

10

"IT'S NICE TO FINALLY MEET the woman who's not only fascinated a good part of Chicago with her sultry talk show, but has also captured Ian's attention, as well."

Ian had known this conversation was coming from the moment he and Erica had arrived at the Winslows' more than an hour ago, and he'd seen Gayle's eyes light up with interest and curiosity. He was more surprised that Gayle had held off as long as she had in directly mentioning his relationship with Erica when he knew how straightforward the other woman could be.

"I do have to say the feeling is mutual," Erica replied smoothly, sincerely, then took a sip of her raspberry iced tea. They were all relaxing out on the terrace after a light lunch of croissant sandwiches and fresh fruit. "Now I see why Ian thinks of all of you as family."

"We can't imagine our lives without Ian in it." Eve Winslow beamed with pride, as if Ian was truly a blood relation. "Both Ian and Adam are like sons to us," she said of Gayle's husband, too. "Once you're a part of the Winslow family, there's no getting rid of us."

David echoed his wife's sentiment. "Besides, I need someone to golf with on Sundays, and these boys keep me young on the golf course," he joked.

"Don't let the old guy fool you, Erica," Ian added wryly. "David takes great pleasure in beating the pants off me and Adam."

Erica laughed, seemingly enjoying the easy camaraderie within the family.

David winked at her. "Like I said, it keeps me young."

Gayle's five-year-old daughter, Shelly, came up to Ian and without preamble climbed up on his lap and settled in to feed a bottle to her doll. The little girl was shy and quiet and a treasure. Ian cuddled her close, inhaling her soft, powdery scent, enjoying his role as uncle. He caught Erica watching him, and smiled at her.

"You seem to have a way with little girls," she commented.

He knew she was referring to Janet, and the way the two of them had bonded so easily. "I have a soft spot for kids in general." And he couldn't wait to have a family of his own one day. While it was on the tip of his tongue to tell her that, he caught himself, knowing it was an insinuation Erica didn't need on top of everything else that had transpired between them in the past twenty-four hours.

After his spontaneous "I love you" last night she'd been more quiet than usual, but she hadn't withdrawn, and he took that as a positive sign. Today their time with the Winslows was going well, despite how nervous she'd been about meeting everyone. Seeing her interact with them and witnessing the undeniable approval from his surrogate family merely confirmed what he already knew…Erica was a perfect fit for him. Like him, she needed a family in her life, and he was more than willing to share his.

"So, what's next for you and Ian after this sexy city nights campaign the two of you are doing?" Gayle asked, her eyes bright and eager for more details.

"I don't think Ian and I have thought that far ahead,"

Erica replied, choosing her explanation carefully. She was keeping the sale of the station in mind, which could mean the end to their on-the-air association if WTLK was bought out by the new heavy-metal group.

They spent the next hour talking about *Heat Waves* and the success of their campaign, and how amused family and friends were to see Ian's picture on billboard ads. Erica never mentioned the fate of WTLK, but Ian knew it was a constant concern for her, as it was for him, especially since the possibility existed that she could leave Chicago to find another job that suited her goals and purpose.

Gayle cast a quick glance at her watch, then looked back at Erica. "The guys are going to head out for their golf game pretty soon. Would you like to join my mom and me for our Sunday afternoon ritual of shopping?"

Erica's gaze automatically sought his, and Ian gave her a smile that conveyed the choice was hers. If the idea appealed and she was comfortable with Eve and Gayle, then go. If she'd rather not, he'd take her back home.

He saw the uncertainties in her eyes turn to longing, and then Erica smiled at the two women who were waiting anxiously for her response. "Sure, I'd love to go."

Eve stood, warmth and caring etching her features. "I was hoping you'd say yes. We'll have such fun. It'll be just like when Gayle and Audrey and I used to go shopping and talk girl stuff."

With Eve's comment, Ian realized that the Winslows had wholeheartedly embraced Erica into the family. And by them accepting her so openly, he felt a sense of peace settle within him. The Winslows had always been genuine in their approval of him, but a part of him had wondered if that approval had hinged on his relationship with their daughter, who was now gone. As if his presence was their way of holding tight to Audrey's memory.

But those doubts and insecurities fled, as did the restlessness that had taken residence within him when Audrey had died. Audrey might have been the catalyst that had brought the Winslows into his life, but Erica was the woman who completed him.

And in that moment, he knew he'd do whatever it took to keep Erica in his life permanently.

ERICA ARRIVED AT Ghirardelli's ice cream shop off of Michigan Avenue ten minutes before she was supposed to meet with Carly, who'd called Erica early that afternoon at home and invited her out for a "celebratory" hot fudge sundae. The excitement in Carly's voice had been unmistakable, and she'd refused to give Erica so much as a hint of what they might be celebrating. If it involved chocolate, Erica figured it was big news. Her first guess was that her friend had finally gotten laid by Dan. And if that was the case, chocolate was definitely the way to honor the occasion.

Erica grinned privately to herself as she stepped inside the cool ice cream shop to wait for Carly, thinking of her own torrid affair with Ian, which was gradually taking on subtle but undeniable nuances of a real relationship. A frightening prospect when she took into account Ian's declaration of love, and how he was slowly integrating her into his life, including making her a part of his relationship with the Winslows. She was surprised to find herself doing the same by openly sharing private bits and pieces of herself. Now there was the future to consider, and that's where her feelings and emotions became divided.

She sighed and absently perused the shelves stocked

with tempting assortments of chocolate confections and gifts, her mind tumbling with the same doubts and concerns that had plagued her for the past few days. There was a part of her that craved what Ian offered since they were so well matched, while another small voice in her head reminded her how hard she'd worked to claim back her independence after Paul. Was she ready to give up her freedom for a man, especially one with traditional values who was searching for a life mate more than a playmate? Could she risk falling into that dependent cycle her mother was in? Her answer was a resounding, firm *no,* but she did give serious thought to the possibility of meeting Ian halfway somehow. Of saying yes to something beyond a temporary affair, a promise to date him exclusively, but without pressure or expectations of anything more.

"I'm glad to see you didn't start without me."

The chipper sound of Carly's voice pulled Erica from her thoughts, and she whirled around to find her friend grinning like a Cheshire cat, and her skin literally glowing. "Believe me, I was tempted." Erica inhaled deeply. "I think I've gained five pounds just by breathing in the rich smell of chocolate in this place."

Carly laughed, her eyes sparkling merrily. "And I'm about to add another five with the real thing. Come on, order whatever you'd like. My treat."

"Your treat, huh?" Smiling at her friend's upbeat, buoyant mood, Erica followed her over to the soda fountain counter. "Wow, whatever news you've got to share must be huge."

"Oh, it most definitely is." Carly tossed the words saucily over her shoulder, causing her chin-length bob to brush her chin. "Big enough to order extra hot fudge on my sundae."

The young woman behind the counter took their orders and minutes later delivered their double-thick sundaes. The two of them carried their bowls to a vacant table, and as soon as they sat down Erica found she couldn't stand the suspense a moment longer.

"Okay, you have to know that I'm dying here," she said anxiously. "Tell me what we're celebrating already!"

Carly thrust out her left hand, which flashed a gorgeous, glittering diamond solitaire on her ring finger. "I'm officially engaged," she announced giddily.

"Ohmigod!" Erica gaped, her eyes widening in shock and disbelief. "Are you serious?"

"As serious as this *one carat* diamond ring Dan slipped on my finger," she bragged. "He asked me to marry him last night, I said yes, then of course I ripped his clothes off and forced him to finally consummate our relationship." She dipped her spoon into her ice cream, a soft, dreamy expression flitting across her face. "I have to say, the man is going to keep me plenty satisfied, in bed and out. He was so worth waiting for."

Erica laughed, and was startled by the stab of envy she experienced.

Reaching across the small table, she gathered her friend into a brief, congratulatory hug. "Oh, Carly, I'm so thrilled for you." And she truly was.

"Of course I want you to be my maid of honor when we get married," Carly said.

Misty-eyed, Erica pressed a hand to her chest, overwhelmed with Carly's special request. "I would love to be your maid of honor."

Carly ate another scoop of ice cream heaped with fudge, whipped cream and nuts, and smiled knowingly. "I'm hoping you'll be next to get engaged...to Ian."

A startling, inexplicable warmth filled Erica at the thought. Mouth full of decadent chocolate, Erica shook her head and swallowed. "I'm not looking to get married, Carly."

"And you think I was?" She followed that question with amused laughter. "You know how many guys I dated before I finally hooked up with Dan. I was looking for a good time, even with him, but instead I discovered that finding the right person and falling in love can happen when you least expect it."

Erica bit her lower lip, then asked a question that had been hiding somewhere in the back of her mind. "And what do you do when love happens when you least expect it?"

She shrugged. "You adjust your life accordingly and make it work," she replied simply.

That easy. That difficult. Erica frowned and shoveled another spoonful of the icy treat into her mouth, wondering if she could adjust her life accordingly and make it work with Ian.

Carly regarded her with concern, seemingly picking up on her shift in mood. "Things are good with Ian, right?"

Erica nodded. She wasn't ready to share the fact that Ian loved her. She was still getting used to that revelation herself. "Yeah, we're great...."

A grin quirked the corner of her friend's mouth. "Why do I hear a 'but' in the tone of your voice?"

Erica dragged her fingers through her loose hair, suddenly feeling very weary. "Maybe because I'm trying to take things one day at a time with Ian. Maybe because I'm torn and confused."

"About?"

"I care about Ian," she said, wanting to make that clear so Carly would hopefully understand where she was coming from. "But with the fate of the station so up in the air and all of us on the verge of unemployment, I've been thinking about sending résumés out to stations here in Chicago. Possibly to some high-profile stations in Indianapolis, too, just in case I can't find anything here in the city. I feel like I can't commit to anything right now."

"Indianapolis?" Carly echoed, a genuinely perplexed look transforming her features. "Ian didn't tell you he—" She cut off the rest of her comment, her eyes widening in sudden realization. Uncharacteristic to Carly's outspoken nature, she ducked her head, concentrated on her sundae and filled her mouth with more ice cream.

An odd sensation pricked the back of Erica's neck, and she didn't like the feeling one bit. "Tell me what, Carly?"

"Um, if you don't know, I'm not sure it's my place to tell you." Carly absently twisted her new engagement ring on her finger. "Dan mentioned something to me, and I guess I should have kept my big mouth shut until he called a staff meeting," she said dismissively.

Erica pushed her half-eaten sundae aside and pinned her friend with a direct look, determined to get the goods. "If it involves me somehow, or even Ian, then as my friend you should tell me."

"It does involve you, and Ian...oh, *damn.*" She grimaced. "I wish I'd never said anything at all."

But she had, and whatever Carly was keeping a secret, it was big and important and Erica wanted details. "Out with it, Carly," she demanded.

"I guess you're going to find out sooner or later," she rationalized. "And it *is* good news."

Erica clenched her jaw with impatience. "Find out *what?*"

"Ian bought the station," she blurted, then grinned as if she'd just bestowed a huge gift upon Erica. "He contacted Virginia on Monday, offered her exactly what she wanted with a huge cash down payment that she obviously couldn't resist, and now it's just a matter of him signing the paperwork and it's a done deal."

Erica sat back in her chair, stunned to the very tips of her toes and unable to believe it could be true. "Tell me you're kidding."

"Why would I joke about something so important to all of us?" Carly looked at her as if she'd lost her mind. "Erica, I thought you'd be excited. Thrilled, actually. Especially considering the success of your show."

A phenomenal success she owed in part to Ian and his nightly calls and their sexy city nights campaign. And now he was ensuring she didn't go anywhere by purchasing WTLK. The solution had been that simple for him. Erica pressed a hand to her belly, feeling as though she'd been delivered a physical blow to her midsection.

"This means we all get to keep our jobs," Carly continued, oblivious to Erica's emotional upheaval, too caught up in the fact that Erica's prince had been the station's knight in shining armor in saving them all from unemployment. "We can continue promoting *Heat Waves,* and for sure you won't be looking for another job elsewhere...."

Carly went on exalting Ian's generosity, but Erica no longer followed the conversation. The only thought filling her head was that Ian hadn't said a word to her about buying the station. He hadn't told her that he was even considering the investment, or asked her opinion on the matter. *Nothing.* He'd contacted Virginia on Monday, and here it was Wednesday and she'd had no clue.

Feeling devastated and blindsided, Erica felt her mind

spin. Every fear and insecurity she'd battled to keep out of her relationship with Ian rose to the surface and nearly strangled her. She was so close to repeating the same pattern with Ian as she had with Paul. Her mother and sister's pattern. Allowing a man to take control. Getting completely lost in the relationship and letting emotions cloud her better judgment so that she hadn't even seen this issue with Ian coming. A decision that put her in the position of relying on him when it came to her job. It afforded him far too much power and influence over her life.

She should have seen the signs, considering her own past lessons learned. She knew better than to become complacent, to let down her guard. But she'd fallen so hard and fast for Ian, trusting him like no other man with her soul, and she'd believed that he'd never betray that trust.

She'd obviously been wrong.

While she struggled for her identity and independence and tried to make the best choices for her future even when faced with the most unexpected, conflicting circumstances, the solution was so simple for Ian. Buy the station to keep her in his life, and take all decisions about her career, her future, out of her hands and put it directly in his, without so much as a discussion of what she wanted.

Icy panic twisted around her heart, nearly suffocating her. If she stayed in Chicago, if she agreed to continue working at WTLK with him as the new owner, she'd all but admit she needed him to take care of her, to secure her job, to be a part of her success. She would be admitting she couldn't do it on her own. He owned the station. Would he own her, as well? Would she be in-

debted to him for his supposed generosity? And where
would that neediness end?

She shuddered, knowing it had to end now or it never
would.

Abruptly, Erica stood and gathered up her purse, startling Carly with her brusque movement.

"Erica...where are you going?"

She jutted her chin out determinedly, defiantly. "To
talk to Ian."

As she left Ghirardelli's and headed over to Ian's office
building, Erica couldn't decide which betrayal hurt the
most...that the man she'd fallen so hard for couldn't be
honest with his intentions, or that her own heart had led
her astray.

"MR. CARLISLE, ERICA MCCREE is here to see you."

The voice of Ian's personal secretary drifted through
the intercom on his desk, pulling him from the stock re-
ports he was reviewing on the Internet. He was completely taken aback by Erica's spontaneous visit, pleas-
antly so, especially since she'd never been to his office
before today. He'd given her a standing, open invitation
to stop by anytime, and he was glad that she felt comfortable enough to take him up on his offer.

He hadn't seen her since Sunday when they'd spent
the afternoon at the Winslows, and he welcomed the rush
of enthusiasm and desire that lifted his spirits and quickened his pulse. "Go ahead and show her to my office,
Penny," he told his secretary.

Saving the documents on his computer, he stood and
reached the door just as Erica entered his office. Knowing
who Erica was from *Heat Waves* and her boss's involvement with her, Penny closed the door after her to afford
them privacy, which Ian appreciated, since the first thing

he planned to do was pin her against the wall and kiss her senseless.

Except the irritable vibes shimmering off Erica and the animosity flashing in her eyes wasn't exactly conducive for a seductive embrace. She was clearly upset, furious if her tense body language was any indication.

Concern immediately edged out more basic, sensual needs. Not knowing the source of her agitation but wanting to soothe her in any way he could, he reached out to gently grasp her arm. "Erica, honey, is everything okay?"

She stepped away from him, evading his touch, eluding him, and his gut constricted at the personal rejection.

Her chin lifted mutinously. "You bought the station," she stated bluntly, her voice sharp with righteous anger.

He swore beneath his breath, annoyed that she'd discovered his plans to purchase WTLK when he'd specifically told Dan to keep the sale quiet until everything was signed, sealed and delivered, which wouldn't be for a few more days. He'd wanted to tell Erica the news himself, under much different circumstances, in a more romantic setting, with roses and champagne to celebrate the acquisition.

This confrontation and her simmering wrath was far from the happy occasion he'd envisioned. "How did you find out?" he asked, just to be sure where she'd gotten her source of information.

"Dan told Carly, and Carly let it slip." She moved around him and into the middle of the spacious room, putting even more distance between them. She turned back to face him, her mouth stretched into a grim line. "I would have rather heard the news from you, and I'm feeling like the last one to know. Why didn't you tell me you were buying the station?"

He exhaled a deep breath. "Because I was waiting for finalization of the paperwork. Quite frankly, Virginia has been a pain in the ass about her terms, which has slowed down the sale on her broker's end. I wasn't going to take anything for granted until I had the acquisition papers in hand." He met her golden-brown gaze, hoping to soften the tension filling his office. "And I wanted the sale to be a surprise."

Bitter laughter erupted from her throat. "You certainly succeeded there. I'm still stunned."

He narrowed his gaze, trying to understand Erica's attitude. "And obviously very mad." Feeling provoked and a bit ruffled himself by Erica's temperament, he couldn't stop the sarcasm from creeping into his voice. "And here I thought you might be…oh, I don't know, happy, maybe? Relieved that the station isn't going to go bankrupt or be bought out by heavy-metal enthusiasts. Grateful that you don't have to worry about being unemployed and hitting the pavement for another job. Thrilled that the success of *Heat Waves* can continue."

"A success thanks to you."

He sighed, knowing this was a very sensitive issue for her. He attempted to alleviate her insecurities. "We've already had this discussion, Erica, before we agreed to do the sexy city nights campaign. Any success you've achieved is yours and yours alone. Me buying the station won't change any of that. If anything, it'll enable you to become a bigger, more recognizable personality in the industry."

She tossed her head stubbornly, and the sunlight reflecting in from the windows twisted gold through the honey-blond strands tumbling around her face. "Don't you think it's more than a little convenient that your buying WTLK keeps me here in Chicago with you?"

"Yeah, I guess it is." He wouldn't deny his more self-serving reasons for investing in the station. The mere thought of losing Erica had made him desperate, and trying to maintain a long-distance relationship with her living in Indianapolis didn't appeal to him. He didn't think she'd want that, either, given the choice. Or maybe she did.

The notion that he might have misread their developing relationship, that he might have misunderstood the intimacy and emotion the two of them had shared, made him bring the question out in the open. "And staying here in Chicago with me is a bad thing?"

"Not if it was my choice to make, but you took any decision I might have made away from me." She crossed her arms over her chest, her gaze obstinate and purposeful. "You never gave me a chance and didn't even ask what I wanted. You just bought the station and automatically assumed that I'd be so overwhelmed with gratitude that I'd stay here in Chicago and let you take care of me. You know what, Ian, I don't need you to secure me a job, and the last thing I want is to be indebted to you."

Growing more piqued with this entire situation, he braced his hands on his hips and let his own annoyance leak into his voice. "You don't owe me anything, Erica. I'm first and foremost a businessman, and I wouldn't have bought the station if it wasn't a solid investment. The furnishings and equipment might need to be updated, and the offices restored, but with your steadily climbing ratings and the overall appeal of your show and the talk-show format, I didn't see it as a horrible thing that buying the station served two distinct purposes, as a business investment and to allow you the opportunity to keep the job you enjoy and love and are so good at. And yes, to keep you in my life, too."

She shook her head in obvious frustration. "And where does it all end, Ian? How am I ever going to know if I'm truly a success, on my own, if you come charging to my rescue every time there's a bump in the road? I would have survived the sale of the station to someone else just fine, in my own way, making my own decisions about my career and future."

He moved across the room toward Erica, closing the space between them, and she stood her ground. "So, it was okay that I offered Tori a job, but I can't do the same for you?" he asked.

"Tori is a different situation," she refuted, bristling. "She needed a job."

"And you don't?" he countered, and before she could argue he plowed forward. "I enjoy helping people I care about, Erica. It makes me feel good, like I'm giving to someone else the opportunities the Winslows gave to me. And I'm fortunate that I'm in a position that I can afford to do it. I offered Tori a job because I believe in her and wanted to give her a fresh start. And I believe in you, too, Erica. There's not a damn thing wrong with taking advantage of a rare opportunity another person might offer," he said, speaking from experience. "It won't make you a needy, overly dependent person like your mother or sister."

Her spine stiffened. "This has nothing to do with that," she said too quickly, too defensively.

"I happen to think this conversation and your stubborn ideals have everything to do with your childhood." Without a doubt, this crisis of hers stemmed from a whole lot of unresolved fears on her part, and he knew she had to come to terms with those insecurities in her own way.

But for now, he tried to bridge the ever-widening gap between them, and subdue the emotional threat she was feeling. "No matter what you might think, I'm not trying to curb your independence or make any decisions for you. That was never my intention. But I can't deny that I do want to make things easy on you and give you every opportunity to be a huge radio personality in Chicago. You deserve that."

The fight seemed to drain out of her, and she glanced away, as if it pained her to look at him.

Very gently, he tucked his finger beneath her chin and brought her gaze back to his, and felt her tremble beneath his touch. The resistance was still there, along with a wealth of vulnerabilities that squeezed his heart like a vise. "Call me selfish," he said softly, "But I love you and I don't want you looking elsewhere for what's right in front of you." Not only a secure, successful job, but him.

Her breath caught, as if she realized what he was asking for. A commitment to more than just her job and *Heat Waves*. He wanted, needed, her to believe in all that they'd shared the past month. Beyond the seduction, despite her fears, the two of them belonged together.

"I can't do this again, Ian," she whispered, her voice choked with the same tears filling her eyes, along with more doubts and uncertainties he couldn't penetrate or soothe. "This isn't going to work for me. With you as the new owner, I think it's best if I hand in my resignation."

A piercing pain shot through his chest, and it hurt for him to draw air into his lungs. "You're quitting?" he asked incredulously. More than her job, his words asked if she was giving up and walking away from them.

She took a step back and nodded, her silence speaking volumes and answering the silent question that swirled between them. "I'm sorry," she said raggedly, then moved around him and headed for the door.

Ian's hands tightened into fists against the urge to stop Erica from leaving and try one last time to convince her that she was making the wrong decision. But because he loved Erica and didn't want to stifle her or hold her back from what she believed she had to do, he let her go…and hoped he survived the second-most-devastating loss of his life.

11

"HOW COME YOU AREN'T debating issues on the air with Ian anymore?"

Erica had known from the moment she'd arrived at Tori's new, fully furnished apartment with two bags full of nonperishable grocery items that it would be only a matter of time before their conversation turned to Ian. Five days had passed since their break-up on Wednesday, and when Ian didn't call the show that night for their normal evening debate, the finality of what she'd done had hit her hard. She should have been relieved that he hadn't called and made things more awkward between them, but instead a deep, consuming emptiness had enveloped her and it had taken every ounce of fortitude she'd possessed to make it to the end of her show that night…as well as Thursday and Friday night. And tomorrow night, Monday, she'd get to do it all over again, for another two weeks until her obligation to Ian and the station was fulfilled.

Tori's question seemed to be the same one on everyone's mind, from Carly and Dan, to her listeners, to the fans who recognized her in the stores and on the streets. Carly and Dan knew the truth and she'd managed to skirt the answer with her listeners, but she wanted to be honest with Tori, since Ian was a common link for the two of them.

She finished putting away the cans of soup in the kitchen cupboard Tori had designated, and turned to her friend. "Ian and I aren't seeing each other any longer. On the air or off." The painful words caused a lump to form in her throat and her chest to expand with a misery that seemed to increase with each passing hour she spent apart from Ian.

Tori frowned in bewilderment. "Why not?"

Erica leaned wearily against the counter behind her and glanced at the small dinette table where Janet was eating a few of the Oreo cookies Erica had brought for her. The little girl was playing with her new Barbie while enjoying her snack, oblivious to the conversation between the adults. She seemed happy and adjusting well to all the changes in her life, and Erica was grateful that the transition had been an easy one for Janet, and Tori, too, it seemed.

Erica wished her own personal transition to a life without Ian was going as smoothly. "Ian and I had a difference of opinion," she told Tori, and explained the entire situation to her friend. Erica told Tori about Ian buying the station, expecting her to stay, and how she'd made the spontaneous, heat-of-the-moment decision to quit *Heat Waves* and search elsewhere for a new job because she refused to depend on Ian for anything.

"Oh, Erica," Tori said compassionately, understanding her fears so well. "You can't be serious about leaving the show and Ian. I've heard you on the air, and I've seen the two of you together, and I can't imagine a more perfect match between two people. It's so obvious that he adores you."

He loved her. He'd said the words twice now, asking for nothing in return but her trust. So simple. So difficult.

And she'd ultimately rebuffed him. Driven by a haunting past she was so afraid of repeating, she'd made a mad dash for freedom. Yet unlike when she'd decided to leave Paul, there had been nothing liberating about walking out of Ian's life. Just pain and misery she'd never anticipated.

She wrapped her arms around her middle, grateful to have someone to talk to who empathized with all the misgivings running through her. "There's no doubt in my mind how Ian feels about me, but I don't want to be indebted to him for buying the station and securing my job. I don't want to need or depend on him for the direction of my career, or anything else, for that matter."

Tori thought about that for a quiet moment, then responded. "If there's one thing I've learned the past month, there's a big difference between needing someone and being needy. Looking back, I can finally admit that my relationship with my husband was controlling and dominating, and I was needy because that's what he expected of me. I fell into a pattern that just seemed to escalate to the point that I had no control in my life. And like you, once I made the decision to leave Rick, I swore I'd never depend on another man. And then Ian came along and offered me a job and a sense of security for me and Janet, and I took it."

Erica chewed on her thumbnail, hearing the other woman's words and seeing the undeniable gratitude shining in her eyes. The same kind of gratitude Erica had refused to feel in regards toward Ian buying the station. Her stubborn pride and a slew of fears seemed to be in control of so many aspects of her life—including denying herself the opportunity to grasp any semblance of happiness when it came her way.

"Look where I am, Erica," Tori continued, gesturing

with a wave of her hand at the nice apartment in which she lived, the stability that was within reach. "I couldn't have gotten this far without Ian's support. Without realizing it, I needed him because he was that stepping-stone to a better life and my personal independence. I didn't lose anything by depending on him and accepting his help but I gained so much."

Erica listened but couldn't bring herself to reply. She was too caught up in the similarities between Tori's situation and her own. And how differently they'd each responded to Ian's offer of help.

"And look at everything you've done for me," Tori added, a smile on her pretty face. "You gave me the strength I needed to believe in myself when I thought all hope was lost. And yes, I do feel indebted to you, but it's a good kind of obligation because I plan to repay you in friendship and by making you proud of me and what I do with my life."

Erica pressed two fingers to her lips, overwhelmed by Tori's declaration and by a tidal wave of emotion that seemed to shake her to the very core. To know that she'd had such a profound effect on Tori's life was humbling. To realize what a strong woman Tori had become as a result of her support was an extraordinary feeling.

Tori grabbed her free hand, her gaze soft and imploring as it latched onto hers. "I guess what I'm trying to say is that there is no control issue with Ian, except maybe in your mind because of what you've been through in your past."

Erica searched the other woman's gaze, seeing so much internal strength in Tori despite the ordeal she'd been through with her soon-to-be ex-husband. Witnessing how different Tori was from her own mother who'd gone through a similar experience was sobering for Erica. The fortitude in Tori was like a bright, shining beacon, while Erica was still cowering from emotional fears and weaknesses she'd always vowed would never dominate her life.

Erica shook her head. How funny that she'd been the one to lend support to Tori all these months, and now it was her friend giving back to her when she needed it the most. "When did you get so smart?"

Tori squeezed her hand one last time before letting go. "When I realized that I can't let my fears stop me from being happy. I did that for too many years with Rick, and while I might be cautious when it comes to certain things, I also know that I have to keep an open mind. Maybe you need to do the same. If you let him, Ian could be the best thing that's ever happened to you."

Ian was the best thing that had ever happened to her. The knowledge leapt from the depths of her soul, strong and sure, along with the love for him she'd been denying for days. He might have started out as a sexy mysterious caller, but somewhere along the way he'd become her lover and best friend. She'd shared more about herself, had opened herself up to him in ways that no other person had ever glimpsed, and he'd accepted her the way she was, flaws and all. Even now, with his silence, he was accepting her and supporting the decision she felt she'd needed to make, no matter what it had cost him personally.

He'd let her walk away. No demands. No ultimatums. And in that glorious moment she knew Ian would never hold her back from her goals and dreams. He'd only enhance everything about her life.

She'd spent the weekend perusing her volumes on sex

and relationships for a subject for tomorrow night's show, and now she knew exactly what it would be. But this time, there was no textbook to help her on this particular topic she'd address on the air and to Ian. All she had was her heart, soul, and her love for him to guide her.

She prayed that was enough.

"THIS IS ERICA MCCREE, and you're listening to *Heat Waves* on WTLK," she said, greeting her listeners for her Monday night show. "It looks like we're finally in for some cooler weather than we've had all summer, which is a good thing because it's been hot and intense for a lot of us, on and off the air."

Erica inhaled deeply, trying to calm the riot of nerves fluttering in her stomach. She was addressing her audience, but her words were meant for one man alone, and she hoped that he was out there listening to her tonight, that he'd realize her entire show was dedicated to him, their relationship and their future together. If he still wanted her in his life after the way she'd rejected his love.

Trying not to dwell on that devastating possibility, she glanced to the booth next to hers at Carly, who offered an encouraging smile. Erica held tight to her courage and her belief in Ian, in them, and continued.

"For the past few weeks we've talked about every aspect of sex and dating and what attracts men and women to each other, which has been fun and enlightening, even for me. I've learned just how powerful and intense an initial attraction can be with the right person and how being that special someone can open you up to all kinds of physical desires and emotional needs. I've discovered that mind sex and foreplay can be erotic and incredibly arousing, and that a woman can have multiple orgasms with the kind of partner who puts her pleasure before his own,'' she said with a thread of amusement in her tone.

"I've come to realize that while sex and orgasms can be fun and satisfying, making love is one of the most emotional, passionate things that can happen between a man and a woman. And then there's love. For some of us that closeness and intimacy comes easily. For others it's a struggle to allow those emotions to surface when we've been hurt in the past or believe that love comes with certain expectations."

She grew quiet for a few heartbeats, letting her listeners absorb her comments and relate to them in their own way. "We've covered attraction, dating and sex over the past month, and as all of you who've been following the sexy city nights campaign know, Ian and I have become somewhat of an item. You've enjoyed hearing about our dates and have been a part of our relationship from the very beginning. I know most of you are wondering why Ian hasn't been on the air with me lately, which brings me to tonight's topic."

She shifted restlessly in her seat, pushing all doubts and uncertainties from her mind in order to concentrate on the most important part of her show—convincing Ian that she wanted to try to make a relationship work with him. He alone would comprehend the underlying message in her words—he understood her so well.

"I thought we could talk about what happens when personal fears get in the way of a healthy, committed relationship," she said, prepared to open up herself in ways that would leave her vulnerable and in doing so would allow her to face her greatest fears. "I'm sure I'm not the only person who harbors insecurities, but mine do run deep, to the point that I let them rule my heart and emotions. I've been afraid to trust, afraid to believe, and I've made assumptions that were not only wrong but hurt the one person who gave me so much and never once demanded anything from me in return.''

She tucked a loose strand of hair behind her ear with a trembling hand. "So, I guess the big question would be, how do you make it up to someone that you really love when you've screwed up?" she asked her listeners, her voice soft and husky with regret. "How do you convince him that you want a second chance to make a relationship work and are willing to meet him or her halfway? That you don't want to look elsewhere for what's right in front of you? Give me a call and let me know what you think.''

Erica broke for a commercial while Carly screened the incoming calls. The phone lines lit up, and her computer monitor flashed the names of the callers. No doubt her listeners would have all kinds of advice for her, and while her request had been made in part for fun, she'd never been more serious about what to do about Ian and how to gain his forgiveness.

Taking a quick drink of water to quench her dry throat, she hit the first line and welcomed the caller to the show. "Hi, Ann, what's your suggestion?''

"How about that old, traditional expression of love?" the other woman said. "Plan a romantic evening, then send him eleven roses and keep the twelfth one to give to him when you see him.''

"That's a nice idea," Erica said, though it didn't work for her, personally. She moved on to the next caller.

"Thanks for calling *Heat Waves,* Bea. You're on the air."

"Bake him some cookies or a pie," the older woman said in a very grandmotherly kind of voice. "George swears that the best way to a man's heart is through his stomach. We've been married for over fifty years, and anytime we've gotten into a tiff I just bake him some kind of treat and all is forgiven."

Erica smiled at the sweet sentiment. "George is a very lucky man. Unfortunately, I'm afraid my attempts at baking would just make things worse between me and Ian."

In the soundproof studio next to hers, she saw Carly snicker, knowing cooking or baking wasn't her forte. Making a face at her friend, she picked up the next line.

"Surprise him with a night of hot sex," Grant recommended. "Ask any guy and he'll tell you that make-up sex is the best!"

Erica rolled her eyes. "Make-up sex is an easy way out," she argued. "I'm looking for something with a bit more depth and emotion to it."

"How about sending Ian a gorilla singing telegram along with a box of chocolates and a note that reads, 'I'm ape over you'?" another caller suggested.

Erica laughed and shook her head. "Ah, that's very clever, but I think this is something I need to do in person, and I'd rather not do it in a gorilla costume."

"You can always show up at his office wearing nothing but a trench coat and a smile," a man offered. "A guy will listen to anything a naked woman has to say."

"I'll keep that in mind for future reference." The calls continued for the next half hour, and Erica enjoyed all the fun, lighthearted and crazy ideas everyone felt compelled to share. But no one's advice struck a chord within her as she'd hoped. She kept holding out for something more genuine and sincere.

Line three blinked, and Erica looked at her monitor to gauge the caller's identity. There was no name on the screen. She glanced Carly's way, but she was busy doing something else and Erica couldn't get her attention to point out the problem. Figuring Carly must have just forgotten to type the name into the system, she pressed the line and greeted the caller. "Thank you for calling *Heat Waves*. I'm desperate for some real, solid advice. Something simple yet effective. How should I tell the man I care about that I messed up and will do anything to make things right again?"

"The answer is easy," a rich, familiar masculine voice replied. "How about just be honest and tell him what's in your heart?"

Erica's pulse quickened as Ian's voice drifted out of the intercom, and that aching, painful longing that had taken up residence within her grew to startling proportions. The understanding, tenderness and caring in his voice was unmistakable. And she knew, despite everything, he still wanted her, believed in her, loved her.

She drew a shaky breath. "I think that's the best advice I've heard all night."

"I heard everything you said tonight, now tell me what's in your heart," he whispered, coaxing her to share this moment with her listeners, since they'd been with them from the very beginning of their relationship.

For the first time in her life, Erica trusted someone completely—with her life, her future and her very soul. Because of that faith, because of Ian, she held nothing back. "My heart is filled with regret, for walking away and hurting you," she said with quiet honesty. "My heart is overflowing with a tenderness I've never, ever experienced before, but I never want the feeling to end. My heart is nothing without you in my life.''

"Do you believe in me?" he asked.

She nodded to herself, no longer clinging to the uncertainties and doubts that had ruled her emotions for too long. "Just as much as you believe in everything I do, and everything I am."

"Do you need me?" he asked, husky emotion deepening his voice.

Oh, yes, she most definitely *needed* this man. "I need your support, your encouragement, and the way you understand me better than I know myself sometimes. I need you to remind me that it's okay to be a little scared sometimes and that you'll always be there for me. I need you in my life, Ian."

"Do you love me?"

"In ways that are frightening, but oh, so wonderful." She blinked back the well of tears gathering in her eyes. "I don't want to cling to my past or fear the future. I want what's right in front of me, and I won't settle for less."

"I take it that means you've decided to stay in Chicago, and that you don't mind me being your new boss?"

She laughed throatily, wondering how she ever thought she could leave this man behind when he was such an integral part of who she was. "I'm staying in Chicago, because it's the only choice I ever could have made. As for you being my new boss...we'll have to discuss what kind of perks and benefits you offer."

"How's this for starters?" The line disconnected just as the door to her studio opened.

Startled, Erica stood up as Ian entered the room, unable

to believe he'd been there at the station the entire time
they'd been on the air. She could only guess that he'd
made the trip over as soon as he'd heard what tonight's
topic was all about. Him. Them. Her wanting him. He
tucked his cell phone into his pocket, came around the
console separating them and stopped in front of her.

With a wicked grin, he framed her face in his hands
and lowered his head and kissed her, long and slow and
deep. A "perk" designed to sway her. His hot, aroused
body pressed her up against the console, and she welcomed his solid weight as his lips consumed hers. She
melted into him, lost in the heat of his mouth, the emotion in his kiss, the tenderness of his touch. Everything
that was now hers, and always would be. When he finally
let her up for air she blushed, though no one but Ian could
see the high color rise in her cheeks.

"Um, we're still on the air," she told him, making
sure he realized that the city of Chicago was listening in
on them.

"Good," he said, smoothing his hands down her back
and over her bottom, making their position a more intimate one. "Because I want everyone to know how much
I love you, and to make sure that they stay tuned for
more sexy city nights to come."

She sighed as he dipped his head and nuzzled her neck,
and she threaded her fingers through his thick, silky hair.
"Aah, another perk." Sleeping and working with the
boss was going to be a whole lot of fun, she decided.

He met her gaze again, his need for her shining in his
vibrant green eyes. "When you're ready, will you marry
me?"

He was giving her time. Time she no longer needed
because a day, week, month or year wouldn't change the

way she felt about him. She slid her fingers along his jaw as undescribable happiness bubbled within her, and it was a feeling she embraced wholeheartedly.

"I'm ready now," she said.

Two months later, she made good on that promise as they recited their wedding vows surrounded by family and friends...and with the city of Chicago listening in on the joyous occasion that was broadcasted live on *Heat Waves*.

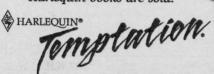

CALL THE ONES YOU LOVE OVER THE HOLIDAYS!

Save $25 off future book purchases when you buy any four Harlequin® or Silhouette® books in October, November and December 2001,

PLUS

receive a phone card good for 15 minutes of long-distance calls to anyone you want in North America!

WHAT AN INCREDIBLE DEAL!

Just fill out this form and attach 4 proofs of purchase (cash register receipts) from October, November and December 2001 books, and Harlequin Books will send you a coupon booklet worth a total savings of $25 off future purchases of Harlequin® and Silhouette® books, AND a 15-minute phone card to call the ones you love, anywhere in North America.

Please send this form, along with your cash register receipts
as proofs of purchase, to:
In the USA: Harlequin Books, P.O. Box 9057, Buffalo, NY 14269-9057
In Canada: Harlequin Books, P.O. Box 622, Fort Erie, Ontario L2A 5X3
Cash register receipts must be dated no later than December 31, 2001.
Limit of 1 coupon booklet and phone card per household.
Please allow 4-6 weeks for delivery.

I accept your offer! Please send me my coupon booklet and a 15-minute phone card:

Name: _____

Address: _____ City: _____

State/Prov.: _____ Zip/Postal Code: _____

Account Number (if available): _____

---

097 KJB DAGL
PHQ4012

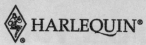